MINOTAUR
MYSTERIES

Other titles from St. Martin's Minotaur Mysteries

ZEN AND THE ART OF MURDER
by Elizabeth M. Cosin
BREAD ON ARRIVAL by Lou Jane Temple
BIGGIE AND THE FRICASSEED FAT MAN
by Nancy Bell
MOODY FOREVER by Steve Oliver
AGATHA RAISIN AND THE WIZARD
OF EVESHAM by M. C. Beaton
DEATH TAKES UP A COLLECTION
by Sister Carol Anne O'Marie
A MURDER IN THEBES by Anna Apostolou
AQUARIUS DESCENDING by Martha C. Lawrence
MY BODY LIES OVER THE OCEAN by J. S. Borthwick
MURDER WITH PEACOCKS by Donna Andrews
A COLD DAY IN PARADISE by Steve Hamilton
CROSSROAD BLUES by Ace Atkins
ROMAN BLOOD by Steven Saylor
TELL NO TALES by Eleanor Taylor Bland
FAREWELL PERFORMANCE by Donna Huston Murray
DEATH AL DENTE by Peter King
JITTER JOINT by Howard Swindle

Minotaur is also proud to present these mystery classics by Ngaio Marsh

BLACK AS HE'S PAINTED
GRAVE MISTAKE
LAST DITCH
PHOTO FINISH

EXTRAORDINARY ACCLAIM FOR THE NOVELS OF ELEANOR TAYLOR BLAND

"She's anything but bland . . . Sharp and sassy and right on the money." —Lawrence Block

"Marti MacAlister is a most welcome addition to crime fiction." —Sara Paretsky

"[Bland is] a fine storyteller." —*Washington Post Book World*

"Solidly plotted police procedurals with interesting people, packaged in careful, understated prose." —*Philadelphia Inquirer*

"Her writing is intelligent, sensitive, and sometimes gritty." —*Quarterly Black Review of Books*

"One of the better new crime writers of this decade." —*Mystery News*

"A well-written standout series." —*Portsmouth Herald*

"Marti is a great character . . . and this entire series continues to provide some of the best who-done-it novels available today." —*Midwest Book Review*

"A strong series." —*Minneapolis Star Tribune*

"[Bland] is a sensitive and hugely promising writer." —*Mystery Scene*

"Bland's heroine, Marti MacAlister, is as grounded in reality as her fictional turf." —*Chicago Tribune*

"Bland handles the evolving relationship between Marti and a white male partner unsure of a woman's place in the police world with sensitivity and humor." —*Publisher's Weekly*

TELL NO TALES
"When the curtain falls, all the important players are in place and the audience is ready to applaud." —*Washington Post Book World*

"The author deftly builds suspense and tension as Marti gets close to some awful truths that will bring death too near."
—*Washington Post*

"*Tell No Tales* is a treat for longtime fans and a good introduction to those who have not yet made her acquaintance." —*Tampa Tribune*

"A rich mystery . . . The author excels at painting everyday, gritty street life." —*Library Journal*

"Continues the tradition of multilevel story lines blending into a wonderful novel . . . The varying complexities ultimately flow into an entertaining book."

—Harriet Klausner, Painted Rock Reviews

SEE NO EVIL

"A compelling page-turner . . . A mood of high suspense right through to the end. . . . Marti MacAlister was named one of the top five lesser-known female sleuths. With this sixth installment of the superior series, it's high time she graduates into the ranks of the best known." —*Booklist* (starred review)

"Bland tightens the suspense with realistic details and subplot twists before wrapping the narrative up in a satisfying solution."
—*Publishers Weekly*

"Fast-paced and edgy . . . Captures both the hope and the despair of life on Marti's beat." —*Minneapolis Star-Tribune*

"A tightly written police procedural . . . Bland pumps up the suspense . . . [and] the surprise ending is even more terrifying."
—*Ft. Lauderdale Sun-Sentinel*

"Bland's sixth case featuring . . . Marti MacAlister explores new depth in the character. [Filled with] murderous schemes in chilling detail and . . . a nameless psychopath [whose] identity is not disclosed until the very end, and the revelation will startle many readers." —*Chicago Sun-Times*

"Bland's blunt honesty about her characters' conflicted emotions makes this the best of Marti's six cases to date." —*Kirkus Reviews*

KEEP STILL

"A deftly written, cleverly plotted joy to read." —*Washington Times*

"Pulls no punches . . . A stellar installment in an excellent series."
—*Booklist*

DONE WRONG

"Marti is a strong, quiet presence, and her story resonates."
—*Publishers Weekly*

"Bland deftly weaves together elements of everyday police work,
back-room politicking, and homely domestic life into a novel that
is both suspenseful and emotionally satisfying."
—*Alfred Hitchcock Mystery Magazine*

"Bland succeeds in further developing a heroine whose life and
work illuminate the black middle class. These novels are not about
race—they are about people and the human condition."
—*Chicago Sun-Times*

**St. Martin's Paperbacks Titles
by Eleanor Taylor Bland**

Tell No Tales
See No Evil
Keep Still
Done Wrong

TELL NO TALES

ELEANOR
TAYLOR
BLAND

St. Martin's Paperbacks

NOTE: If you purchased this book without a cover you should be aware that this book is stolen property. It was reported as "unsold and destroyed" to the publisher, and neither the author nor the publisher has received any payment for this "stripped book."

TELL NO TALES

Copyright © 1999 by Eleanor Taylor Bland.
Excerpt from *Scream in Silence* copyright © 2000 by Eleanor Taylor Bland.

All rights reserved. No part of this book may be used or reproduced in any manner whatsoever without written permission except in the case of brief quotations embodied in critical articles or reviews. For information address St. Martin's Press, 175 Fifth Avenue, New York, NY 10010.

Library of Congress Catalog Card Number: 98-46974

ISBN: 0-312-97113-3

Printed in the United States of America

St. Martin's Press hardcover edition / February 1999
St. Martin's Paperbacks edition / March 2000

10 9 8 7 6 5 4 3 2 1

In memorium

MARLON LONNIE
December 31, 1974–March 28, 1998

The innocent cry out for justice.

"Without memory there is no healing,
without forgiveness there is no future."

Archbishop Desmond Tutu

As always, this is dedicated to Ted Chichak, with great affection and much appreciation.

There have been several changes in my professional life. I would like to thank Sally Richardson for her thoughtfulness and concern; my former editor, Anne Savarese, for seeing the possibilities, I miss you; my new editor, Kelley Ragland, for making this transition so easy; David Goldberg, my former publicist, for facilitating my appearance on CBS News Sunday Morning; and Naomi Mendelsohn, my new publicist. I would also like to thank my copyeditor, Christine Aebi.

For technical assistance, I would like to acknowledge: Dr. Edmund R. Donaghue, chief medical examiner, Dr. Robert J. Stine Institute of Forensic Medicine, Chicago, IL; John A. Rorabeck, forensic analyst, deputy coroner, Lake County, IL; Capt. Frank Winan (ret.), Sgt. Michael Blazencic; Sgt. Portia Wallace, Lake County Sheriffs Department; Monique McIntosh, Lake County State's Attorney; Timothy Mooney, Stage Two Theater, for information on the history of theater in Lake County and the Genesee Theater; Margaret Kaiser, Betty Kaiser, Norma Cribb, Diane Dixon, Laura Hiney, Cheryl Ptasienski; Sandy Correa, Waukegan School District 60, and Tim; Devon Nelson, Ralph Zahorik, *Waukegan News-Sun;* Edward Gilbreth, Pat Christianson, Virginia Gerst, Dwayne Coclough; Sylvia Johnson, Staben Center; Cynthia

Alexander, Staben House; Patricia Jones, Waukegan Township supervisor.

To some very special people at CBS News Sunday Morning: Doug Smith, Anthony Mason, and Tom Vlodek.

To Hugh Holton, Gary Phillips, Gar Anthony Haywood, and Richard Yarborough. Thanks for being there when I needed you.

Congratulations to Dawn Taborn.

To superfans Judy Duhl, Ruth Walker, Judy Stewart, Bonnie Claeson, Willaida Jernigan, Marcella Hardin.

As Barnabas Cheney looked out at the night, snow blew like a curtain of white against the darkness. Angels, swift in flight, caught the currents of the wind and soared high above the impermanence of mortals, fleeing the persistence of this orb of rock and water as it turned its back on the ordinary lightness of day. The days went by unwept, unvoiced, but night, he loved the night.

"Lincoln Prairie," the conductor said. His voice was loud, as if Barnabas was not the only passenger in this car and there were others who needed to be awakened.

"Lincoln Prairie," the stern-faced conductor announced again.

Barnabas thought about getting up without moving. The pane of glass was cold against his face, a pleasant coldness, not touched by the warmth within the train. He felt loath to move, but he did so when the wheels began to whine as they locked on the rails. As soon as he stepped off the train, snow swarmed about him, stinging his face. The wind whispered as it snaked around the corner of the station, then hissed as it scoured snow from the walkway and cleared a swirling path before him.

"They make a noise like feathers," Barnabas said. He heard Estragon answer, "Like leaves."

"We are no longer alone . . . waiting for the night . . . waiting for . . . waiting . . ." He pulled his coat closed and fumbled for the buttons, then stopped for a moment under a light, surprised that there weren't any buttons. He would have to remember. . . . The train whistle blew and the train began moving away. The wind blew his coat open and he tried to button it. Still standing there, he looked down and saw that there were none. Barnabas pulled his knitted cap down until it touched his neck and reached just above his eyes. He pulled on his gloves and moved quickly away. The snow was higher than his shoes. The wind kept blowing his coat open and there were few buildings to shelter him as he walked. No one was about, not even a cop car passed him. Except for the wind, it was quiet.

Instead of turning down the street where he lived, Barnabas continued walking around the block. He slowed down, spread his hands in front of him, fingers splayed, and began a slow waving motion with his arms. "Alleluia, oh, praise You, I praise You," he sang over and over until he had made a complete circle around the block.

He walked the length of the yellow-brick two-story commercial building where he lived, dipping and waving and bowing toward the storefront windows, then unlocked the door and made his way in the dark to the wide staircase that took him one level below the street. He paused there, looked around the huge open room without windows—a storage area for the antique dealer who rented space on the first floor—then negotiated the maze of boxes and furniture and appliances until he reached the narrow stairwell that would take him to the subbasement two floors below.

Barnabas turned on a small lamp and an electric heater. His room was partitioned off with sheets. He went to his desk without taking off his coat, waiting for the place to warm up, but pulled off his socks and his shoes and slipped on his sandals. He sat at the desk, pulled some bread out of his coat pocket and opened his Bible, but he felt too tired to read. Instead, he put his head on the desk.

When he woke up, someone was there. He could see their feet where the sheet stopped short of the floor.

"Is that you, Grandfather?"

The sheets parted.

"Who? . . . What?"

He started to get up, then ducked when the man picked up the lamp and swung it at him.

1

Marti bounded up the hill, plunging into the snow as she raced Ben to the top. Halfway up, she leaned against the trunk of a pine tree and gulped in deep breaths of cold air. The new snow sparkled in the bright sunlight. The sky was a clear, cloudless blue. To the south, ice rimmed the edge of the pond where earlier she had seen a family of deer. Canada geese, permanent residents that would never fly any farther south, swam near the center. Tall pines were grouped along the hill like stands of untrimmed Christmas trees. She felt a rare sense of freedom. Everything and everyone she could possibly worry about seemed far away.

At the foot of the hill, near the pond, the white clapboard inn where they were staying was still holiday-festive, with red bows and wreaths on the windows and doors. It was just a quiet inn in Wisconsin. Homey, with logs crackling in the fireplaces, poinsettias on tables and sideboards, and a tall tree with wide branches in the front hallway, trimmed with Victorian lace ornaments and porcelain angels. Bayberry candles, with small flames flickering in green-and-gold globes, scented the air.

She hadn't realized how stressed out she was until they came here. She had spent most of yesterday sleeping. It had snowed all day and into the night, and when she had looked out the window this morning, she'd felt a wonderful sense of isolation. Four other couples shared their lodgings, each as intent on privacy. The locals had burrowed in for the winter. The big ski resorts were farther north.

"The guys say it's sort of like an old folks home," Ben had told her before he made reservations. "A great place for mature couples like us." He'd laughed, a deep, rumbling chuckle. "My first choice was Cancún—swimming, hiking, scuba diving, sailing. Then I thought, Maybe Florida, just as much sun, a few more clubs, dancing until daybreak. Then we had that fire at the tire place that burned for a day and a half. And there was that snowmobile accident, with all of those deep dives in a cold lake. And finally the green-goop alert, with four pumpers and a hook and ladder on standby while the Bomb Squad blew up that amateur scientist's concoction because the kids' parents thought it was an explosive. That's when I remembered this place, and I thought, Hot tub, breakfast in bed, candlelight, and time, lots of time to relax, talk, listen to music, make love. Something about that seemed so much more romantic."

"A much better idea," Marti had agreed. She hadn't been able to face a week of being a tourist, either. The thought of being someplace where teenagers and twenty-somethings were the hired help and not the clientele was appealing. The young woman who brought their meals was pleasant and helpful without being familiar and chatty.

Time was the ultimate factor. With her working long hours whenever she had a homicide, and Ben working forty-eight on and forty-eight off, they always seemed to have so little time alone together. Neither of them could take much time off for a honeymoon, and she didn't want to go too far from home.

This was only the second time they had left their suite. At first, the great outdoors seemed less interesting than mulled wine, warm oil massages, the glow from the fireplace, and sharing a bed; but there was something intriguing about the stillness, hilly white expanses of snow, glimpses of deer, geese overhead, and rabbits that scampered about. She couldn't remember the last time she had been anyplace where it was this peaceful. Everything was good. Being with Ben was good.

Their decision to get married on New Year's Day had not been as abrupt as it had seemed. They sat down to Thanksgiving dinner and she looked around the table—at Ben, at his son, Mike, at her two children, Theo and Joanna—and she realized that after four years of being a widow, she wanted to be a family again.

"I don't want to be alone anymore," she told Ben later that evening. She had that same sure, quiet feeling that she'd had when she decided it was time to marry her late husband, Johnny.

"Does this mean marriage?" Ben asked.

"I think so."

"Tomorrow?"

"No, silly."

"Next week."

"I think it's going to take a little longer than that to get everything organized."

"Not if we keep it simple," Ben said.

"Even if we keep it simple, which I intend to."

Later, they called the children into the den.

"Ben and I have decided to get married."

Mike's eyes got wide and he grinned. He was shorter than Theo, and chubby, although he was losing weight. He laughed a lot, like his father. "Yes!" he said, and jumped up and hugged her, then his dad. "Yes!"

Neither Theo nor Joanna said anything. Theo's angular face, so much like Johnny's, became a brown mask. Like Johnny, he rarely let her know how he felt or what he was thinking. She had learned to decipher Johnny's nonverbal clues. Theo was often an enigma.

"Where will we live?" he asked finally.

Marti wasn't sure why that was important, or if it was. "We haven't decided. We have to look around."

"I want to share a room with Mike."

At least he liked the idea of having a brother.

Mike grinned in agreement.

"Does this mean you come with us when we go camping, Ma?" Theo asked. "Or can we still got without you sometimes?"

"I don't think too much will change."

"Good."

She wasn't sure what that meant and didn't ask.

Joanna didn't say anything until the boys had run from the room. An even six feet, she was two inches taller than Marti, and when she stood up, she seemed taller. She walked to the window, the round, full features of her face just like Momma's in profile. "Well," she said. "I'm glad, I think. We'll see." Swinging her long auburn braid over her shoulder so that it hung down her back, she strode from the room.

This blended family was definitely not going to be anything like the Brady Bunch, Marti decided.

After the kids were in bed, Marti called Momma and Ben called his parents. Like Mike, they seemed pleased.

Now they were both wearing plain gold bands.

"Gotcha," he yelled, still at least twenty feet away. He tossed a snowball that didn't even land close to were she was standing. A startled goose honked, then gave her an arrogant stare.

"Cops run faster than fireman," she yelled as he got closer.

When Ben reached her, he said, "Smart firemen let cute cops win."

"You're a paramedic, too. Will that get me mouth-to-mouth resuscitation?"

He brushed snow from the strands of hair that weren't pushed under her cap, then leaned down and kissed her. He was a big man, tall and muscular, and perhaps because he was aware of his size, he was gentle.

"We've been here since Sunday, three days already," he said.

She laughed.

"And no call from Vik," they said in unison. When he laughed, even his eyes smiled.

Her partner, Detective Matthew "Vik" Jessenovik, had been less than happy about their marriage. The day before the wedding, the guys at the precinct had taken bets on the day and the hour that he would find sufficient reason to ask her to return early. That hadn't happened yet. Their kids hadn't called, either. Momma was visiting from Arkansas and everything at home was just fine. She had four more days to make love, sleep in, have breakfast in bed, and play in the snow. She leaned against Ben, felt his arms around her. "God, this is good."

Ben hugged her tighter. His face was cold against hers. "Still want to go to the top of the hill?" he asked.

She thought of the heat from the hearth and the warmth of their bodies beneath the blankets and other fires they had only just begun to ignite. She giggled. "Maybe later."

Later, lying beside her, Ben wondered how much more time he and Marti would have before Job Interruptus sent them back to the real world of homicide and arson, a life that he knew would be disorganized and unpredictable. When he'd mentioned that to his father, the old man had laughed. "Just what a man needs when he reaches middle age, a woman to fire him up again and enough kids around to keep his mind sharp." The "middle age" part had jolted him, but Dad was right.

If anyone had told him four years ago that they would be here together today, he would have said, "Impossible." Marti didn't even like him then, as far as he could tell. They met at a PTO potluck supper. Theo and Mike had become best friends. Mike was the class bully then and Marti didn't want him to play with her son. She didn't even pretend to be friendly. Even then, he had wanted her, but mostly because that seemed so unlikely. She was pretty in an earthy kind of way—"healthy" his mother would say—with that generosity of features God blessed some black women with: full lips, wide oval eyes, along with big legs, broad hips, firm breasts—everything he liked in a woman.

He still wasn't sure how he had managed this. He probably hadn't. Ever since his father had admitted he was always two steps behind Mom, and said that trying to figure out where she was heading next was why he'd put up with her all of these years, Ben had decided that understanding a woman, in addition to being almost impossible, might not be all that necessary. Marti had convinced him that the old man was right. As well as he thought he knew her, he sure couldn't explain her in any way that would make much sense to anybody else. Marti. He held his hand

7

close enough to her mouth to feel her breath warm on his fingertips. An old Fats Domino song came to mind. "Yes it's me and I'm in love again . . ."

Heavy draperies darkened the room and flames danced in the fireplace. The light floral scent of Marti's cologne mingled with the pine and berry scents of the deep-bowled candles centered in wreaths of holly. Her hair, auburn in the bright sunlight, but darker now, was damp with sweat. The sheet had fallen away from her shoulder and he could see the small uneven birthmark on her smooth amber skin just above the swell of her breast.

My woman, he thought. This is my woman. Would she contradict him if he said that aloud? He didn't think she thought of herself as belonging to anybody but herself. "You got yourself an independent woman this time," his mother said, concerned because his first wife, Carol, hadn't been. Then Mom smiled and patted his arm. "She reminds me of myself when I was younger." That comment stayed in his mind, made some subtle change in the way he saw Marti, and after awhile, he realized it was true. He liked that. His parents had been married for forty-five years now.

"That's my woman." How often had he heard Dad say that? Even now the old man had a way of leaning back and cocking his head to one side and looking at Mom as if she still looked exactly the way she had when he'd married her. The way he would look at Marti one day.

He leaned down, inhaled the scent of her, touched the birthmark with his fingertip, felt the moist softness of her skin. My woman, he thought, hungry for her again.

•

Vik plugged in a small radio and tuned in to an all-news station. The office was quiet without Marti, too quiet, and she'd only been gone three days. That was a hell of a way to begin the New Year, getting married. Of course, with the way last year had ended, with that dipshit bungling a home invasion, he couldn't blame her for wanting to have a man around the house. Even so, she'd been doing just fine on her own. He hated to admit it, but she did deserve a week off, as long as there were no dead bodies to interrupt her trip. The sooner what's-his-name, the paramedic, got used to being married to a cop, the better. Cops didn't have a high divorce rate for nothing. Not that he wanted Marti to get divorced, but being a cop's husband had to be a hell of a lot worse than being a cop's wife. Women were more used to having a man in charge than vice versa.

He turned up the radio. Where were Slim and Cowboy? What the hell was the point in sharing an office if you didn't even bother to show up in the morning? What did vice cops have to do in the daytime anyway besides talk about last weekend's hooker roundup and how many johns got their names in the *News-Times*? They were probably in court. At least Cowboy had made coffee. Vik poured a cup and poked at the doughnuts that had been here since yesterday, then chose the one that seemed the least stale. When Mildred felt better, which would be soon, he was going to go back to eating breakfast at home.

After he went through his in basket, he organized the files for upcoming court cases and went through them, making sure nothing had been overlooked. He reached for the phone but didn't call home. He had promised Mildred that he wouldn't worry. Why didn't it ring? He needed a fresh case to work on—with Marti. The lieutenant had said he would have to work with Lupe Torres if something came up, but he didn't intend to. Lieutenant or no lieutenant, the next body they found, Marti came home. Not that Lupe wasn't okay, as female officers went, but she had no sense of humor, and she preferred to have lunch at the Spicy Tamale and not the Barrister, and she expected him to do his share of the driving. He stared at the phone, almost praying that it would ring, but nothing happened. They hadn't had a real stiff in almost a month, just routine death investigations and a couple of holiday suicides. Where were the serial killers when you needed them?

It was after three when the phone rang. A mummy had been found at the Geneva Theater.

"A mummy! You mean something from one of those magic acts they used to have when vaudeville shows played there?"

"I'm afraid not, Jessenovik," the sergeant said. "This one is human."

Before he left, he unfolded the afternoon edition of the *News-Times*. There it was, page one, the third installment of the number-one story this week, downtown revitalization. ANOTHER STEP TOWARD DOWNTOWN COMEBACK? read the headline right above a picture of the Geneva.

"More likely another setback," Vik muttered. All it had been so far was talk for three or four years now. That and wild ideas, from a lakefront parkway and cutesy little shops to restoring the theater district. He could remember when that place was alive with people, the days when they used to "Scoop the Loop" in their cars. Now Scooping the Loop was an annual Christmas-time event and downtown didn't exist anymore, and never would again.

"A mummy," Vik said, shaking his head as he followed the uniformed cop into the old theater. "What next?" He had never seen one. What the hell did they look like? Did they smell?

"Madam Senator was very upset," the uniform said. "With that, and the nest of mice we disturbed in the room behind the stage where they kept the costumes . . ." He stifled a laugh. "You should have seen everyone hopping around. I thought one old guy was going to pass out. Kept saying this was not the theater he remembered, that the place was too far gone."

"Damned mummy," Vik amended. A state senator and officials representing the county had been here as part of the tour, as well as local pols. So much for getting restoration funds from the state.

The place had been closed up for years. Vik began sneezing as soon as they stepped into the lobby. He had one vague memory of standing by the case with a poster of the *The Orient Express* years ago, waiting while his father bought tickets to an Abbott and Costello movie. The carpet hadn't been worn as thin then. Otherwise, except for dust and age and this closed-in smell that had his nose clogged up, nothing had changed.

"You think Jack Benny ever played here?" the uniform asked.

"How would I know?" His father had seen Benny when one of his movies premiered here. He'd told Vik about watching the motorcade with Benny, Rochester, and Dorothy Lamour almost every time they drove down Geneva. Dad even knew Benny's cousin, the one Benny stayed with when he came to town. Not that Vik would ever tell anyone that, at least not anyone other than Marti. They might think he was old. "So, where's this mummy?"

"Wait 'til you see this. Some kind of hidden room. This place is full of odd rooms and storage places. It's weird-looking with that dome ceiling and those box seats jutting out from the walls, enough to give you the creeps. One of the ladies almost fell into that hole in front of the stage."

"That's the orchestra pit, kid."

Vik followed him up to the projection room. "A grand place," his father used to say. "Your mother and I came to see vaudeville shows here while we were courting."

A grand place it still was. Vaulted ceilings with all the curlicue plasterwork. Long red velvet curtains on either side of the stage. And real seats with real padding, thick enough for comfort. They didn't recline, and you would have to squeeze in if you weighed too much, but they weren't molded plastic with a thin vinyl-covered pad, either.

"Here, sir."

"What? Oh."

The uniform pointed to a narrow walkway behind the projectionist's booth.

"Wait 'til you see this. It's like something out of *Tales from the Crypt*."

There was a deep but narrow closet, with a door as seamless as the wall, and no knob.

"Senator Sutton leaned against the wall right there, sir, and fell into the room. Not much more than a broom closet. See how the body is propped up against the back wall? The senator touched the thing, turned to see what it was, and let out one hell of a scream."

"Why don't you call the precinct and tell the sarge we need a detail out here to search the building," Vik said. Maybe they would find somebody else. "A while back, they found a body over at the Rialto. . . ."

"That incident where some guy shot his girlfriend?"

"No, that just happened a couple of years ago. She didn't die. I was talking about the Rialto."

"The Rialto?"

"Right. It's the Palace now. Four blocks south of here. The other side of the street." Peach-fuzz kid didn't even know this town. He didn't add that the homicide had happened when his dad was a cop.

Dr. Cyprian, the medical examiner, was kneeling on the floor. Vik stood in the doorway and tried to look over his shoulder. There was no unusual odor that he could detect. From what he could see, it looked like a skeleton with leather stretched over it. Except for the grin, and the dark hair.

"Hispanic or African-American?" Vik asked, not sure if the brown skin tone was the result of the mummification process.

"Black female."

"Age?"

"Can't tell yet, Jessenovik."

"Any injuries?"

"None that I can see."

"Could she have died recently?"

"This doesn't happen overnight."

"How much time are we talking about, then, given these conditions?"

"You're going have to wait for the reports."

"What else is new?" He heard footsteps.

"Sir?"

It was Lupe. "It took you long enough to get here," Vik said. The only reason he'd called her in was because they had never had a case like this before. "Take a look."

"Awesome," she said. "This really looks weird, like something out of *Tales from the Crypt.*"

Vik wondered what *Tales from the Crypt* was. He wasn't going to ask, but that was the second time he'd heard it since he'd been here.

"It's not a kid, is it, Jessenovik? Dead kids are going to take getting used to."

Vik turned toward her. There was a hardness in the set of her jaw that hadn't been there three years ago, and her eyes were like black stones. Even though she wasn't more than five six, she stood there as if the equipment she was carrying weighed three pounds, not twenty. She had grown up in the job, become someone he wouldn't be afraid to have watching his back.

"Looks like a short adult to me," he said. Looking at Lupe, you wouldn't think anything would bother her, but he had never known a cop who got used to seeing dead kids. She would have to figure out how to cope with it.

"Does MacAlister have to come back?"

"No." He had checked with the lieutenant, who told him Marti was not to be called in unless the body was still warm and the victim damned important.

"Good. After all, she just left."

After Cyprian and the evidence techs were through, Vik told them to go ahead and take the body. "No purse," he said. "No ID."

"No photo ID. No driver's license," Lupe added. "No I LIKE IKE button, no platform shoes, no Grateful Dead T-shirt—nothing that would tell us a thing."

"Now what does a young cop like you know about stuff like that?" Vik asked. "How about stopping for burgers?"

When they went back to the precinct Vik checked out missing persons in the computer database. He requested a list of African-American females. The list went back five years. There were twenty-five names. Lupe began contacting relatives to see which of the young women had returned without their being notified.

"This is a waste of time," Vik said. "We don't even know what we're looking for. When did she die? I bet Cyprian could have told us something, estimated how long it had been there . . . something."

"She," Lupe said.

"Look, kid, you can't get personally involved with these cases. *She* is dead. And you'd better hope we don't have to look up, chase down, and interview everyone who has reported a black female missing for the last twenty years in order to figure out who *she* is."

Darkness had come by the time the coroner Janet Petrosky called. The coroner was an elected position in Lincoln Prairie. Janet was not a physician.

Vik listened, then slammed down the receiver after Janet hung up. "They're not releasing any information until a radiologist from Cook County comes in and looks at the X rays they took of it."

"She, sir, she."

"A dead she. A very dead she. If you're going let it get to you every time—"

"Okay, okay." Lupe grinned. For a moment, she looked like a teenager and made him think of his daughter. "We all know that you never allow yourself to get personally involved in a case, Jessenovik."

"Let's just hope it's the only body we find in there."

"Do you think we've come across a nineteenth-century serial killer? Another Jack the Ripper? Maybe—"

"The building hasn't been there that long, Torres. Years ago, a body was found in the Rialto Theater, but they got the guy."

"The Rialto is the Palace now, right?"

At least this kid knew something. Vik started to tell Lupe about the case, then checked his watch. It was time to go home. Mildred's sister was staying with her while he worked, but even though they were sisters, they didn't get along that well.

"How's your wife?" Lupe asked as they walked to the parking lot.

He wondered why he thought nobody knew. This was a police precinct, after all. Everybody always knew everything.

"She'll be okay."

"I've got a cousin who got MS when she was thirty. She's fifty-seven now. Still hanging in there."

Yup, everyone knew. They even knew what was wrong.

Vik sat by the bedroom window. He hadn't had time to take the Christmas decorations down. The crèche was still up out front, and here, in the backyard, reindeer and Santa in his sleigh were outlined by bright lights. It was dark inside, except for the moonlight, and so quiet that he could hear Mildred's soft, even breathing, interrupted by an occasional gentle snore. Her legs had given way again today. She had fallen down the three steps leading to the basement. Her thigh was bruised and there was a bump on her head, but it could have been worse. She could have fallen down an entire flight of stairs, from the second floor to the first. He would have to get the bed moved downstairs tomorrow. Stephen could come over after work, and Krysta's husband could help him. They would get things moved downstairs. When the weather got warm, he could enlarge the den. No, by then Mildred would be okay. She would be well again long before spring. The MS flared up every three or four years, the medication controlled it, and Mildred was her old self again. It would happen this time, too. Mildred would be just fine, real soon.

He looked about the room. He and his father had made that hope chest at the foot of the bed, drawing the pattern, cutting the wood, assembling and sanding and varnishing it during that long winter before he and Mildred were married. It was so cold that year that Fox Lake froze over and they went skating every Sunday for a month. Mildred, slender and graceful and strong in her red skating outfit—even now he could see her, head back, arms curved like a ballerina, blond hair flowing, spinning and jumping on the ice.

They had so much snow that year. Instead of cutting across the

15

field, he'd had to take the long way to Mildred's house. Mildred and her mother had been working on the wedding ring–pattern quilt that still covered their bed. Such old-fashioned things to do, and not that long ago, only twenty-eight years. One night, just before the wedding, Mildred had been so quiet, so sad. When he asked what was wrong, she began crying. "I won't be with my mother anymore," she said. "My quilt is the last thing we'll ever do together."

"You'll still do lots of things, especially cooking." At least he'd hoped her mother would give her a few more cooking lessons, but he understood what she meant each time he worked on that hope chest with his father. Nowadays, leaving home and getting married was no big deal. When they were younger, Stephen and Krysta couldn't wait to be on their own. Having raised them, after countless disagreements with Mildred and a few good arguments, all that along with MS and the job, he could understand why people were so quick to get divorced. But he could not imagine this room, or this house, or his life, without Mildred. They had slept in this room for over twenty-seven years. The house was small and sometimes they talked about buying something bigger, but they never did. Tomorrow, he and Mildred would move downstairs. Tomorrow night for the first time since their honeymoon, except for vacations, they would not sleep in this room. But it was just temporary. Just until they were sure Mildred could get around without falling. Not having to climb stairs, and having a walker to steady herself, would mean that Mildred could be independent again. She needed that, more than she needed to sleep in this room every night.

Mildred stirred and reached out for him. "Matthew? You're home?"

"I didn't mean to wake you up."

They spoke to each other in Polish, just as they always did.

"I'm glad I'm not alone."

He went over and got in beside her. "I'm right here, *moja serce.*" My heart. He always called her that, but he never would have said it aloud if he had to say it in English. He touched her cheek, warm and flushed with sleep. There was just the beginning of fine lines at the corners of her eyes and mouth from a lifetime of smiling.

"Hold me."

He could tell by the tone of her voice that she wanted more than that.

"You're not feeling well." He stroked her hair, short now and just beginning to gray, but as soft as when she was a girl and it hung long and blond down her back. "The doctor says lots of rest."

"And exercise, Matthew, moderate exercise."

How she loved long walks in the Wisconsin woods. "You fell today."

"Yes, and perhaps I will fall again. And soon it will be a walker, and eventually it will be a wheelchair. But now, tonight, it is none of these. Now, tonight, I am whole."

Now, tonight, she was a girl again, the girl he had crossed that field every night to be with. *"Moja serce,"* he said again. And he held her and loved her against the day when he could not.

2

Marti and Ben returned to Lincoln Prairie the following morning. Vik called the inn a little after seven o'clock. A body had been found in a building on River Street and the lieutenant wanted both of them to handle it. Marti sat on the edge of the bed with the phone in her hand until the dial tone stopped and a recorded message began.

"I'm not ready to go home."

"Me neither." Disappointment was etched in Ben's voice.

"We knew this could happen."

"It's okay."

"No. It's not okay, Ben. We just got married, and we can't even have a week to ourselves." Ben wasn't a cop. He was familiar with her schedule, or the lack of it, but he really hadn't lived with it yet. Three days. So little time to begin a marriage. She turned to him. "What if this is as good as it gets?"

"Look, this isn't totally new to me. Carol and I were both in the army when we first got married." Carol had died in a car accident. And she had gotten out of the army soon after they married, staying at home and raising their son, Mike, until her death.

"But then she stayed at home," Marti reminded him. "I'm not going to do that."

"Look, I'm not even going to come home every day. You're going to have to get used to my being gone two days at a time, maybe three if we're shorthanded."

Marti's first husband had been a narc. They were both on the force in Chicago when he was killed. There were times when he was undercover and she didn't see him that often. She would adjust to Ben's schedule, just as she had adjusted to Johnny's. Would he adjust as easily to hers? Would he understand that she needed to be a cop just as much as he needed to be a fireman and a paramedic?

Ben pulled her down beside him. "This wasn't too bad, lady. I say we try to be grateful."

"I have to go back," she said.

He stroked her hair. "Strange, isn't it? The compulsion. Most people shy away from the dead, at least until they're presentable. Or if you want to see them move really fast, yell 'Fire.' And then there are folks like us. We run toward it."

She kissed him. "Thanks."

It was only a two-and-half-hour drive. Breakfast consisted of sandwiches from a fast-food place. They spent most of the time talking, not about anything important, just odd things—how he felt the first time he suited up for a varsity football game and walked behind the band to the field; her only part in a school play and how she forgot her lines. All memories that would get pushed aside and crowded out by things that were more important, trivial things they might have told each other tomorrow or the day after but that they were trying to cram in now, the small stuff that was the prelude to secrets they had hoarded for years.

As they pulled up across the street from the yellow-brick building, she reached over and squeezed his hand. "I didn't want it to be over so soon. It was like . . ."

"Paradise?" Ben prompted.

"It was good to get away, have some time alone," she said.

"Heavenly, maybe?"

"I thought I would miss the kids more than I did, worry about them, but I didn't."

"We'll have to remember that, make times for ourselves."

"I'm a cop. Even if we do make the time, it will probably end up like this."

"We did have three days," he reminded her. "That was almost as much as we asked for. And I do believe we made every minute count."

"Is half a loaf always going to be enough?"

"That depends on what we consider half a loaf."

Marti looked at the unmarked car, the two squad cars, and the coroner's vehicle parked across the street. Vik had said the victim was male; his family was wealthy and lived in Lake Forest. The first uniform on the scene had said his head had been bashed in. She could feel the adrenaline pumping. "I've gotten spoiled since I've been here, Ben. This is my homicide, and I get to work the whole case. I'm not sharing it with teams on two other shifts, and Vik was right to call me. I would have felt cheated if I'd missed anything."

"That's because you're a good cop."

"That's me, a good cop, a good mother . . ."

"And now a good wife?"

She sighed.

"I intend to make sure that the wife part is the easiest."

"I love you," she said.

"Me too."

Marti got her camera bag out of the trunk and waved as Ben pulled away from the curb. She paused outside the building, which took up half a block and fronted on two streets. Nobody had shoveled the snow, but a path had been trampled down. *Merchants Hall, 1925* was chiseled in the cornerstone of the arched doorway. Storefronts were lined up on either side. Most of them were empty. Downtown Lincoln Prairie had completed the transition from thriving to "Let's go to the mall." There were no onlookers. A uniform was just inside the door. Marti went in out of the cold.

"Beautiful," she said, noting the elaborate plasterwork on the walls, the tarnished brass sconces that must once have burned gas. She loved these old buildings. "Where's Jessenovik?"

"Downstairs, ma'am."

The heels of her boots clicked against the marble floor. She pushed open a double door and walked down a wide oak staircase with carved handrails, wondering why a building this solid hadn't been torn down. Then she smiled. That sounded just like something Vik would say. The stairs led to one big room filled with all kinds of junk. As her eyes adjusted to the darkness, she identified a path of sorts. There was nobody here. She went toward the sound of voices and located a rear door and more stairs. She paused a moment to get oriented. The back of the building faced the ravine where the Lincoln Prairie River, which was little more than a stream, flowed east to Lake Michigan. Instead of constructing this building on steel girders, the way two buildings on Geneva had been constructed, they had built from the ravine up, which meant there was more than one floor below street level. Walking down the narrow flights of stairs was like going to a dungeon. She got out her flashlight. Bright lights two flights down told her she had reached the scene of the crime. That and Vik's voice. She smiled as she saw his craggy face in profile, prominent salt-and-pepper eyebrows, wiry and thick, nose skewed from a break when he was kid. He needed a haircut. His hair had a tendency to unruliness even when it was cut short. This morning, it looked as if he hadn't combed it yet. His scowl was fierce and habitual. He seldom smiled. Tall and thin, shoulders hunched, he had assumed what she called his "vulture position" as he waited for Dr. Cyprian to finish up with the body. She had missed him. Be damned.

Dr. Cyprian was kneeling beside the body. All Marti could see were brown sandals at least two sizes bigger than the victim's feet, faded jeans, and an olive drab coat that didn't look warm enough for the weather.

Vik turned toward her. "You're back!"

She wasn't sure if the relief in his voice was caused by the interruption of her honeymoon or the fact that he wouldn't have to work a homicide with Lupe. Although Torres was a good cop, Marti and Vik were a team.

"What have we got?" she asked.

"Barnabas Cheney, age sixty-seven," Vik said. "His family owns this building. They used to own a lot of the buildings around here. They got rid of the rest of them before property values began falling, kept this one, for some reason."

Marti glanced around. The room they were standing in consisted of one wall and three sheets rigged to the ceiling beams. A small microwave was on a stack of books, and two mattresses were stacked on the floor. A small electric heater was turned off. A pair of blue canvas shoes that looked wet were lined up in front of it. Had the heater been on before the man died? Had he turned it off? Why? A cardboard box held a jar of instant coffee and several cups with dried coffee at the bottom. Clothes had been tossed into boxes and were in a heap on the floor. Notebooks were stacked on a desk, along with a supply of pens and pencils, an open Bible, and a plastic bag with three kaiser rolls. Beside the desk, a bookcase held dozens of books, mostly paperbacks. A floor lamp was plugged into an extension cord and provided enough light to read by. A chair had been knocked over. Based on the position of the body, Marti guessed that the man had been sitting there.

"The weapon, I bet," Vik said, pointing to an old-fashioned iron-based lamp that was on the floor.

"Looks heavy enough," she agreed. Vik had not been allowed into the area yet, and Cyprian, who seldom had much to say, hadn't reached a point where he was ready to talk.

"There's dried blood on it," Vik said. "According to the uniform who called it in."

"Reaching, aren't you?" Marti teased. "This might turn out to be accidental."

"How do you figure that?"

"Well, he's got his coat on, Jessenovik. And this concrete floor—he could have slipped and hit his head."

"After he took off his shoes? And on a lamp that just happened to be on the floor?"

"Only if it's dried blood and not rust. He could have tripped over his sandals."

"Marti, someone bashed his head in."

"Right. You couldn't wait to call me, Vik, admit it."

A flush crept up the back of his neck. "The victim is well connected. As soon as the lieutenant knew that—"

"Don't try to explain. I get it."

Another twenty minutes passed before Dr. Cyprian relinquished the body.

"The blow caught him on the side of the head, left temple."

"That's it?" Vik said.

"Yes. I cannot give you any indication of time of death. The body is in full rigor, and lividity indicates that the body has not been moved. There is a cold draft near the floor, which is also cold and could prolong rigor. Stomach contents will tell us something perhaps. We shall see."

"But it was a blunt instrument," Vik said. "That lamp."

"You will have to wait for the reports, but yes, there is a dent in his head that should match up quite nicely with the base of that lamp."

"Jeez, the man was real talkative for once," Vik said as Cyprian went upstairs. "I couldn't get anything out of him yesterday."

"A wedding gift," Cyprian called down.

"Yesterday?" Marti said.

"We found a mummy in the old Geneva Theater."

"A mummy!" The Geneva was part of a building five blocks north that along with the Merchants building to the south formed the boundaries of what Vik called "downtown." "I remember someone finding a mummy while I was on the job in Chicago. It didn't turn out to be a homicide, though. An undertaker fell in love with one of his clients and hung him in his closet."

"Jeez, Marti, is there anything that hasn't happened in the big city? Maybe we'll get lucky and this one won't be a homicide, either."

"What did Dr. Cyprian say?"

"Nothing. Not until a radiologist from the Stine Institute gets here from Chicago to take a look at the X rays—somebody who works with the forensic anthropologist they bring in from Iowa."

"I'd rather have a cautious Cyprian than inaccurate information and a wild-goose chase. That mortician in Chicago lied his butt off before he got around to telling the truth."

Marti took out her camera and checked to see how many exposures she had left. She would finish off this roll of color film, the one with the pictures of the geese by the lake and Ben standing beneath a fir tree and she and Ben by the fireplace, taken by the waiter who brought room service. She shot around the victim until that roll of film was used up.

After she finished taking pictures, she knelt beside the body. An unwashed odor, the sour smell of perspiration, was stronger than the smell of feces and urine. He needed a shave. There was a small small scar shaped like a half-moon between his eyebrows, a scar that had faded until it was almost the color of his skin. An injury incurred a long time ago, a childhood injury perhaps. He had dirt in the creases in his neck, and a wax buildup in his left ear. The whole left side of his skull was caved in. He had been hit by someone using their left hand. Cheney.

"Do you know the family, Jessenovik?"

"No, they stayed in Lake Forest, just owned property here."

"Who found him?"

"Someone called it in from a pay phone in Milwaukee."

"That's different."

"I know," Vik said. "It seems strange that anyone would come down here to visit. Maybe whoever did it wanted us to find the body."

"Well, normal rigor begins in about two hours, is complete within another two to six hours, and lasts twenty-four hours. . . ."

"Given ideal conditions."

"If we ignore things like heat and cold, that means four to twenty-four hours. Maybe we have a witness. What time did we get the the call?"

"A little before six."

Vik had taken the time to make sure it wasn't someone's idea of a joke before calling Marti.

"So, it's Wednesday. This happened maybe early yesterday morning, or sometime Monday night."

"Maybe," Vik said, cautious, as usual. "It's cold down here, slows decomposition."

After the body was removed, they went through the boxes of clothing. Most of it was dirty; all of it smelled. There were seven notebooks. The pages had something written on them, but the handwriting looked like Sanskrit with a few words in English here and there. Nothing made any sense. The Bibles, ten in all, were dog-eared, with loose pages. Those that were inscribed had family names other than Cheney. When they explored beyond the perimeters of the room, they found a bathroom with toilet, sink, and shower, but little else. Unlike the upper level, there wasn't much more down here than dust, mice, and cobwebs. The building was well constructed, dry, with a closed-in smell but no mold or mildew odor.

"And he has family still living," Marti said.

"There are a few of them still around."

The Merchants building fronted River Street and Geneva. The second floor was vacant, as were most of the storefronts.

Vik pointed to one with the windows boarded up. "That used to be the Greyhound bus station."

Two of the storefronts were occupied. The antiques store had a BACK AT sign in the window, with the hands on the clock pointing to 1:00 P.M. Aunt Lindy's Jesus Mercy Resale Clothing Store was open for business. Sweaters and children's clothing were folded and stacked on tables; coats, dresses, blouses, and jackets hung on racks, and an assortment of hats and purses were on the shelves that lined one wall.

An elderly woman greeted them. Before they could ask any questions she explained that she hadn't arrived until after the uniformed cops were there. She was a short, skinny woman with a potbelly. Her kinky gray hair was cut in a short Afro and her dark skin was smooth as a child's even though, Marti was certain, she was at least seventy-five. She was dressed as if she was going to church—thick stockings, low heels, dark blue suit, frilly blouse, and a small hat that she had taken off but was still holding in her hand.

"Are you Aunt Lindy, ma'am?" Vik asked.

"Yes, and I thought I was about to faint when I got off the bus and saw that police car. I thought someone musta broken in here. Although Lord knows, if they did, I sure wouldn't begrudge them nothing they took. We got so many homeless people wandering around town, you can't help but worry if they're warm when the weather gets this cold." She cocked her head to one side and looked up at them. "Hard to believe you're here just 'cause old Barnabas is dead, even if his people is rich white folks."

"Did you know him?" Vik asked.

"Course I did. Strange him just dying like this. I ain't never known him to be sick. Musta been a heart attack or something."

"When's the last time you saw him?"

"He come in here once in awhile during the summer. Don't see him none this time of year." She folded her arms, careful not to crush her hat. "Did you say you were detectives? Ain't never known a detective to come 'cause a man dies of a heart attack."

"We handle all death investigations, ma'am," Vik said. "That includes anyone who hasn't been in the hospital for twenty-four hours before they depart."

"Well, I'm glad you got no other reason for being here." It was more a question than a statement.

Aunt Lindy reminded Marti of one of the church mothers she'd grown up with, nosy and into everyone's business. She wasn't even tempted to tell the old woman what she was trying to find out. "Can you remember the last time you saw him, ma'am?" she asked.

"Mostly, old Barnabas kept to himself. He was hardly ever around here, and I didn't usually see him when he was. If he needed something, he hadn't got to do no more than walk to the bank on the corner of Jefferson. Didn't see him hardly none at all; won't be seeing him no more. It's a shame about that. Don't know of nobody in his family with no heart trouble." She looked about the room, then sat in a chair and put her hat on her lap. "I think his people just didn't want this place empty with him here. They needed someplace for him to stay. And of course, old Barnabas, he knew me. Wasn't like him to say nothing to strangers. I think they was worried he'd be here and take sick or need something and not have nobody to ask for help. The old man let me rent dirt cheap, and Jeremiah never upped it. I suppose with Barnabas dead, they won't have no reason to keep it. They done sold just about all the other property they had around here." ·

"How long have you been here?" Marti asked.

"Oh, it's been seventeen, eighteen years now, ever since I retired. Course with this talk of bringing this part of town back, maybe they'll hold on to this awhile longer, just in case they can get some money out of it."

"Do you see much of the Cheneys?" Marti asked.

"No. Not since the old man died and Jeremiah moved to Florida. Ain't nobody left in these parts but the grandchildren and the great-grands, and they ain't too close by."

"You seem to know the family pretty well."

"Worked for them thirty-five years before I started this. I was the laundress. Full-time job, too, just keeping up with their dirty sheets and underwear. Never did see folks what had to have their bed linens and blankets changed every day, and those mile-long tableclothes, as well."

"How well did you know Barnabas?"

"Knew him before he got real crazy in the head, but he never was quite right. Laughing and talking to himself before he was out of grade school, and sitting and staring off for hours at a time. Course nobody didn't want to see that something was the matter. His momma was a little strange herself, if you ask me. She was the one what had to have everything washed all the time. She got to stay home and act silly right up until she got sick and died. They shut Barnabas up someplace for awhile. Not here. Sent him to Europe to one of them fancy crazy houses. A sanatorium. The way they said it was like I would say *hotel* or *vacation*. It wasn't until the old man got sick that they let him out. He wouldn't never harm nobody. He just wasn't right in the head."

"Did you ever see him with anyone?"

She chuckled. "Old Barnabas didn't need nobody besides himself to make conversation. Couldn't hardly follow what you were saying when you did talk to him, and as likely to walk away or burst out singing or praying or laughing as to answer you. I will say one thing for Barnabas, though. He could quote you the Bible a good ten or fifteen minutes before he stopped making sense. He ran them Jehovah's Witnesses right from around here. I ain't seen nary a one in five, six years now."

"How did he get along with his family?"

"Barnabas always been in his own world, never had much to do with nobody. Couldn't tell the old man that something was wrong with him, though, at least not until Barnabas got real bad about bathing and changing his clothes and talking to himself and answering back, and got to keeping everybody up all hours of the night with his preaching and clapping and singing. The old man was his daddy, after all. Once Barnabas got be a nuisance, even he had to agree to him being put away."

"And his brother?" Vik said.

"It wasn't like him and Jeremiah was close, born eight years apart and all. Jeremiah was the youngest, so most of what would have gone to Barnabas went to Jeremiah instead; plus, he got to be in charge when the old man got sick. He couldn't have felt too bad about that."

Marti wondered what Barnabas had gotten from the old man. Someone had cared enough about him to see that he was in a safe place with someone familiar nearby.

"Everything in this part of town is commercial," Vik said as they went outside. "I had a couple of uniforms go to both grocery stores and the bars and whatever else was open, just in case Cheney went there. I told them to check on deliveries, too. Maybe a truck driver passing through early saw something. They haven't come up with anything. There's nothing else here but the public-aid office and the Salvation Army store. Cheney didn't need to go to either place."

Marti pulled her hat over her ears and wrapped her scarf around most of her face. There wasn't much wind, but they were close enough to the lake to feel its icy effects.

There was an entrance to the Merchants building on the corner of Geneva, but that only accessed the first and second floors. Cheney would have had to use the River Street entrance to get downstairs. A bridge on Geneva spanned the ravine. There was a vacant lot beside the River Street side of the building, and a parking lot across the street. Nobody was hanging around waiting to talk with them, but they found half a dozen vagrants in the immediate vicinity. They spoke to the man sitting in a doorway first. He gave them a blank stare and spat into a cup a few times. The next man muttered something unintelligible and appeared to be drunk. Marti jotted down their descriptions while Vik tried for a name. Each man was his own little island, either not interested or not able to rejoin the rest of the world, at least not today.

"We'll have to come back with a morgue shot and show it to these guys, if they're still here," Marti said. She didn't think they would have much luck when they did. By the time they got into the car, her nose felt frostbitten and her feet, despite boots and two pairs of socks, were cold, and she was dressed more warmly than those they had spoken to.

The antiques dealer still had not opened his store. Marti and Vik checked out the owner's home. It was a white-framed duplex two blocks away. There was no answer when they rang the bell.

"No garage, no car parked outside," Vik said.

They swung by the store again. There was still no sign of Armstrong, the owner.

"Maybe someone offed him, too," Vik said.

"We don't have probable cause to go in."

"Yet," Vik said, rubbing his hands together. "We'd better notify Cheney's family. Either they are going to want to keep the whole thing quiet or they're going to to want the perp apprehended yesterday. Either way, this case is going to be political."

"Piece of cake," Marti said. In Lincoln Prairie, "political" covered everything from *The Social Register* to ethnic and religious groups to politicians and their friends and relatives. There was no machine, just numerous individual and organizational wanna-be's. "Where to?"

Vik pulled out his notebook. "We can take Sherman Avenue. I've got a proper east Lake Forest address."

East. Old money. According to Vik, people with new money lived on the west side of town.

The Cheney estate took up half a city block. Surveillance cameras were mounted at the entrance. The gates were open, the gatehouse empty. They drove through a forest of oak trees for several minutes before the Georgian mansion came into view.

"They've sold off most of the property," Vik said.

"Don't tell me," Marti said. "The family fell on hard times."

"A wealthy person's equivalent to hard times."

A maid, complete with black dress, white apron, and frilly cap opened the door. She spoke with an accent—Irish maybe, or French.

She admitted them to the foyer. It was dark inside, and not just because the lights were out and the curtains drawn. The paneling was dark and the wallpaper a dull flocked gold; Oriental runners covered the hardwood floor.

"You did not call before coming," the maid said. "I will have to find out if someone can see you." There was bench in the hallway near the staircase. She motioned them there.

"I guess coppers don't qualify for the parlor," Vik said.

Marti tried not to stare at a light fixture. "That's just green glass, right?"

"No. It's real jade. I forget the story, but there is one."

"Jade light fixtures in the foyer?"

"Old man Cheney, the grandfather, was loaded, something to do with railroads and the old stockyards."

The man who came down the stairs was tall and blond. Marti

guessed that he was in his mid-thirties. He bore no resemblance to the dead man.

"Jonathan Cheney," he said without extending his hand. "What do you want?"

"Are you related to Barnabas Cheney?" Vik asked.

"He's my uncle."

"Well, I'm very sorry to have to tell you this, but your uncle is dead."

There was no reaction.

"He was found dead this morning."

Cheney blinked.

"In the subbasement of the Merchants Hall."

"I see."

"He didn't die of natural causes."

With that, Jonathan Cheney raised his eyebrows.

"When is the last time you saw your uncle?" Vik asked.

"Oh, but I haven't. Not in years. When I was a boy. I couldn't even tell you what he looked like now."

According to Jonathan Cheney, he lived on the family estate with his wife and two children. His sister lived in Winnetka, another North Shore bastion of the wealthy. She was vacationing in California. His father, Jeremiah Cheney, had retired with his second wife to Florida. Jonathan's mother was deceased.

"When is the last time any member of the family saw him?"

"I couldn't tell you that absolutely, but I'm certain that no one has, not for a long while."

"Was there any particular reason for that?"

"Of course. Uncle Barnabas was crazy."

"Makes sense to me," Vik said as they walked to the car. "Everyone knows that there are no crazy people in Lake Forest. They export them all to Lincoln Prairie. What would the neighbors think if they saw Uncle Barnabas out wandering around? When was it when they stopped locking them up in the nuthouse, the early eighties?"

Marti got behind the wheel. "Let's wait until we see if crazy

31

Uncle Barnabas has any insurance policies, bequests, trust funds, or other assets and find out who the beneficiary is. These large estates aren't always what they appear to be. Old plumbing, old heating systems, wiring that doesn't meet code. I wouldn't want to have the upkeep on that house." She turned the key in the ignition. "If someone felt the need to keep up appearances and there was this well-endowed loony old uncle . . . who knows?"

Marti drove slowly along the streets of Lake Forest. As she passed wide snow-covered expanses of land and tall snow-laden fir trees, she thought of Wisconsin and felt sad. "Anything else happen while I was gone?"

"It was only three days," Vik said. "Nothing much, unless you count the alderman who got a speeding ticket and wasn't wearing his seat belt. That and the mummy. Slim and Cowboy were in court all day yesterday with one of their bigger cases, a john with a preference for male hookers under seventeen. They used one of the sheriff's men as bait."

"What do we know about the mummy?"

"Not much. Black female, that's about it."

"Anything in the personal effects to determine how long she could have been there?"

"Not that I could tell, but this can't be anything recent. The theater's been closed up tight as a drum for years."

"But it's part of a building that takes up an entire block, with occupants—businesses, a restaurant, apartments. Maybe someone figured out how to get in."

"We had a team in yesterday and we've got another one in there today. Nobody has come up with anything, no more mummies, no secret entrances, no break-ins, nothing but mice and dust."

"So let's hope it was an isolated incident. How carefully did you check the missing persons reports?"

"We can go back twenty years on microfiche. Lupe sent for hard copies of what they had. We've got five years on the database. There wasn't much that applied."

"It would be nice to know the age of the woman, how she died, and time of death." Marti braked at a stop sign. "They can find out some things from X rays, and they can use the amino acids in the teeth to estimate age—that's about all I remember from the case in Chicago."

"We came up with twenty names, eliminated seven by making a phone call, couldn't locate anyone else. It might not be a long list, but we could be looking at a lot of legwork if we have to start checking them out."

"I'm going to take a look at what we've got when we get back. I want to take a look at the mummy, and the theater, too. Can we still get in?"

"I've got a phone number if the search teams are through."

She turned north on Green Bay Road. "Maybe it's something that happened way back, the thirties or something, whenever the theater first opened up."

"The lieutenant said the same thing."

"The Geneva. Is it built anything like the Merchants Hall?"

Vik snickered. "The Geneva makes the Merchants building look like a dump."

Marti thought of something she had read in the newspaper a few months back. "Isn't the Geneva the theater where some woman was found dead years ago?"

"No, that was the old Rialto. The guy who did it is still in jail."

Now she remembered the gist of the article. "No, he's not. It was in the News-Times around Thanksgiving. Some kind of human-interest story. The guy is out on parole. He's staying at that transitional housing facility where Isaac the Wino is."

Marti slowed as she approached the bridge just before West-leigh Road, then stopped for a red light. She wanted to ask Vik about his wife, Mildred, but when she'd mentioned her on the way here, he had seemed reluctant to talk. Instead, she said, "It's hard to believe those old buildings on Geneva are still standing."

"I thought they would raze the Merchants building when they had the fire in the bowling alley," Vik agreed.

"Bowling alley?"

"Yes, just below street level. When you reach the bottom of that big flight of stairs."

"That room where the junk is?"

"Next time we go in, I'll show you. The walls on one side are still black from the smoke."

"And you bowled there, I suppose."

"Everyone did."

They drove in silence until she came to a Dunkin Donuts. "Coffee?" she asked. Vik nodded.

She went to the drive-up, ordered jelly-filled doughnuts for Vik and a couple with chocolate icing for herself, then pulled into a parking space. "So, how's Mildred?" she asked when the coffee had cooled.

"Not good."

She waited. He ate his doughnuts. "She went to the doctor yesterday. The medication isn't working. Not yet anyway. I've got to move her downstairs, and convince her to use a walker. Sometimes her legs just give out from under her."

Marti was convinced that anyone who had put up with Vik for twenty-seven years deserved an award, not multiple sclerosis, but she had talked with Mildred often enough to know she was content. "Does she need someone to stay with her?"

"Her sister comes over."

"I thought they didn't get along."

He finished his coffee and crushed the Styrofoam cup before opening the window and tossing it in the nearest trash receptacle. "I thought so, too, but I'm beginning to think they enjoy disagreeing, or maybe they've just gotten used to it. Saturday night, they agreed that they didn't like one of those talk shows, so they switched to a game show, and two minutes later they were arguing about that." He stared straight ahead. "I guess it's time we went back and talked with that antiques dealer. Funny his place wasn't open. It's not like he'd make appointments with the customers."

"Business in that part of town can't be that good," Marti agreed. "Maybe discovering a mummy will generate a little interest."

34

"I'm sure it will," Vik said. "But I think it will be more like notoriety than fame."

"A mummy—who would have thought? I bet everyone in the precinct volunteered to search the building."

"No, but at least half the department has gone to the morgue."

"Remember when we found that skeleton awhile back? Everyone thought they knew who it was. It turned out to be an Indian-American."

"Damned shame this isn't," Vik said. "This is just another reason for everyone to stay away from that part of town." He sounded sad.

3

The antiques store was open for business when Marti pulled up in front. The sun hadn't managed to break through the cloud cover all day and now it was beginning to get dark.

"I wonder if this gentleman—" Vik said.

"Mr. Armstrong."

"Yeah, maybe Armstrong can tell us what Cheney had in that place. There has to be a reason why he's dead, and greed is as good a motive as any."

"We saw what he had when we got there."

"Not a hell of a lot."

"And the place has been secured since we found the body, so nothing has gone missing since then." It was difficult to think of Cheney as anything but a reclusive old man without friends. The house with jade light fixtures was light-years away. "From the looks of it, he wasn't interested in things other people would consider valuable."

"Maybe our Mr. Armstrong will know. After all, he is an antiques dealer."

"If we find any antiques in that subbasement, Vik, I'll bet Armstrong will be just as surprised as we are."

Mr. Armstrong had so much furniture jammed into the large storefront that the front door didn't open all the way.

"If he gives us a hard time, I'm going to threaten him with the fire marshal," Vik said. Books, vases, statues, dishes, and lamps covered every available surface. Everything was covered with dust.

"Yes, yes, come in." Armstrong negotiated a jagged aisle with armoires and desks on either side. He was of medium height, slender, with horn-rimmed glasses and a hearing aid. The expression on his face went from anticipation to dismay as he came closer. "Cops! You're going to scare my customers away. Someone just died in this building. You're endangering the curiosity seekers. Nobody likes cops."

Vik sneezed twice and blew his nose. "We thought you might know if Mr. Cheney had anything valuable down there. With all of this stuff you've got here—"

"Antiques," Armstrong corrected. "And collectables." He fussed with a large silver cuff link with an onyx stone.

Vik sneezed again. His eyes were beginning to water.

"Whatever, Mr. Armstrong. In any case, you've got access to the basement and lots of old ju— stuff down there. . . ."

"Antiques."

"And you've got this weird old guy way down in the second subbasement, who is also the rich owner's son. Now it makes sense to me that you would be just a little bit curious about this guy, that's all, maybe just take a look at what he kept in his room."

Mr. Armstrong squared his shoulders. "I am a reputable dealer."

"I'm not saying you'd steal from him."

"Well, you certainly seem to be implying that."

"Look, Mr. Armstrong. Try to see this from our point of view. You've got a basement full of junk—"

"Anti—"

"I know, I know. But you must have been curious. Everyone is."

"We need to know what was in that room, and if it's still there," Marti said. "Even if it looked worthless to you."

"Well, the meters are down where he was," Armstrong said, hedging. "Water, electric, gas. So sometimes I've got to go down there with a meter reader. And sometimes the curtains weren't closed, but I never saw anything in there that was worth anything."

"So," Vik said, "if you went down there with us now, you might be able to tell if something was missing?"

"Uh . . ."

"Right, Mr. Armstrong?"

"Yes. I think I could. Maybe."

He followed Vik down the three flights of stairs. Marti brought up the rear.

Armstrong paused when they reached the curtained-off area, then went in. He drew back when he saw the dark circle of congealed blood, then looked at the desk and gasped. "The watch. It can't be gone. He did have a watch on him, didn't he?"

"Describe it," Vik said.

"A fob watch, his grandfather's, made in Switzerland, real gold, told time to the second for over a hundred years. It was beautiful." He stepped over the uneven circle of blood and walked to the desk. "He always kept it right here, with the case open. He did have it with him, didn't he? Or the family has it?"

Vik didn't answer.

"We'll check it out," Marti said. "Is there anything else?"

"No," Armstrong said. He looked around and paused very slightly when he came to the microwave. "No, there's nothing else."

"Mr. Armstrong . . ." Vik said as he turned away.

"What?"

"I need to know where you were last night and this morning."

"I had some errands to run."

"And you won't mind telling us where."

Armstrong ran his fingers through his hair. "Last night, I was home alone."

"What did you do?"

Vik took notes as Armstrong described his evening. "And today, sir?"

"I looked at some goods for the store."

"We'll need to know where."

"Look, these are people who sell to me. You go around asking questions, and they'll start wondering if I'm legit."

"It might not come to that, sir."

Armstrong gave them three names and addresses. "Is that all?"

"For now."

"It's a damned shame when a citizen doesn't even have the right to privacy. This country is going to hell in a handbasket. The state has too much power," Armstrong declared, and walked away.

Vik shrugged. "It sounds like he really wanted that watch," he said without waiting until Armstrong was out of hearing range. "Not that that it had to be the only thing of value down here, just the most valuable, at least to him. It would be nice to know where the watch is."

He gave Armstrong time to get upstairs, then said, "I can't tell if he's upset about the watch or whatever was on that microwave. Something was there, that's for sure."

"Maybe he has it and he's afraid we'll find out," Marti said. "Not that I know how we'll ever figure out what it is. We'll have to talk with Jonathan Cheney again."

"If Armstrong did do it, and he can't fake an alibi, maybe that will give him enough reason to tell us."

"Meanwhile, we can have the locals rounded up and brought in," Marti said. "Maybe we'll get lucky and one of them will have the watch."

Vik gave her a look that suggested she must be joking. "No vacations and ski resorts here, MacAlister; it's business as usual."

It was the first reference he had made to her marriage since he'd interrupted her honeymoon. He hadn't called Ben by name since they became engaged. If they hadn't decided against having someone give her away, she would have had to ask him at the last minute. Her brother had been snowed in in Colorado. When she told him that at the reception, he didn't answer. He did shake Ben's hand after the ceremony, but did not add one word of congratulations. Maybe this meant he was adjusting.

Marti made a quick call home to let Ben know she would be working late, then had the men they had spoken with on the street rounded up and brought in. This time, when they talked with them, they had a morgue photo of Cheney. Two were too drunk to respond to anything. The man who had stared at them and spit into a cup became stressed and kept saying, "Thy word is a lamp unto my feet and a light unto my path." Only one gave any indication that he recognized Cheney. He gave his name as Edward Logan.

"You know him, Mr. Logan?" Marti asked.

Logan shook his head. "Seen him, that's all."

"Where have you seen him?"

"Train station."

"The train station?"

"Yeah. I'd rather ride freight trains myself."

"The Metro station at the end of Jefferson Street?"

"Yes, ma'am."

"When's the last time you saw him there?"

The man scratched his beard, "Warm. It was warm. Musta been summer, I guess."

"What about since it's gotten cold?"

"Don't see him none now. He don't be where I go."

Cheney didn't need soup kitchens or warming places or shelters. "You haven't seen him at all?"

"Don't go down by the train station in the winter. Too cold. They don't let you come in."

"Where do you live?" Marti asked.

"Around."

"We're going to detain you for a couple of hours."

"I already missed supper. Won't have no place to sleep if I don't get to the shelter by eight."

"We'll make sure you have a place to stay."

"I ain't no criminal. Ain't done nothin' wrong. Don't want to be having no record for having to sleep in jail when there ain't no need to."

"If you didn't do anything, you don't have anything to worry about."

Marti offered him a choice of fast food, then sent out for pizza.

"They probably feed them better at the shelter, if what Mildred donates is any indication," Vik said. "Hope you got him one with three toppings."

Vik dispatched a uniform to the train station with a morgue shot and instructions to see that everyone who worked there as well as all employees who came through on the trains took a look at it.

"Maybe we've missed someone," Marti said. "Let's talk with the beat cop." They called in the request and met with him in the parking lot across from the Merchants building. Marti rolled down her window. The uniform rolled down the window of his squad car. He was an older cop, beginning to gray at the temples. She recognized him from previous cases she had worked in the area, which meant he'd been on this beat for a while.

"These are the guys we talked with," she said. As she read off the names, the beat cop nodded. "A watch that belonged to the victim seems to be missing. Nobody knew anything about it. Can you tell us if we're missing someone who usually hangs out here?"

"It's hard to say, MacAlister. Second shift is when most of them are trying to find food and shelter for the night. They keep track of which church is serving food and where the beds are. When the weather is bad, like now, I circle around looking for strays, someone new in town, the ones who get obnoxious and get put out, and the drunks and addicts—they're the most at risk for hypothermia if we don't get them into a cell or a hospital bed. Off the top of my head, everyone was present and accounted for last night and the night before."

"You would have noticed if someone wasn't?"

"I would have noticed if it was someone I see most of the time. I ask around if someone's missing, just in case they've gotten too drunk or too high or too crazy to get in out of the cold. This is a designated community policing area. We pay a lot of attention to the resident transients. With those who are just passing through, it's different. I can help them, but it's not like I'll get to know them."

"What about Edward Logan?"

"Ed? Damned shame about him. He's okay except for the paranoia. Just doesn't trust nobody. He lived with his grandmother until she died last year. Now nobody in the family will take him in."

"We're holding him."

"Why?"

"He recognized Cheney."

"The man's got no priors, MacAlister. He's just got some kind of chemical screwup in his brain."

"I hate to remind you of this," Vik said, "but people we think of as normal lose it and kill people sometimes. We haven't caught him yet. That doesn't mean he hasn't done anything."

"I feel pretty sure about Ed."

"Somebody felt sure about John Wayne Gacy."

"Can you let him go on my say-so?"

"Can you still get him into a shelter tonight?" Marti asked. He was persistent.

"No problem. And thanks."

As they pulled away, Vik said, "That man is a social worker. This isn't community policing; it's community baby-sitting. What we need out here are cops."

"What we've got here, Jessenovik, is a whole population of people with no place to go. We don't have places for people like Logan anymore. Somebody decided it was cheaper to let them roam the streets, and now somebody's got to keep a handle on it. Guess who?"

Ed Logan was late getting to the shelter, but nobody had taken his spot. He pulled his mat over to the corner, got his blanket out of his backpack, and sat with his back against the wall so that he could see if anyone came toward him. He could find someplace to sleep during the daytime; night was when Satan came out. He never slept when it was dark unless the angel came.

Why were the cops asking him about Dancing Man? He hadn't hurt Dancing Man, too, had he? If he could just remember stuff better. He had seen him at the train station, and he knew for sure that it was summer, just like he told them, but there was that night when Satan got into the church and sat right on the edge of his mat and he had to sneak out through the bathroom window and sneak back in toward morning. What night was that? Had Satan got hold of him again that night? Was it the night he had seen Dancing Man going round that building casting devil spells? Was it cold when he saw him? Was there snow? All he could remember was his feet being cold. The pain in his head started up again. He squeezed his eyes shut as pain spread from the back of his neck to his temples. His arms felt numb. When everything got blurry, he saw the angel guarding the door. It would be safe to sleep tonight, if the pain went away.

Lt. Dan Dirkowitz was waiting in their office when they got back to the precinct. He had his feet on Vik's desk and was sipping a cup of Cowboy's coffee.

"What have you got on the Cheney case?" he asked. The lieutenant had earned the nickname "Dirty Dirk" while playing linebacker for the Salukis of Southern Illinois University. Whatever that meant in relationship to the way he played the game, he insisted on fair play here. All of their written reports went to his desk. Beyond that and weekly briefings, he seldom requested a meeting unless the case was political or of personal interest or concern. He rarely came to them.

Vik gave him a rundown.

When he was finished, the lieutenant said, "I'm getting phone calls from a few people, including the governor and a senator. It looks like we've got a member of the family yanking strings. Let me know if anyone interferes, blocks, obstructs, or otherwise gets in your way. If they're uncooperative, do your job. I don't just want this case closed; I want it solved."

Before going home, they stopped by the addresses Armstrong had given them and confirmed that he had been at two of the three places, though he had shown up at both a little later than he'd said.

The woman he was to have seen first, Mrs. Stazlowski, was on her way out when they arrived at her apartment building. Her blond hair was pulled back in a chignon, and she was wearing a full-length mink coat.

"No, he didn't show up," she said. "Not that that surprised me. I've met dealers like him before."

A car pulled up and man got out and held open the door on the passenger side.

"She's definitely out of Armstrong's league," Vik said as she hurried toward the car. "And he missed his appointment with her. Let's have another talk with him."

The lights were on in Armstrong's side of the duplex. There was a dead bolt and a strike bar but no chain on the door.

"We need to talk with you about your appointment with . . ." Vik consulted his notes. "With a Mrs. Stazlowski to look at some lamps."

Armstrong ran his fingers through his hair. "Yes. Well, I . . . it's garbage pickup day in Highland Park. I went there instead. They throw out some good stuff sometimes. I found two tables and brought them back. By then, it was too late to see Mrs. Stazlowski. I called and made another appointment."

"And where are these two tables, sir?" Vik asked.

"Upstairs."

"Why didn't you take them to the store?"

"Oh, I . . . um . . . a lady was looking for some the other day. I thought I'd clean them up. . . ."

"Mind if we take a look?"

"No, no." He ran his fingers through his hair again. "Come up, come up. Place is a mess. Always is. No time . . . I don't have time to clean up."

The place was a mess, at least what Marti could see of it. Sofas and chairs pushed against the wall, tables and dressers stacked on one another, small appliances. And portable televisions, CD players, and VCRs.

"What are doing you with all of this electronic stuff?" Vik asked.

"I . . . I . . . just fix it and sell it."

44

"Where do you get it?"

"Oh, out of the trash, and people sell it to me cheap."

"I don't recall seeing any merchandise like that in your store."

"Oh, I sell it from here. People know me."

"Look, Mr. Armstrong, this looks suspicious to me," Vik said. "I hope you understand, sir. I'm going to have to have someone come in here and check these against our theft and burglary reports."

"But, but . . . I'm a respectable businessman. How am I to know if something is stolen?"

"You'll have to sort that out with Theft Division, sir. We're here to talk with you about a homicide. Now, where are those tables?"

"Here, here. They're up here."

They followed him to an upstairs bedroom. A path had been cleared in the center of the room and an unmade bed was by the window. The rest of the space was taken up with odds and ends of furniture. Armstrong pointed to two square coffee tables stacked one atop the other. Marti reached up and wiped her finger across the top one and came away with dust.

"It looks like these have been here for a while, sir," Vik said. He opened one of the drawers. "And see, it's dry. There's too much snow out there for these to have been picked up today." He open the drawer to the other one. "Did the lady want to buy these copies of *Playboy*, too?"

"I . . . I . . . I overslept. I was up late last night repairing some televisions."

"Oh, and where are they?"

"I . . . I . . . I want a lawyer. I'm not saying anything else."

"But we haven't charged you with anything, sir."

"But you're insinuating."

"No, sir. We're asking a few logical questions. There are things here that need explaining."

"Well, I'm not explaining anything else until I talk to a lawyer."

They waited until the team from Theft arrived and identified enough stolen goods to take Armstrong in for questioning.

"Hold him as long as you can," Marti said. Sometimes being in jail encouraged people to be creative about getting out. Armstrong could be looking at less time for manslaughter than for theft. Closing the Cheney case without too much of a public display would make the lieutenant happy, too. If they could just identify what had been on that microwave. With all of the junk in this place, they could have looked right at it without knowing what it was.

Marti stopped at the morgue before going home. The mummy was so unlike the bodies she was accustomed to seeing that it took her a moment to allocate to it those same human attributes. This woman had been alive once; she had either straightened her hair with a hot comb or relaxed it with chemicals. It was difficult to determine a style, but it was cut above the shoulder and at an angle. There was something about the slant of the cut—it would come to her. The victim had pierced ears and wore large gold hoop earrings. The hands of her watch had stopped at 11:32, but the glass that covered the face of the watch was not shattered or cracked. It was wound by a stem. A jeweler would come in to appraise the rings on her fingers. One looked like cheap glass. The one with the blue sapphire had a silver setting that looked Victorian. Perhaps when they had a few leads, someone would be able to identify them.

Janet Petrosky came in as Marti was leaving.

"Sad, isn't it?" she said. "To have been closed up in that closet for who knows how long with nobody knowing she was there and maybe nobody to miss her."

Marti had a momentary image of the girl pounding her fists against the seamless door in the unused theater until she collapsed against the wall and died.

Janet looked at the mummy with a brooding expression. "I wonder how long she was there, if there's someone out there wondering what happened to her. So many people just walk away without anyone ever bothering to look for them."

"How much can she tell us?"

"Enough, I hope. This radiologist, a Dr. Pickus, will be here sometime tomorrow. She's already sent instructions on the X rays she wants taken. She's worked on quite a few cases requiring forensic anthropology."

"She?"

Janet smiled. "Meline Pickus."

"In that case, I'll make sure Vik comes along."

Marti drove the route to the new house with the same familiarity that she had driven to the street her children called "the gingerbread village." Their new house was a redbrick quad-level. They had installed a customized security system that everyone knew how to use. The trees closest to the house had been cut down, along with two that obstructed the view from the street. Lights lit the walkway; sensor lights came on as she soon as she pulled into the driveway. She opened the garage door with a remote control. The garage was detached, with a small apartment above it; a connecting walkway had been built to the house. Their new German shepherd had a doghouse in the fenced-in backyard. He was a guard dog, not a pet. Bigfoot, their Saint Bernard–sized mongrel, who was a pet, lived inside.

Marti liked the new house. It had been on the market for a while because it was older and big, with six bedrooms. The couple who had lived here had been the original owners. They had retired and wanted go south. Ben had resuscitated the man following a heart attack a couple of years ago. They hadn't had any problem striking a deal. Managing a family, the house, and a husband still seemed overwhelming, but she'd get the hang of it sooner or later. At least tonight she wouldn't have to worry about dinner. Momma was still here. It was after eleven. The children would be asleep.

For a moment, before she opened the door, she thought of a bright yellow kitchen with Boston ferns hanging at the window. Then she went inside. Her kitchen was wallpapered. Joanna had hung colored sun catchers at the windows. It smelled of garlic and oregano. The sink was clean and there was just a hint of a murmur from the dishwasher. Marti lifted the lid from the pot and inhaled the aroma of Momma's spaghetti sauce. Ben must have loved it. If she had cooked, it would have been Ragu. Not for the first time, she wished Momma could stay.

She checked the board by the refrigerator. She had missed Joanna's basketball game, but the tournament wasn't until next week. It had been Cub Scout night for Theo and Mike. They were working on their Readyman badge and Ben was teaching them first aid. Goblin watched her from just inside the pantry. They had acquired Goblin last year. Marti called to the cat, but she didn't come. Within a few days of her arrival, Goblin had gone from friendly but shy to wary and skittish. Now she stayed out of sight until late at night. Marti found the remains of a baked salmon in the refrigerator and tried using a piece to tempt Goblin closer. The cat kept her distance and waited until Marti gave up and put the fish in her bowl. Marti poured a cup of coffee, then went down the half flight of stairs to the family room, puzzled by the cat's behavior.

Ben and Momma were watching a boxing match on TV. Momma could remember fighters she had never heard of and quote statistics on everyone fighting today. Looking at Momma in profile was like watching Joanna. Momma had let her thick auburn hair grow long enough to pull back. Her hazel eyes framed with tortoise-shelled eyeglasses. Like Marti, Momma was healthy.

"No, no," Momma said. "Lead with your right, fool."

Ben looked up at her and grinned. "What's the body count, Officer Ma'am?"

"Just the one. And a mummy they found a few days ago."

"A mummy. Now that sounds interesting."

"I'll let you know. We've got an experienced radiologist coming in to look at the X rays. Hopefully, we'll get enough to find out who she is."

Marti put her mug on the table beside the chair where Ben was reclining, and went over and gave Momma a kiss on the forehead.

Gas-fed flames burned low in the fireplace. The two upstairs fireplaces were real, but Marti had insisted on having one that required no maintenance.

"Decaf?" Momma asked.

"Whatever was in the coffeepot."

"Decaf." She sighed.

Marti agreed. She could have used a little caffeine.

"Oh Lord," Momma said. "He keeps dropping his left. Look, he got nailed again."

Marti sat on the floor with her back resting against Ben's legs. Ben finally had someone else in the house who liked boxing. Wait until he found out Momma liked wrestling, too.

When the match was over, Ben said, "If you ladies don't mind, I have a few things to do upstairs. Can I get you some more coffee?"

"Something with just a little caffeine," Momma said. "Some of that instant I put on the second shelf and dared Joanna to throw away."

"Me too," Marti said. She wanted to be wide awake when she went to bed.

"I bought some butter, too, Marti, but Lord knows, I'm not taking that child shopping again."

"Joanna is so . . ." She hesitated. Momma wasn't from the school that tolerated children telling grown folks what to do.

"You have a lot of patience with that child, Marti, even when you're tired. And Lord knows, she needs it. She's just tricking herself into thinking that she can keep you alive with all this food foolishness, but she'll grow up enough to get over it before too much longer. I'm glad you just did the usual moping when your daddy passed."

Marti knew she should be way past the time when she needed approval from her mother; even so, she wanted to hug her. "Joanna usually lets me know what's on her mind. Theo is the one I worry about."

"Just like his daddy, looks, attitude, and all. It always did worry me that Johnny held so much in, but he was always so good to you and the children. It would have been good for him, though, if he could have confided in you more."

Now how did Momma know that? Marti sure couldn't have told her. She hadn't even realized it until after Johnny was killed in the line of duty.

"I thought I knew more of what was going on with Johnny. With Theo, I can't even pretend. Ben's got him talking a little bit more and Mike helps him lighten up."

"Ben is a lot different from Johnny, but then you've grown, too."

"Ben is so easygoing, it's scary. Johnny was more . . ."

"Johnny was such a strong-willed person, I'm surprised you two got along so well."

Was he? She didn't remember him that way.

"You gave in to him a lot. That used to worry me, too."

Was Momma right? It had been easier, letting Johnny make the final decisions. Marriage with Ben was going to be a lot more democratic. Did she want that?

"There seems to be more give-and-take between you and Ben."

"I'm not sure I know how to be married to someone who's not a cop." Why had she done this? Now there was someone else with wants and needs, someone else to add to this juggling act, which had been unmanageable even before she got married. "The divorce rate among cops is astronomical. It's scary."

"At least you've known Ben for a few years, had enough time to become friends; that's what got you and Johnny through the rough times." Momma chuckled. "Lord, child, I can remember when Johnny first moved to Washburn Avenue. He hadn't been there three days when he made you that scooter out of a couple of pieces of wood and an old skate. You weren't but eight years old, and the two of you were inseparable after that. It worried me, you two being that close. If he hadn't gone into the army . . ."

"What?" Marti prompted. She could see Johnny now, the way he'd looked the first time he came home in his uniform. Johnny always looked good in a uniform.

"It was just that it gave him some direction. Johnny never did know what he wanted to do with himself. You were always going to be a social worker or a schoolteacher. Johnny just couldn't seem to find himself, at least not while he was in school. Too much going on at home, I suppose, what with his daddy drinking and all. Getting away for those few years was the best thing that ever happened to him, even if he was in a war."

Johnny was so different after Vietnam. He knew what he wanted to do, be a police officer. She had never told Momma how much she'd worried about what he would do when he graduated. He'd always stayed in the church and off the streets, but he didn't have trade or skill when he graduated, and if he couldn't find a job . . .

"It surprised me, his becoming a police officer," Momma said. "Born to it, wasn't he? Funny the way the Lord leads you to what you're supposed to do."

Yes, funny. Johnny was the one who had urged her to join the force, too. Now she couldn't imagine ever wanting to do anything else.

"You have got your hands full now, haven't you, sister? A second marriage is a lot different from the first, even when there aren't any children."

"Don't remind me. They say you learn from your mistakes the second time. But I've got a strong hunch there were mistakes with me and Johnny that I'm not even aware of."

Marriage hadn't been that easy the first time, and she had known Johnny for years. Why had she done this? Now what was going to happen?

"Things will work out just fine, child. They will work out just fine."

She was glad Momma thought so, but Momma hadn't spent much time with Ben, hadn't seen the two of them together for more than an hour at one time. If Momma had worried about her and Johnny, as well as she knew him, then what could she know about this?

51

"Maybe," Marti said. "Maybe."

"Marti, if you and Johnny could make it, young as you were, you and Ben are going to be just fine."

She and Johnny had waited almost six years to become parents. They'd had time alone together. Now there were three children involved. What time she and Ben had at home had to be shared with everyone. How could she manage it all?

"How have you been, Momma?"

"I'm well, child, just fine. My arthritis kicks up sometimes and I've got me some reading glasses, but other than that, I'm just fine."

Momma did look good, a little thinner maybe, and tired around the eyes, but well. They hadn't spent any time together since she moved here four years ago after Johnny died, except for phone conversations. Momma had already been living in Arkansas for two years with Great-Aunt Sadie. She had never found time to visit and knew nothing more than that Aunt Sadie lived in a town with a population of 329. She could not imagine living in a place that small and didn't have a clue as to how Momma managed. Right now, she was trying not to think about how tired Momma had seemed when she first came here and how much she had perked up since she had been with the children. In their family, you did not put your elders in a nursing home. Momma was the only one without family responsibilities, so the care of Aunt Sadie had fallen to her. Momma went without complaining, knowing someone else would do the same when it was her time, but that meant Marti, and her children, had to do without her being around. And her children did need their grandmother, and about as much as she needed a mother.

What would she do on Sunday, after Momma left, when there would be nobody to tell her things would be all right? When was she going to get too old to need her mother's reassurances? Not that she would ever say this to Momma; it would only make her feel bad. She was a cop, for God's sake, and she'd be forty soon. That was too old to be needing your mother, but right now, she needed help as much as Aunt Sadie did. Not that she could tell anyone that. It wouldn't be fair, asking Momma to move from one place to the other just to assume another set of burdens.

"How's Aunt Sadie doing?" she asked.

"She's had so many strokes, she's bedridden now. The last one took what was left of her speech, but you should see her smile when I sing to her."

"Do her children come to see her very often?"

Marti would never palm off the care of her mother on some other family member.

"She doesn't know them most of the time. Neal and Dora both live in Little Rock. Neal is a minister. I'm not sure if Dora works anymore since she got married again. It must be an hour-and-half drive. They come every once in awhile."

"Does Aunt Sadie know you?"

"Sometimes."

"Here's Ben with the coffee." Marti was getting annoyed, hearing all this.

"Oh, I almost forgot. If you look in that Tupperware container on the counter, you'll find some pound cake. I would like just a little slice of that."

Marti followed Ben upstairs. She gave him a pinch on the butt as he reached the top step, then a quick kiss. "I've made no plans to be too tired," she told him.

"Cake," he said, grinning.

"That will do, for now. You and Momma seem to be getting along okay." This had to be an adjustment for him, too.

"I was a little nervous at first. . . ."

"You? Nervous?"

"Well, I'm the second husband. She's got someone else to compare me to."

She took a step back and looked at him. "No comparisons," she said. How quickly she had idealized Johnny when he died, forgot every fault. Ben must have done the same thing with Carol. Maybe Carol was still perfect to him. Carol had stayed at home.

She wasn't exhausted and stressed-out when her husband came home. "No comparisons," she said again, and hugged him.

She cut them both a piece of pound cake, then fixed Ben some coffee and sat with him for a few minutes, catching up. Then she took two thick slices downstairs.

"Do you think you could make a couple of sweet potato pies before you go and maybe some fried-apple pies and banana pudding?"

Momma laughed. "Lord, child, you'll have Joanna helping me pack. I made some collard greens and corn bread yesterday, and you could see from the way her mouth was set that she was counting up the cholesterol."

"Just don't let her watch you when you bake. She has no idea of how much butter and how many eggs the pies take. She's been using this grape-seed oil for cooking. Costs a fortune, but it makes life a lot easier if you want to fry something. Use it for the fried pies. That will give her less to complain about."

"Is that child interested in boys yet? That'll take her mind off of what everyone eats."

"You haven't met Chris?"

"Not yet."

Maybe they had broken up. Not that she wanted Joanna to date just one boy. It was just that she knew Chris, and he knew her. She didn't have the time right now to achieve that same understanding with someone else.

"Joanna needs more to occupy her mind, Marti. When you were her age, you were more involved with the church."

"And for several reasons. Not the least being that I had to go when you did. And that was the best way to get to see Johnny. But times have changed. Not necessarily for the better."

If Momma stayed here, she would find a way to shift Joanna's interests to something else. Joanna would have someone else to confide in, too, someone who would tell her the truth without hurting her feelings too often. And there was that apartment over the garage. Momma would have a place of her own and not have to stay with an invalid day in and day out.

"Please try to bake before you leave. You know what kind of cook I am. Ben cooks a lot better than I do."

"Check the freezer. I've got a few things put away there that should get you through the next couple of weeks. You might have this murder figured out by then. You've got your hands full here."

Momma didn't say anything else for a while. They had sat together like this when she was a child, Momma occupying herself with hand sewing or reading while Marti sat nearby doing her schoolwork. They'd listen to "Gangbusters" or "Gunsmoke" or "The Shadow" on the radio, have something cool or hot to drink, depending on the time of year, and talk about just about everything.

"Me and Ben had a nice visit today. We both know you got enough on your plate for two people, but things will work out, they surely will."

Because it was Momma saying it, Marti feld comforted and reassured.

Marti called the medical exam-
iner's office at the Robert Stine Institute in Chicago as soon as she
reached her office the next morning. Dr. Pickus would be arriving in the afternoon. There was a message from Vik; he would be
late, but Mildred was all right. Another message from Lieutenant
Dirkowitz. He wanted to see her. There was no mention of Vik,
but she called to make sure he wanted to see her alone before
walking over to his office.

Offices with windows were at a premium in the precinct. The
window in Marti's office faced the flagpole. Dirkowitz had a view
of the lake. Today, the sky was a darker shade of gray than the
water. She hoped that didn't mean more snow. The lieutenant
leaned back in his chair when she came in. He locked beefy fingers behind his thick linebacker's neck. The wall behind his desk
was referred to as "the wall of infamy" by those who were Re-
publicans, and "the wall of fame" by the Democrats. Not only
did Dirkowitz have a picture of himself as a teenager with Walter
Mondale, as well as one with Bill Clinton, but in the past year he
had added photos with Al Gore and Hillary Rodham Clinton.
The going joke was, "Where's Buddy? Where's Socks?"

Dirkowitz sat up and flexed his fingers. "Well, MacAlister, nice
trip?"

"Fine, sir."

The apple-shaped grenade that he usually played with and

then dropped to signal that the meeting was over remained on his desk. She wondered if that meant this was unofficial.

"That was quite a get-together you and Ben had New Year's Day. Great way to begin the New Year."

"Thank you, sir." He had euphemisms for wedding and honeymoon, too.

"Sorry I had to ask you to come back. Have we got anything on the mummy?"

"Not yet, sir."

"But we do know that it is a black female. Anything else?"

"Cyprian estimates her age at seventeen to twenty-one because the wisdom teeth were about to erupt. We've got someone coming in from Chicago this afternoon who might be able to provide us with more information."

"I wish we had found it someplace else. Just when it looks like we might have someone in Springfield interested in downtown revitalization, something like this has to happen."

He had been born and raised here, the same as Vik.

"We're not releasing anything on this until we have more information. There will be a mention in the News-Times, but hopefully none of the news services will pick up on it. The faster we can get this resolved, and the less publicity we get, the more likely it is that the Geneva will get some restoration funds. Fortunately, the senator is on our side and she's downplaying the entire incident. Have you got Lupe Torres involved? She was backup while you were gone."

"Torres checked through some missing persons reports without coming up with anything. Basically, she was just looking for an age match. It'll be pretty much up to us to come up with a reasonable estimate of time of death."

"Vik seems to work well with Torres, and you've worked with her before."

"She can handle Vik, Slim, and Cowboy."

"That's good." He hunched forward.

Marti waited.

"I'm not sure how Vik's wife is doing, MacAlister, but Torres might have to work with you on this, too. That was the main reason why I asked you to come back. We have to have at least one experienced homicide cop on duty."

"Is there something wrong with Mildred that I don't know about?"

"As far as I know, this is a routine MS episode that's not responding to treatment yet, but I want Vik to feel that he can take time off when he needs to. I also understand that your family situation has changed. And I owe you for coming in." He tapped the gold band on his finger. "This is my third marriage. It ain't easy."

"Tell me about it," Marti said. Her stomach lurched into a sluggish churning.

"Torres is authorized to work overtime. I'll leave it to you and Jessenovik to figure out how to utilize her. I'm hoping this will give you some flexibility in grabbing a little family time, and also make it easier for Vik to take Mildred to the doctor or whatever. Keep me advised on what you get on the mummy. Let me know when you begin making inquiries so I can be prepared for any questions from the press. Be discreet. Let me know if anything develops."

Vik came in a little after nine. The bags under his eyes were darker than usual and he yawned as he fixed a cup of coffee.

"How's Mildred?"

"She'll be okay. It's just taking longer than usual. The medication won't kick in, one leg keeps getting weak, and her sister was running late. I was afraid she would need something, try to get it, and fall. It looks like she's going have to use a walker for a while."

"You haven't spent much time with her. I'm sure she needs that, too." She hoped he wouldn't need too much nudging to let Lupe help out. "Does her sister mind spending the day with her?"

"No, she loves it. They both do. It gives them someone to argue with, but that's okay, once Mildred gives in and starts using the walker, Helena will be able to stay home and drive her own family nuts." Vik snapped a pencil in half and sat staring at his cup. "This is the first time it's been this bad, this long," he said in a quiet voice.

"Then I'm glad you stayed home this morning and spent a little time with her. It makes more sense than coming in and worrying."

He pushed the cup with two fingers until it was centered in the middle of his desk. "Maybe."

"Look, Vik, we both at least need to try to spend a little more time at home. My mother is here only until Sunday and I've hardly seen her. Lupe's still authorized to work with us. I asked her to come in when her shift is over so we can bring her up to speed on things."

Vik nodded and ran his fingers through his hair. He needed a haircut. A few more minutes of that and it would be totally unruly for the rest of the day.

"Cut that out, Jessenovik."

He reached for some reports.

"Vik, Lupe is a good cop. I've never worked a three-cop team before, but I think we should think of it that way, break her in." She almost held her breath, expecting opposition.

"Got any ideas as to how?"

"No," she admitted. "Nothing specific. We'll have to feel our way through it. The thing is, it's a way of freeing up a little time maybe. If she's trained properly, so that we know we can rely on her, then at least in an emergency we've got someone who can come in and take up some of the slack."

"It's not a bad idea."

Marti looked at him for a minute. She had expected an argument. He had to be more worried about Mildred than he was letting on. She took out her notebook, went through what she had written, and made a short list. "Let's begin with the mummy. I've got to make a quick trip to the theater as soon as I get a chance. The hair made me think of something, but I can't put my finger on it yet. There is a ring with a distinctive setting.

As for Cheney . . ." She pulled a report from her in-basket. "No prints on anything, a few smudges. Sounds like someone wiped everything clean. Interesting. We need a better description of that watch, Vik, and we need to find out if Cheney had anything else of value. We still haven't heard anything from their lawyer. Not a word about what he was worth or who gets it." She put in a call to Jonathan Cheney and was told that he wasn't at home.

"So much for that. Armstrong went to court this morning and pleaded innocent to receiving stolen goods. I would have another little chat with him before he makes bail if I had some idea of what was on that microwave."

They swung by the train station to see if anyone had recognized the morgue shot of Cheney.

"Brick," Vik said, as if it were a dirty word. "The old place was like something out of a movie. Those benches with slats of wood. A high counter, closed in with a window. My dad and I used to take the train to the city to watch the Cubs play when it was still the Chicago Northwestern. Steve and I did the same thing."

Marti didn't say anything. Everyone needed memories, and going into that old theater and the Merchants building with its burned out bowling alley all in the same week had sent him on a real nostalgia trip.

Half a dozen people were inside, most of them reading newspapers. The seats were molded plastic, the counter little more than waist-high. When Marti walked over, she saw a man sitting at a desk near the wall.

"Sir?"

In profile, he was a young man with a long nose and a receding chin. He was reading a magazine and ignored her.

"Sir!"

"Just a minute."

"Now," Marti said. "Police."

He looked up at her. His receding chin was further emphasized by an overbite.

"Oh that," he said when she asked about the picture. He rummaged in a cluttered desk drawer and pulled it out. "Someone left it here yesterday or the day before."

"Have you shown it to any of the train crews?"

"Not yet. It's too cold. They don't want to come in here. I don't want to walk out there."

Vik cussed under his breath. "When were you planning to show it to them?" he asked. "Next summer?"

"Hey, look, this is a busy place."

"Yes," Vik agreed. "I can see that. You always have this many people waiting for the next train?"

Two of the customers had stopped reading their newspapers. The other four either weren't interested or were pretending not to be.

"This place is so busy, MacAlister, that at least half the trains making the Chicago to Kenosha run don't even stop here anymore. Let me see a schedule."

The clerk tossed one on the counter. Vik held out his hand until the man picked it up and placed it on his palm.

Vik scanned it. "We'd better get a uniform over here to handle this," he said. "No point in asking a boy to do a man's work."

"Now just wait a minute."

"No," Marti said. "You wait a minute, Mr. . . ." She checked his name tag. "Langley, Norbert. This is police business. We requested your cooperation. You declined. That will be communicated to the appropriate personnel."

"But . . . but it's freezing out there. The windchill hasn't gotten higher than five above in a week."

Marti showed the picture around. Everyone shook their head. Nobody asked any questions. As they headed out the door, the clerk called out, "They didn't say anything about it being important."

"Maybe the officer thought he was dealing with someone with

a little intelligence, or at least some common sense," Vik called back.

As Marti stepped outside, the wind whipped across her face and slammed the door shut.

When they got back to the precinct, there was a message from Jonathan Cheney and a phone number with a Chicago area code.

"Mr. Cheney. I understand your uncle had a watch that belonged to his grandfather."

Cheney cleared his throat. "I'd have to check with my father on that."

"Do you know of anything else he might have had that was of value? Something smaller than a microwave."

"I don't have a clue. I'm sorry. I'll talk with my dad."

"Could you do that right away, sir, and get back to me as quickly as possible? Oh, and one more thing. Your attorney has not contacted us yet."

The phone rang again almost as soon as Marti hung up. It was Janet Petrosky. Dr. Pickus would be arriving at four.

When Lupe came in at half past three, after working a full shift, she seemed more energized than tired. "I need some decaf."

"We don't have any."

She helped herself to Cowboy's potent brew anyway. "What do you want me to do?"

Marti hesitated. "You've worked with us before and done fine, but I think it's time we tried something different, to work more as a team, and we're going to have to feel our way through it."

Lupe positioned a chair between Vik's desk and Marti's, straddled the seat, and waited.

"Working a homicide is like . . . doing a puzzle, except you begin with an empty box and a body. You add the pieces as you get them. They're in no particular order, and some don't belong in the box at all. Eventually, you get enough of the right pieces to figure out what happened, who did it, and why."

"And that means you two have to look at all of the pieces. What if I have some that you don't?"

"All three of us have to look at all of the pieces. That's what we have to work out."

"Sounds great!" Lupe said. "What do we do? You've worked shift on cases, Marti, been off duty when some were solved. We have to do it all here."

"We talk," Marti said. "And bring you in on as much as possible, which is why you're going over to the coroner's office with us. You're a cop, Lupe, not a secretary or a gofer. We're going to give you a lot of the grunt work, but we'll have to make time to bring you up-to-date on both cases. You're going to have to read through all of the reports, all of the case notes, and make notes of your own. You're going to have to bring us current on everything you're doing, and make sure we know everything you find out."

Lupe grinned.

"Whatever happened to that partner of yours, Torres?" Vik asked. "The dumbshit hotshot you used to ride patrol with?"

"Burdette? He's still assigned to a squad. He's got the best record in the department for number of traffic tickets written, and the worst for convictions."

"And you're assigned to community policing. You could have gone to the Narc Unit or the Gang Unit."

"I go into the community just like cops did years ago. I know the kids on my beat; I recognize the strangers. The people who live there trust me enough to tell me what's going on, who's doing what. The crime stats on my beat are down significantly. It's probably a lot like the way your dad policed when he was on the force."

Vik didn't say anything. Marti gave her a thumbs-up.

They were on their way out when Jonathan Cheney called to say that he would be picking his father up at the airport in two hours. "Jeremiah Cheney wants to meet with us at eight," she told Vik.

Dr. Pickus was a tall, slender woman with silver-gray hair. She was wearing jeans, jogging shoes, and a bright green cable-knit sweater. When they went into the conference room, she was standing with her back to them, clipping X rays to a viewer as she consulted with Dr. Cyprian. The physical evidence was in plastic bags at the far end of the table.

"That's Dr. Pickus?" Vik said. He looked so surprised, Marti was glad she hadn't told him Dr. Pickus was a woman.

"And she works with not so recently dead bodies?" he added. "Odor, insects, and all?"

"Sometimes," Dr. Pickus said without turning around. "Most of my patients are live ones."

As Marti sat down in one of the functional but reasonably comfortable chairs grouped around a long table in the conference room, she wished she could put her head down and take a nap. Lupe jiggled her leg. Marti knew the feeling: wired—hyped—too much street life; too much caffeine; and now another high, a postmortem of sorts on the mummy.

She stifled a yawn and Vik leaned toward her. "Too much nightlife, MacAlister?"

She assumed that was another euphemism.

Lupe grinned.

Marti fixed a cup of coffee.

It was another ten minutes before Janet Petrosky came in, made introductions all around, and dimmed the lights. Dr. Pickus folded her hands on the table and began. "I'll try to keep this brief and as nontechnical as possible. Dr. Cyprian and I concur with these findings, which are preliminary. These are the mummified remains of a black female. Through X rays, we have determined that the medial clavicle epethius is not closed. This is the middle portion of the collarbone and closes at age twenty-five. Closure of the cranial sutures also occurs at about twenty-five and has not here. We can see that the third maxillary molars, the wisdom teeth, were about to erupt. This should occur between the ages of seventeen and twenty. Based on the status of the third maxillaries and the root formation of the second molars, we are estimating her age at seventeen or eighteen, given a maximum range of seventeen to twenty-five. We also identified a fetus in utero. Usually, a fetal skeleton can be identified at about four months. Based on that and the size of the fetus, we're estimating that she was five months pregnant. There is one other thing that I would like to show you."

Janet Petrosky turned on the slide projector and pulled down a screen.

The first slides were of the head. Again Marti noted the angular cut of the hair, which had been straightened and parted on the side. The hair was longer at the front, where it touched the the side of her face, and shorter by about an inch at the sides and back.

"We need photos of the way the hair is cut," Marti said. A hairdresser should be able to date the style.

The next shots were close-ups of the neck.

"There was no break in the skin surrounding the neck," Dr. Pickus said. "But if you look at the skin, here"—she used a pointer—"and here, this wrinkling, and the indentations on either side indicate pressure—thumbs, I'd guess—something that didn't break the skin."

"Are you saying that she was strangled?" Vik asked.

"I cannot see any indications of hands having encompassed the throat, although that is my best guess. Someone was facing her and pressed here, on either side of the neck."

"Could the indentations be caused by the mummification process?" Lupe asked. Vik gave her an approving look.

"I've never observed anything like that and I am familiar with mummies. We'll send copies of these to Dr. Geoffrey Gless in Iowa. He's the ultimate expert. Right now, he's in England working on a case with Scotland Yard, but he should be back next week. Unless he contradicts, I'd go with manual strangulation as cause of death."

"I wouldn't have been able to tell there was anything unusual about the neck," Marti said. "Will it stand up in court?"

"Yes, and we'll have comparison slides and photos that can be shown."

"So now all we have to find out is time of death."

"We'll do more testing," Dr. Pickus said. "But that will take time, and you already have some clues." She reached for the evidence bags. "Red pants, narrow leg with three-inch slits that begin at the hem and were positioned at the instep. One paisley blouse, and ladies—check it out—a girdle with garters. The stockings didn't hold up too well, so they were probably nylon. Also, one wide black belt, twenty-four inches long. And the bra. About as restrictive as the girdle. Shoes, or what we used to call 'flats,' size five and a half."

"She was killed during the summer," Marti said.

"That tells us a lot," Vik said. "We tend to have summer for at least a few weeks every year."

"The clothes could have been in and out of style two or three times if we go back far enough," Lupe said. "I've got a picture of my mother wearing pants and shoes like those."

"When was it taken?" Marti asked.

"Early sixties, before hippies. Can she have been dead that long?"

"Sure," Dr. Pickus said.

"Can we prove it?" Marti asked.

"We'll run tests on the fibers. The body mummified instead of decaying because of the dry conditions in that room and also because there were no breaks in the skin to cause odors or otherwise attract insect activity. If that part of the building was kept at a constant temperature without too many fluctuations, we could estimate how long the process took. We still can, even if there were wide fluctuations in temperature, but that requires much more information. The fastest, most logical way for you to determine when she died is by using the physical evidence, the clothes, and her jewelry. She was wearing these rings."

Dr. Pickus passed them around. "The setting on the silver ring is quite distinctive."

Marti was certain that the blue sapphire was real. It would have cost less than a stone like a diamond, but the cut was exquisite and the color a cornflower blue. The other ring had a tarnished setting with a fake red stone and glass chips on either side. Why would the victim wear one expensive ring and one cheap fake?

5

A light dusting of new snow covered the street and blew in little swirls as Marti turned into the Cheney driveway at five past eight. Tree branches were outlined in white against the night sky, and it was quiet, that deep woods quiet that comes with snowy nights. Marti thought of the inn in Wisconsin with more than a little regret.

"You okay?" Vik said.

"Just fine."

The driveway had been plowed and salted. This time, there was a guard at the entrance.

"Mr. Jeremiah is expecting you," he said after taking a close look at their IDs. "I'll phone ahead."

They were shown into a large room with a blazing fireplace and wall-to-wall books. Small sofas and chairs were scattered about. Even in the dim light, the man who sat by the fire looked older than Barnabas Cheney, even though chronologically he was younger. His face was drawn, his eyes sunken, and his hair grayer.

"Now, Father," Jonathan Cheney said as he followed close behind them. "You're sure you feel up to this?"

"I'm fine, Jonathan. Leave us alone." Before Jonathan could turn away, the old man raised his hand in a beckoning gesture. "No, perhaps you should stay. There might be something that you should know about."

"Thank you for flying in to talk with us," Marti said. "I appreciate your concern." She also wondered why he felt it was necessary to do so.

Two wing chairs were grouped about the fire. While Marti and Vik sat down, the younger Cheney pulled over another chair and joined them.

"My family is concerned because I just had another round of chemo four days ago and it's very fatiguing. However, I did feel it was necessary to speak with you in person. So much is lost, talking by phone."

"But Dad, you could have—"

"You may only listen, Jonathan." He turned to Marti and Vik. "I would offer you refreshments, but the smell would make me quite ill. I might not have the energy to talk very long, either, so I'll get to the point. Barnabas and I have had no direct contact for the past fifteen years. He was eight years my senior, so we weren't as close as we might have been, but we got along as well as any brothers would. I was always the smaller boy and Barnabas often took up for me. According to my mother, from the time he was five or six, he was a dreamer, frequently staring off into space, often to the chagrin of his teachers. He was never particularly moody, though. Much later, while he was on medication, he told me that even then he had heard voices, but that he'd thought everyone did."

Jeremiah Cheney paused. He seemed tired by the effort to speak. Jonathan looked anxious but said nothing.

"By the time Barnabas reached high school, his attention span was so short and his interests so . . . different that Dad had a tutor live in."

"What were his interests?" Marti asked.

"Anything to do with religion, including studying the Talmud, the Koran, and learning Greek, Hebrew, and Aramaic. He also enjoyed calculus and physics. After he was committed, the doctors measured his IQ at a hundred and seventy-five. Mentally ill people are usually quite bright. Barnabas was very easily bored and jumped from one subject to another, something the tutor could adjust to. In any case, he got a diploma and there was the question of what to do with him. He traveled for a while, mostly isolated places in the Northwest. When he returned, he joined an amateur theater company. At that point, everyone was so worried that nobody cared what he did, as long as it kept him occupied."

Jeremiah paused again, but this time there was a bemused expression on his face. "God but he was good. As soon as he came onstage, he became his character totally. If the madness hadn't overcome him, there is no telling what he could have done. As it was, within nine or ten years, he was institutionalized. It became too real for him. Spies were after him, the Mafia; men were on the rooftops with rifles; hit men were following him in cars. It wasn't until he got out Dad's gun and shut himself up in the attic that the decision to send him away became unavoidable. None of us felt good about it."

He wiped tears from his eyes. "It broke Dad's heart, I think. He never wanted to admit that anything was wrong, and when he was forced to, it just took something out of him."

He closed his eyes and leaned his head against the back of the chair.

"If this is tiring you . . ." Marti began. She had a few questions she wanted to ask him.

"No." He shook his head, and continued. "We sent him abroad. When he was deemed fit to be released, he came back . . . to this country, but he never came home. He stopped taking his medication; he stopped caring about who we were, until one day I don't think he knew who we were. He was locked into who he had become."

"Is that when he went to live in the Merchants building?" Vik asked.

"We didn't banish him to the Merchants building, Officer. He ended up there. He needed a place to be safe. . . ." Jeremiah's voice broke. He took a deep breath. "He said we were not his family. He said Jesus was his family. He said his name was Micah, not Barnabas. We set up a bank account for him; we moved Aunt Lindy into that storefront so that he would at least see a face that was familiar if he needed to. We didn't know what else to do."

He slumped in the chair with his hand on his forehead. "There was no legal recourse. Barnabas was not really a danger to himself or anyone else. No one cared about him but us, and there was nothing more we could do."

"Mr. Cheney," Marti said, "as far as we can determine, Barnabas was an eccentric, reclusive old man who wouldn't harm anyone. He didn't didn't deserve to die the way he did. We'd like to do something about that."

"Why? We lost Barnabas years ago. We lost him because legally we could do nothing to help him. And now the law wants to find out who killed him? The law killed him, years ago."

"Did he have a watch that belonged to your grandfather?"

"Yes." There was a catch in his voice, and as he looked at Marti, a curious expression spread across his face. She couldn't tell if it was hope or fear.

"Can you describe it?"

"Solid gold. Made in Switzerland. Scrollwork on the case, and Grandpa's initials—J.S.C. Josiah Solomon Cheney. There's . . . there's probably an insurance photo. Dear God, could he have kept it?"

"We're certain that he did. Someone saw him with it."

He rubbed his chin. "Grandfather's watch. Jonathan will ask our attorney if there's a photo."

"Could you do that right away?"

Jeremiah sighed. "How quickly the law intervenes when there's no longer any reason for intervention. Yes. Jonathan will see to it."

"Could you tell if he had anything else of value, something smaller than a microwave?"

Jeremiah frowned. "A microwave?"

"There was something sitting on his microwave. It isn't there anymore. We need to know what it was."

"I don't know." He thought for a while. "Could it have been the picture of Grandfather? If he kept the watch all these years, then maybe he kept the picture, too."

"Can you describe it?"

"It was an oil painting, a portrait of Grandpa, not a photograph. Small, five by seven. It belonged to my grandmother. Barnabas took it with him when he went abroad. I can't tell you if he still had it, but that was the last any of us saw of it."

"Was it valuable?"

Jeremiah covered his eyes. "I hope so," he said. "God, I hope so. If he held on to that picture after all of these years . . . then maybe . . . but perhaps not."

"Is there anyone who would know its value?"

"If it's worth anything, it'll be on the insurance inventory list," Jeremiah said. "Please," he added, urgency in his voice, "find out if he kept the picture. That would mean much more to me than finding out who harmed him."

"Call your attorney," Marti said. "Now. See if we can get a description of the frame and an approximate value." She hesitated. "As long as you're calling your attorney, here is one other thing. We need to know if your brother had an estate, and, if so, who his beneficiaries are."

"I can answer that. There is a trust set up for Barnabas, a way of taking care of him. At death, it reverts to my father's estate, is held in trust, and divided equally among the surviving heirs."

She would check further, but it didn't sound like anyone would profit immediately or directly from Barnabas's death.

"Now, as for the portrait. My attorney is at home now. He would have that information at his office."

"A small item like that can be sold very quickly. It may already be too late."

Jeremiah picked up the phone. He explained the situation, listened, then said, "He's got the inventory on his computer. He can read off a description. Will that do? The photographs are in his office safe."

Marti nodded and took out her notebook. Before they left, Marti again thanked Jeremiah for seeing them. He looked pale and exhausted. She called in the description while they were still at the Cheney residence, then confirmed that Armstrong had made bail. Next, she requested a search warrant for his apartment from the state's attorney.

"Let's call Lupe in for the toss," she said as they cleared snow from the car. "Looks like it's going to be a long night."

Vik agreed. "We'd better phone home."

"Is your sister-in-law still there?"

"No, Stephen will stay tonight until I get home."

Marti wanted to ask him more about how Mildred was doing, but she was sure he was either tired of being asked that or didn't need to be reminded.

"Stephen and Krysta's husband moved some furniture for me," he said. He drummed his fingers on the dashboard for a moment, stopped, then said, "We had to move the bed downstairs to the den. She fell down that half flight of stairs that goes to the basement."

Marti reached out and touched his hand. "It gets better."

"Right." Vik sighed. "I know. In God's own sweet time, it does. It's just never taken this long before."

The toss was under way by the time Marti and Vik returned to the duplex where Armstrong lived. Armstrong was sitting on the sofa with his head in his hands. He looked up when Marti and Vik came in.

"Not you two again," he said. "I'd never been arrested in my life until now. Why me?"

There was so much crammed into the apartment that after two hours, they still had not found the painting.

Marti remembered the way Armstrong had looked at the microwave, where the picture most likely had been. It was important to him. She wasn't surprised that they hadn't found it. She went back to the bedroom. It was almost impossible to tell it had already been tossed, since it had been so messy to begin with. She stood in the doorway and looked about the room, certain that the uniforms had gone through everything. Maybe if she began by focusing on what was in plain sight. She poked around for a few minutes, went through the stacks of magazines again, checked the

73

mattress. There was no carpet to roll back. She pushed the tables out of the way and went into the closet. When she came out, an old clock radio vintage 1950s caught her eye. It was right by the bed, but it wasn't working, and it was the only thing in the room that had ever been dusted. She picked it up. It felt heavier than it should, but maybe not. Nothing moved inside when she shook it. The cord was intact. Curious, she used the tool on her key chain to loosen the screws. The frame and painting were inside.

"I don't know anything about it," Armstrong said. "I don't know how it got here. I didn't steal it. I didn't."

A uniform came over and handed Vik the plastic bag containing the painting and the clock radio, gutted of its insides.

Armstrong trembled. "It is so beautiful," he whispered. Tears brimmed in his eyes.

"See you at the county jail," Vik said. "It looks like you're going to be arrested again."

"But I didn't do anything."

"Right," Vik said. "We know."

Snow was still falling when they went outside. "I'd like to question him in the morning," Marti said. "Give him a few hours in a jail cell to rethink his position. What do you think?" It was snowing harder. "I thought we weren't going to have any significant accumulation. At this rate . . ."

Vik got out the scraper and began cleaning off the car. "Armstrong's denying everything. Emotional. But he hasn't asked for his attorney yet. We couldn't find any priors on him, so he doesn't have much experience with the law. Either we talk to him now, at which point he'll clam up and insist on seeing his attorney first, or . . . I don't know."

Marti drove to the county jail. By the time Armstrong was brought into the small interrogation room with the benches and table bolted down, he looked almost green.

He sat with his head down and his hands in his lap, shaking his head. "Not me. Not again."

"Do you want to tell us how you got that portrait?" Marti asked.

"Cheney sold it to me."

"Try again," Vik snapped. "Look, mister, it's damned near midnight, and I'm getting fed up with your lies and your denials, and the phony crying act. Nobody is buying any of it."

"But, but . . ."

"No buts, Armstrong—"

"Look, Vik," Marti said. "Take it easy on the guy. He's an antiques dealer. He knows something valuable when he sees it and knows how to come by it legitimately."

"Sure, like he came by those CD players and VCRs. Antiques dealer? Hah! He's a two-bit crook."

"I didn't kill him," Armstrong said in a small voice.

Marti sat across from him and leaned toward him. "Do you want to tell us what did happen, Mr. Armstrong?"

"I didn't kill him," he repeated. "He was dead and there wasn't anything I could do to help him, and he didn't need the picture anymore. The frame is solid silver. And, it is so beautiful. I wasn't going to sell it, I swear to God. I wanted to keep it, look at it. It is so beautiful."

"Come on, man," Vik said. "You expect us to believe this?"

"It's the truth, I swear to God."

"You have lied to me ever since I laid eyes on you. Why in the hell should I believe you now?"

"Vik," Marti said. "Give the man a chance. Tell me about what happened, Mr. Armstrong. Why did you go down there?"

"I went down there a lot. A couple of times a week, just to look at it. Can't you see how beautiful it is? The frame is over a hundred years old, made in France. The only place I've ever seen anything like this portrait is in a museum. And Cheney, where he comes from, it was nothing. That, the watch—he was used to all of that, lived in a house full of it—didn't care enough about it to clean and polish it. He didn't care about anything, not even himself. He sure didn't care nothing about the guy in the picture."

Marti didn't agree. That and the watch were all Cheney had

kept of his family. Marti hoped that would give Jeremiah Cheney some comfort.

"What happened?"

"I don't know. I didn't hear anything or see anyone. Nobody but the meter readers ever go down there, and he kept his room closed off with those sheets. The upstairs doors are kept locked. I don't know what happened."

Armstrong was getting himself in deeper with everything he said. Marti was ready to read him his rights and formally interrogate him.

"Tell us about the picture frame."

"It was there. Like it always was." Tears flowed down his cheeks. "And he was there, but there was all that blood. He wasn't alive. He didn't need it anymore. His family didn't even want him, so what would they care about a picture frame? They'd throw it away or sell it. I'd never see it again. It is so beautiful. I had never held, never touched anything that beautiful or that valuable before."

"Valuable," Vik said. "That's it, isn't it, Armstrong? All this talk about beauty, and you're just a common thief who saw something that could be worth a lot of money and decided you had to have it, no matter what."

"No, no, I didn't. I didn't. I've looked at it for years. Why would I take it now, unless, unless Cheney—"

"Armstrong, I'm reading you your rights, pal. Pay attention."

An hour later, they were still without a confession. Everything Armstrong said was being recorded. He had agreed to speak to them without an attorney present. His exact words were, "No, I'll call her in the morning. I can't afford to wake her up and pay night rates over something I didn't do."

Again, Vik asked Armstrong to tell him what had happened. Armstrong looked exhausted, but he had given up the crying routine.

"Cheney was always up and out by the time I got there in the morning. I went downstairs, just to take another look at it. . . ."

"What day was this?"

"Tuesday. It was Tuesday."

The day the mummy was found at the Geneva, the last full day of Marti and Ben's honeymoon. The anonymous call on Cheney came in early Wednesday morning.

"And . . ." Vik prodded. Fatigue edged his voice and the pouches under his eyes were darker and puffier than usual.

"And he was there, dead, like I said. So I took it." His voice went up half an octave. "I took it. I took the picture frame. I took it. I did not kill him for it. I took it because he was dead."

"You expect me to believe that?"

"Yes."

"Why?"

"Because it's the truth."

"Are you sure you can tell the difference?" Vik itemized the lies Armstrong had told them so far.

"I'm telling the truth." Armstrong put his head on his arms.

Marti leaned toward him. "You might feel better if you told us the whole truth."

"I couldn't call the police. I couldn't be the one to find him. I couldn't even go back there after lunch. That's why I didn't go to the shop yesterday morning. I knew he was down there."

"You knew he was dead because you killed him," Vik said.

"No, no. Why didn't I just leave that picture frame alone?" Armstrong sobbed. "Greed," he said. "Greed. And now they're going to give me the chair for it."

Marti suppressed a giggle. She had to be overtired, if Armstrong's histrionics were getting to her. She nodded to Vik. They had enough to have an intelligent conversation with his attorney.

"See you in the morning, Mr. Armstrong."

"Thank God we're finally packing it in for the night," Vik said. "I'm too damned tired to make a call on this one."

"Me too," Marti admitted. Their cars had been parked in the precinct lot since morning and were covered with four inches of snow. She decided she had just about enough energy to clear the windows. "If nothing else, we can charge him with obstruction of justice and failure to report a death to the coroner. From the sounds of it, he looked at that frame for years without taking it. There would have had to be something to make him act now."

"Man's a voyeur," Vik agreed. "Probably got more out of looking at it than stealing it."

The streets were dark and almost deserted as she headed home. She was tired enough to fall asleep at the wheel. Instead, she opened the window just enough to let in some cold air and turned on the radio. She made several turns before she noticed the vehicle about six car lengths behind her. Something about it seemed familiar. It was an older model, big, dark. She turned at the next light. Before she was halfway down the block, she could see the other car in the rearview mirror. She turned again and slowed down. This time, the car kept going straight. She circled around, positioning herself to drive toward the car, but she couldn't find it. Most of the houses in the neighborhood had garages. Whoever it was must have gone home.

Stephen opened the door when Vik got home, and took his coat.

"Thanks, son."

He was lucky. His kids had turned out pretty much the way he wanted them to, even though he wished Krysta was a doctor instead of a housewife and Steve had become an engineer instead of a computer analyst.

"Thanks for staying. Your mother likes having you around. We don't see enough of you." He patted Stephen on the back. Vik had pretended to be annoyed when at fourteen the boy shot up three inches taller than he was, but secretly he'd been pleased. With his height and that straight brown hair that would not curl and those gray eyes, Stephen looked just like his grandpa. Dad had been pleased, too.

"Is your mom all right?"

"I don't think she was too happy about moving downstairs."

"Of course not, but it had to be done." He hated to admit it, even to himself, but he was glad he hadn't been here to see the look in Mildred's eyes when that bed came downstairs. "Better than finding her at the foot of the stairs one day with her neck broken."

"Aunt Helena made sauerkraut and sausage."

Vik walked ahead of him to the kitchen. Helena was a damned good cook. Too bad about her personality.

While he warmed dinner up in the microwave, Stephen poured coffee and cut two slices of apple pie and wedges of cheddar cheese. "Ma refused to let us move your table or your recliner out of the den, and Krysta insisted that Ma had to have her rocker downstairs. We got it all in there somehow. It's pretty crowded, but we pushed what we could against the wall and left enough room on either side of the bed for her walker."

"Has she used the damned thing yet?"

"Yeah, she did. Surprised me."

The fall must have scared her. He bit into a mouthful of home-made sauerkraut and cut a hunk of sausage. The sour, spicy cabbage had a bite to it. "I hated to do it, but it's temporary. She'll adjust."

"Is it?" Stephen asked.

"Is it what?"

"Temporary."

Vik scooped up more sauerkraut, chewed slowly, then said, "I hope so."

"Dad," Stephen said.

"What?"

"You doing okay?"

"Of course I am."

"No, I mean really. You can't be with her; you've got to work. Are you okay?"

Vik stabbed a hunk of sausage. "No," he admitted. "Don't tell your sister, or your aunt Helena, or anyone else, but no, I'm not okay."

The house was dark except for lights in the kitchen and den, when Marti pulled into the well-lit driveway. She had wanted to spend a little time with Joanna. The boys seemed okay, but Joanna hadn't fixed her any decaf coffee since she'd gotten back from Wisconsin. Worse, Joanna hadn't said a word this morning when Marti had spread butter on her toast instead of jelly.

As much as she wanted to believe that Joanna's sudden silence was the result of something that had nothing to do with her, silence from Joanna was rare and never indicated anything straightforward like resentment or anger. In silence, Joanna was as inscrutable as Theo, and even more difficult to communicate with. Why couldn't Johnny have been more like Ben? Open, talkative. She'd never have to wonder what was on Ben's mind. Maybe that wasn't such a good thing, but on nights like tonight, it would make life a hell of a lot easier. By the time she went through the walkway from the garage to the house, she had a headache.

Warm southern aromas greeted her as she went into the kitchen. Without taking off her coat, she lifted the lid from one pot, then another. Smothered cabbage, corn bread, fried chicken, gravy.

Ben spoke from the doorway that led to the den. "It's not as bad as it looks. Half the cholesterol, I promise."

"Now if it's only half as good as it smells."

Ben chuckled. "Momma Mac compromised. Smoked turkey in the cabbage, canola oil for the chicken, and my special low-fat gravy for the rice."

"Momma Mac?"

"Sure. Big Mac and Momma Mac." He took a plate from the cupboard. "Exhausted Mac, from the looks of it. Come on and sit down. I'll fix you something to eat. Momma Mac wanted to put it away, but there is something about coming into a room that smells this good and lifting those pot lids and inhaling that aroma that a microwave warm-up can't come close to. So I stashed the pots in the refrigerator and got the fire going under them as soon as you pulled into the driveway. It's amazing how much you, your mom, and Joanna look alike and how differently you cook."

Marti sank into a chair and let him bring dinner. "Did you talk with Joanna today?"

"She had a game. Came in, made a salad without dressing and a tuna fish sandwich without mayo, and said she had to study. Maybe she broke up with Chris."

"I don't think she's speaking to me; at least she didn't seem to be this morning."

"Joanna never has much to say in the morning anyway, which is probably good—she looks damned cranky."

"I've made coffee with caffeine two days in row."

"Hmmm." Ben considered that. "This could be serious after all. Do you think it's got anything to do with us?"

"I don't know. Lately, there's no pleasing her, and I'm not sure that where my personal life is concerned I should have to. She is still the child."

"Spoken like a true cop. Too bad it doesn't work that way. Not only do we want them to have everything we didn't have; we want them to be happy."

Marti rubbed her neck where it ached.

"I've got something for that." He came around behind her and began kneading her shoulders. "So, Officer Mom, are we worried about Joanna or not?"

"I just can't seem to get it right where that girl is concerned." She leaned into his hands. "And I am so damned tired. Already. I've only been back a couple of days and I feel like I did before I left."

"Testy."

"Ben!"

"What are the odds we can make it to her game day after to-morrow?"

"Not as bad as they could be." She told him about Lupe.

"Good, we'll shoot for that, but we won't say anything, just in case. Maybe by then she'll tell you what's on her mind. One thing about Joanna, she's not good at extended sulking. Takes after her mother."

"You think so?"

"I think a nice hot shower is in order. These muscles are really tense."

"Do I get a massage in the shower?"

"You get whatever you want, but only if you sleep in until eight and miss roll call."

"We're assuming I can stay awake."

"Know what? It's okay if you can't. I'm not going anywhere."

Marti wondered about that: A lot of cop's spouses walked after a few years of these hours, and besides that, as much as she loved them, her kids were no prize. And, after Sunday, Momma wouldn't be here to cook.

6

Marti awakened to Ben humming softly as he moved about the room getting dressed. She stayed still and kept her eyes closed. It had been a long time since she had a man in her bedroom. The musky scent of his cologne wafted from the pillow and seemed to surround her. For a moment, it seemed to weigh down on her. Johnny would have been shaking her awake by now. Ben was so easygoing, so far. She thought of an old Marvin Gaye song that had irritated her so much from the first day she heard it that it took the edge off of whatever sadness she might have felt when he got killed. "Wake up, wake up, wake up" would play in her mind over and over, spilling over into resentment from when Johnny would wake her up during the night. She had forgotten that. How much more had she forgotten? How long before Ben began waking her up when she fell asleep after sixteen hours on the job? Sleeping alone had been easier.

"Psst," she said as Ben opened the door.

He came over at sat beside her without closing it. "Morning."

"This isn't easy," she said. "None of it."

"Having second thoughts?"

She looked up at him and realized how much she wanted him to be there.

"Not those kind."

"What kind?"

"I'm not twenty-something anymore. I can't do all the things I did the first time to keep you happy. You might have to be in charge of that yourself."

"Marti, listen. I've been married, and widowed. Since then, I've sowed enough wild oats for several people. You females tend to have the edge when it comes to maturity, but somewhere in there, I hope to God I became man enough to be able to live with a woman, day in, day out, with all the ordinary stuff thrown in along with the kids, as well as the aggravation. I'm serious about growing up, and, so far, I'm enjoying this. Especially your insecurity, Officer Ma'am."

"Insecurity!"

"Oh, I remember. Big Mac. Five ten, a hundred and sixty pounds, carries a Beretta, and nobody who wants to live messes with her."

"You've got that right."

"Yes ma'am." He grinned and gave her a bear hug.

She said a quick prayer that the honeymoon could survive two homicides, a lot of overtime, and an almost forty-year-old bride who fell asleep last night before even a quick kiss. For the first time since she'd gotten back, the sun was shining. She hoped that was a good omen.

Theo and Mike were eating pancakes when Marti went downstairs. She gave each of them a kiss.

"Did you guys see any deer?" Mike asked. He was a round-faced, chubby ten-year-old who had gone from the class bully three years ago to a child who always seemed to be smiling.

"Lots," Marti said. "They shied away when we got to close, but they weren't really afraid."

"Highland Park voted not to shoot their deer," Theo said. He was taller than Mike, and thin, with Johnny's smooth brown skin and aquiline face, thin lips, thin nose and dark deep-set eyes. "We need more forest preserves for them. Developers are taking their land and they have no place to go."

"That's why we have so many skunks in the neighborhood," Mike added. "And raccoons."

Their fifth-grade teacher, an older woman whom Marti had disliked at the beginning of the year, was getting them involved in current events and social issues as well as ecology and endangered species and a whole range of interesting concerns. School had become exciting for both of them and the complaints about homework were down.

Joanna sort of stumbled into the room while Marti was making coffee. Marti waited for a remark about caffeine, but there was none. She felt disappointed. What was wrong with this child? She went over to her and brushed strands of auburn hair away from her face.

"Umm," was all Joanna said. Now that Joanna was two inches taller than she was, Marti had to look up at her unless she was wearing heels.

"Where's Grandma, Joanna?" she asked. "Is she up yet?"

"She gets up at five. She's usually washing clothes by now," Joanna mumbled. "Whether anything is dirty or not." She rubbed hazel eyes the exact shade as Momma's and swung one braid over her shoulder so that it hung down her back to her waist. Marti could remember doing that when she was a teenager and Momma refused to let her cut her hair. Joanna liked having long hair, and she looked so much like Momma. What was she going to do when Momma was gone? Even Ben liked having her here.

Joanna scowled as she shook cereal into a bowl and added cranberries and bananas.

Marti went to her. "You okay?"

"Umm."

"Maybe we can talk tonight."

Joanna's arched eyebrows questioned that, and Marti knew she was right. The odds on her getting home any earlier tonight than she had last night were remote.

"We live in hope," she said. At least Joanna's silence didn't seem to be directed at her. Maybe it did have something to do with Chris.

There was a loud knock on the kitchen door, and when she opened it, two boys—a big stocky boy who looked to be Theo and Mike's age and a tall, slender boy a couple of years older—grinned at her.

"Morning, ma'am. I'm Peter," the younger boy said. "Are you the police officer?" he asked.

"Yes."

"Wow, a cop and a fireman right next door. Are you working on that case with the mummy they found in the theater? Was it there a long time? What does a real mummy look like?"

"Would you like to come in?"

"Oh, yes, ma'am."

The older boy said, "I'm his brother, Patrick. I'm just dropping him off."

"I don't need dropping off. He wanted to meet you."

Marti held out her hand. "It's nice to meet both of you."

She gave Theo and Mike a peck on the forehead, and Joanna accepted a hug. Ben held the door open. "See you later, big boy," she said, giving him her best Mae West imitation. She winked and kissed him on the cheek. "Uh-oh, time for a shave." She vamped out the door.

Vik was at his desk when Marti walked into the office at 8:30. The two vice cops they shared the office with were there, too.

"Coffee, Marti?" Slim said. Slim was tall and slender with skin a shade lighter than caramel. He had a widow's peak and, when he smiled, which was often, dimples. He was also liberal with his Obsession for Men cologne and Marti found the smell annoying. "You look like you could use an eye-opener. Too much morning-after-not-enough night before?"

She debated answering him, decided that would just fan the flames, and poured her own coffee.

"Umph," Cowboy said. He spoke with a drawl that was thicker than a Texan's, even though he'd been born and raised right here in Lincoln Prairie. "Damned if she ain't coming in late already. Looks like Big Mac ain't what she used to be."

"Married life can do that to you, especially if you're a cop married to a fireman," Slim agreed. "You know what they say about firemen. Forty-eight on duty at the fire station, and forty-eight off duty with the incoming duty shift's significant others."

Cowboy put his size twelve boots on his desk, leaned back, and cocked his five-gallon hat back on his head so that a shock of blond hair showed. "Big Mac just might be putting first things first here. I, for one, can appreciate that. Why worry about a dead corpse lying up in the morgue when you got a live one right beside you?"

There was an edge to their comments that took away any humor they might have had, as if they were jealous lovers, rather than cops taking small talk too far.

"If nothing else," Slim said, "having a man around the house takes care of any worries the little woman might have about a home invasion."

Marti bristled. That was a bit too close.

"What's this I hear about you two losing that case yesterday?" Vik said before she could say anything. "Something about the judge calling it entrapment?"

"He was just having a bad day," Slim said. "He came to work too early. Didn't take care of business at home first like Big Mac here."

"Hmm. Entrapment. And the case was thrown out. Nothing like that has ever happened to Marti," Vik said. "There might be something to solid detective work that you two are missing out on as you sit here running your mouths."

Marti busied herself gathering up the paper clips mixed in with the pencils. Vik was getting subtle in his put-downs. It must be from working with her.

"Speaking of which, MacAlister," Vik said, "I thought it might be a good idea to show Jeremiah Cheney that frame. We are bas-- ing this arrest on a verbal description."

"How many solid silver frames with that much detail and the portrait of a man who looks amazingly like all of the Cheney men do you think would have turned up at Armstrong's place?"

"I know, but the man did come here all the way from Florida, and he is sick."

"So, let's do it," she agreed, trying not to think about how much time it would take to drive to Lake Forest and back. "It's the only way he'll get to see it anytime soon."

Vik was getting soft. It had been obvious last night that the portrait, and the fact that Barnabas Cheney had held on to it all these years, had an importance to his brother that far exceeded its material worth.

"And," Vik went on, "I advised the state's attorney's office that we would be holding Armstrong for twenty-four hours without charging him. They want to go with the obstruction and failure to report a death charges, along with the theft charge. They don't think we have enough to make a homicide charge stick."

"I agree. Too much is still circumstantial. His lawyer called, asking to see us, and I told her we'd get back to her. I want to talk with that Stazlowski woman again."

"The customer Cheney didn't see the day he found the body," Vik said. "That crossed my mind, too. She was in a hurry, and we caught her on her way out. It wouldn't hurt to talk to her again."

Marti dialed the woman's number but didn't get any answer. She went through her in basket and pulled out the reports. "Nothing new on the mummy case?"

"Torres should be in in about half an hour for a quick recap of what went down yesterday," Vik said. He looked from Slim to Cowboy. "You two might want to stick around and take a few notes."

To Marti's surprise, Cowboy and Slim were still there when Lupe came in.

"You make this?" she asked Cowboy as she sniffed the coffee.

"Who else?"

"Oh well . . ." Lupe shrugged. "It's almost as good as mine."

"I think we still know who's the best."

"At what? Entrapment?"

Marti grinned. Their story had made it around the precinct with all due speed and Slim and Cowboy deserved every comment, joke, and snide remark it would generate. They had gotten careless, and cops couldn't do that, not even vice cops setting up a john.

Vik began with the Cheney case. "Motive is the stickler in this one. We know how he died, and we have a lot more opportunity than the facts suggest. Even though Cheney was in a secured building when he was killed, the lock on the front door could be opened with a credit card, a set of picks, whatever."

"What about Armstrong?" Lupe asked.

"We're holding Mr. Armstrong for twenty-four hours. The state's attorney's not ready to go with a murder-one charge. Do you know anything about him?"

"It's not my beat. And there's a Robin Hood aspect to that kind of theft that seems to make it okay. Most of the stolen goods that are brought in stay in the neighborhood, and it seems more like a community service than a crime."

Vik grimaced. "Time was when people wanted their neighborhoods crime-free."

"They still do," Lupe said. "We're just getting down to their definitions of crime. What else you got?"

"One question is whether it was a crime of opportunity or premeditated," Vik said. "Did someone see the watch, decide Cheney was any easy mark, and pool? Does the motive have nothing to do with what he had, the watch or the frame, or go deeper than that? We interviewed Aunt Lindy." Vik filled Lupe in on the old woman's background. "We questioned local businessmen. We rounded up the local street residents, and one of them did recognize Cheney. We sent a morgue shot to the train station, based on what he told us."

"We've got a locked door," Marti said. "And a complete lack of identifiable fingerprints, even Cheney's."

"It sounds like you both think it was deliberate," Lupe said. "Premeditated. You don't think someone found out who he was, figured he might have something down there that was worth something, and picked the wrong time to find out?"

"Given his lifestyle, that's tempting," Marti said. "It looks like some planning was required and some knowledge of Cheney's background and habits, but according to Aunt Lindy and the victim's family, Cheney wasn't likely to strike up or even be able to maintain meaningful conversation."

Marti got another cup of coffee. She liked the way Lupe was probing rather than going for superficial answers. Even Slim and Cowboy had shut up and were paying attention. "This could have been a crime of passion," she said. "Even though there is only one blow to the head. The problem is that, as far as we can tell, Cheney didn't interact with anyone often enough to provoke any passion."

"So," Lupe said, "we're either dealing with someone in the indigent population, a psycho, drug addict, whatever, maybe someone who set Cheney up as a mark, or we're dealing with someone like Armstrong, who might be smart enough to try to cover his tracks by wiping away the fingerprints and telling enough of the truth to mask some of his lies. What about family? Isn't that the first place you look?"

"We looked at them in terms of motive, because the family is apparently wealthy. We've determined so far that he had had no contact with them in years, and his share of the money reverts back to a trust and is equally divided among the survivors."

"It looks like that brings us back to Armstrong," Lupe said.

"According to Armstrong," Vik said, "he found Cheney dead Tuesday morning but didn't report it. That does not tell us who called it in on Wednesday. The grandfather's fob watch does exist and is still out there somewhere. We don't know if Cheney carried it around with him or kept it in his room."

"So," Marti said, "we remain at square one. This was either deliberate or a crime of passion or opportunity. We have some parameters for opportunity, but not a clue as to why someone would plan to kill him."

"I think Armstrong is your strongest suspect," Lupe said. "That frame really was an antique, probably the only legitimate one Armstrong ever got his hands on. If we act on the assumption that everyone is capable of murder—"

Marti interrupted Lupe at this point. "We still have a specific victim, and specific suspects and specific circumstances. We still have a lot of puzzle pieces. Some them will be extra."

"We can see that Armstrong is emotional enough to act impulsively," Vik said. "What we can't figure out is why he would find it necessary to kill Cheney. Even if Armstrong stole the damned frame, what would Cheney have done about it? He was an old man. Would he even have had enough of his faculties left to figure out Armstrong could have been the thief?"

"We don't know enough about Cheney," Marti said. "He's the only one besides the killer who can tell us who did this. We have an elderly, mentally ill recluse and a lot of assumptions about people like that and damned little information. The brother's and Aunt Lindy's recollections were too nonspecific."

Vik agreed. "You're right, we don't know enough about him."

"We don't have to dig too deep if Armstrong did it, but if he didn't . . ." Marti made a few notes. "Okay, on to the mummy. Black female. Between seventeen and twenty years of age when she died. Approximately five months pregnant and therefore sexually active." A thought struck her: Is that what's wrong with Joanna? Has she or hasn't she? Good Lord.

"Marti," Vik said.

"Oh. Clothing indicates that she died during the summer. She seems to have liked jewelry. Her hair was cut above shoulder length and on a slant, longest near the face, shortest from the ears and behind the neck. We have not established when she died." They had to figure that out, and the clues were scant. "Physical evidence is all we have to go on right now."

"Maybe I can do some research on the clothing?" Lupe suggested. "Locate the shoe manufacturer? Maybe there's some way to trace the silver and sapphire ring."

"Think about the hairstyle, too," Marti said. There was something familiar about it.

"How about lunch?" Slim suggested.

"No way," Vik said. "You know what they say about manure. It sticks. I'm not going to be seen in public with you for a while."

"We could order in," Marti suggested. She put in another call to Mrs. Stazlowski and again got no answer, then got a call from the county jail. Armstrong's attorney was with him and they wanted to see the officers of record.

Armstrong's attorney was a slender, freckle-faced women with one of those honest, open faces that often indicated a dangerous opponent in court. She was fairly new in town but had won her first five cases and was gaining a reputation as a tough negotiator. Armstrong might have lucked up.

"Well, Officers, I can't argue your *right* to hold my client," she began. "But I certainly can't see any *reason* for it, based on the evidence I have. Is there something you're not telling us?"

Marti smiled. Vik scowled. Neither of them answered. This one was clever. They'd let her do the talking.

"I have not ascertained that your questioning of my client last night was within legal boundaries, so I will not comment on that at this time. However, I do expect you to charge him in court tomorrow morning as relates to Mr. Cheney's death, or to release him today, since theft charges are already pending."

Marti didn't respond. Attorneys could expect whatever they wanted to.

"Well, since neither of you seem to have anything to say, there's no point in prolonging this. Is there anything you would like to ask my client while I'm here? Assume that this is your last opportunity to do so. I've got a busy day ahead of me and he's been instructed not to say anything unless I'm present."

Marti looked at Vik and shrugged. He shook his head. "Nah."

Armstrong looked as if he had just won the lottery.

Marti and Vik went back to the office. Slim and Cowboy were still there, eating pizza, another sure sign that they were catching it for not being smart. She helped herself to a slice of mushroom and sausage.

Vik got on the phone, then said, "Armstrong's attorney is right out of the public defender's office in some postage stamp–sized town downstate and using Lake County as her stepping stone to the big time. She sure improved Armstrong's mood. Not only did he not shed a tear; he was damned near grinning from ear to ear. I don't know what it is about him, but he irritates the hell out of me."

Vik's talkativeness wasn't lost on Marti. He was either worried about something or upset about it, and the something was most likely Mildred. Then again, he had come to work before she had, after staying up just as late, so maybe lack of sleep was compounding his concerns.

"A little overconfidence on his part, Vik, and another day in jail might not be such a bad combination."

"Well, it looks to me like we're going to have our hands full today. We just might have to pick some inconvenient time, like after lights-out, to question him again. We might even have to get that lawyer of his out of bed, since she's so busy today. She's too cocky to suit me, thinks she's holding all the aces on the Cheney case."

The more Marti thought about it, the more she agreed. "It might not be a bad idea to flex a little muscle."

"Damned right. There has to be a little give-and-take in these adversarial relationships or the whole damned judicial system will get bogged down due to lack of common courtesy."

"And effective communication is a must," Marti agreed.

"One late night, at our convenience, might get her attention."

Slim sauntered over. "Are you two going to play good cop/bad cop?"

Vik rubbed his hands together. "Who knows?"

Vik called before they drove to Lake Forest. Marti signed out the portrait. Jonathan Cheney met them at the door himself and actually smiled when he admitted them. "This news about his grandfather's portrait has really made my father feel better. He even ate a little breakfast."

Jeremiah Cheney sat near the fire blazing in the huge fireplace. He was wearing a black turtleneck under a beige fisherman's-knit sweater and had a plaid blanket tucked over his legs.

"It has to stay in the bag," Marti said as she handed him the portrait.

His Adam's apple bobbed as he looked at it and he brushed tears from his eyes. "When he was a boy, Barnabas traveled abroad with our grandparents. Grandmother had this commissioned while they were visiting France. It was while they were away that they first noticed that something was different about Barnabas." He wiped at his eyes. "For him to have kept this all of these years . . . He said we weren't his family, that he had no family. But he kept this. Somewhere inside, he must have known. . . . Can I put it in the casket with him?"

"I'm sorry, sir," Vik said. "I don't know when we'll be able to return it."

He held it away from him and studied it for a moment. "Well then, this will have to be enough. I have something for you, too."

He handed Vik a bulky manila envelope.

"The photographs you requested, a few playbills, names of old acquaintances, medical records, and everything I could think of that might be important, in chronological order, along with whatever names, addresses, and phone numbers I had or could dig up."

"He's been working all morning on this," Jonathan said. "And now he's going to take a nap."

"Thank you," Marti said. The man did look exhausted.

"I hope I wasn't rude last night. You're not responsible for the laws that kept us from helping him. And I do believe you're serious about finding out who did this. Our attorney has blanket permission to cooperate fully. If there's anything else, Jonathan will be here. I've got to go back into the hospital in Florida tomorrow evening."

The call came while they were driving back to Lincoln Prairie. A train conductor had recognized Cheney's photo. They would hold the train until Marti and Vik could get to the station.

"Who knows," Vik said, "maybe this train conductor saw

Cheney talking with whoever offed him and we'll luck up and solve this one fast. If not, I think we should talk with Aunt Lindy again, and with all this information the brother gave us, we can get Torres started on something. Somebody has to know something about Barnabas that will help us figure out who did it. Maybe we'll find them right in here." He patted the envelope. "I've been thinking . . ."

Marti clocked him at six minutes, at least one over his limit, then said, "What's wrong with Mildred?"

He shut up and didn't even clear his throat.

"You moved the bed downstairs," Marti prompted. "Is she using her walker?"

"We had to," he said. "I put it off as long as I could, but she isn't getting any better yet, so I had to." He was silent for a few minutes, then continued. "When she woke up in the den this morning, she told me she didn't think the medication was going to work at all this time. She was really depressed. Mildred is never depressed."

"Mildred has to get depressed, Vik. She might not have let you see it before, but this has to be depressing for her. You did what you had to. Both of you know that. What does the doctor say?"

"That we have to wait."

"So that's what you do. And you come to work and worry a little less about her falling at home. And maybe in a few days, she'll be able to have some time to herself without Helena baby-sitting."

"She needs that," Vik agreed. "Helena's a pain in the ass. If Krysta wasn't pregnant again . . ."

Marti thought of Momma living with an invalid in Arkansas. She could see the change in Momma since she'd been here, from a kind of weary resignation when she arrived to singing and rattling pots and pans in the kitchen. Today she was going shopping with a church sister she'd just met.

"Illness in the family is something you deal with. It isn't easy for anyone." Except for her great-aunt's two children, and one of them a preacher. How dare they assume that because Momma was a widow with grown children, she didn't need a life of her own? How dare they take such advantage of her? Why did Momma let them? Old debts, she supposed, or promises, old ties, like Barnabas's tie to the man in that portrait. Family was family, after all, and turning your back on them was no easy thing.

They reached the train station in record time, as much because her stomach had decided that a slice of pizza was just a snack as because the roads were clear and well salted. The train's engine was humming and smoke curled from under it as it sat on the tracks. The doors at the center of one car were open. The glare of bright sunlight reflecting off of the white snow hurt her eyes. She put on her sunglasses as they walked to the train. A conductor was standing inside.

"Are you the one who recognized the photo?" Vik asked as they climbed aboard.

"I was on the ten-twenty out of Chicago Monday night. The guy in the picture got off here."

"Ever see him before?"

"He rode back most every Monday night, often enough to be considered a regular. I never thought much of it when he didn't. Looked like a transient type, one of those street people. Mostly what got my attention was the smell. Hard not to notice him."

"Did you ever see him talking with anyone?"

"No way. He knew the rules. We've got respectable people riding these trains. Crazy folks got their rights, too, but they ain't got no right to make a nuisance of themselves. As soon as he started up with that gibberish or reading or preaching or whatever, we stopped the train and put him off. He was always well behaved when he rode with me. I don't allow nobody who disrespects the other passengers to ride."

"Did anyone get off the train with him Monday night?"

"No, there was just him."

"Did anyone meet him?"

"Place was deserted. Nothing met him but wind and snow."

"Did you see anyone following him?"

"It was snowing like hell Monday night and close to midnight when we pulled in. He was the only one who got off the train. Only one I saw anywhere around here. We lay over for twenty minutes. I watched him go up the road there, heading south." He pointed. "I didn't see nobody else around, not following him, not hanging around outside, not nowhere. Too much snow. Too windy. Too damned cold."

Not for somebody, Marti thought. But who? And why? She didn't feel as though she was any closer to those answers than she had been when she'd first viewed the body.

They stopped at the Barrister for lunch. After they ate, Marti put in another call to Mrs. Stazlowski and caught her at home. She begged off seeing them, saying she was on her way out, but Marti insisted that she wait. This time, they entered the apartment building and rang the bell to apartment 2C. The woman told them to come up. A buzzer admitted them to a dimly lit foyer. The carpeting was thick and scenes of foxhunts, English manors, and misty moors hung on the walls.

Mrs. Stazlowski kept the chain on the door and demanded their IDs before she let them into the apartment. Reed-thin, she wore a knit suit that outlined the hollows at her hips. Her deeply tanned face was etched with fine wrinkles. Her blond hair was pulled back in a chignon. Marti wondered how old she was and looked at her hands. Late fifties, at least.

As soon as she stepped into the living room, Marti knew she could be onto something. Small collectables cluttered every surface.

"What were you going to sell to Mr. Armstrong?" Marti said. According to Armstrong, he was intending to look at lamps.

"Sell? I was going to buy."

"What?"

"I, well . . . he didn't say. He just said he had something he was certain I would like."

"What had you bought from him in the past?" Marti asked.

"Just small things."

"Like what?"

"Oh"—she looked around—"this."

Marti followed the woman to a writing desk. On it was a delicate porcelain statue of a woman holding a child by the hand, painted in peaches, blues, and grays.

"Is it worth much?" Marti asked.

"That's a bit personal."

"Is it?"

The woman hesitated. "Let's just say that Mr. Armstrong didn't appreciate its value, shall we?"

Marti walked over to a pair of miniature paintings arranged on the table behind the sofa. A man and a woman gazed at each other in profile. The frames were gold.

"I bought those in the city, from a reputable dealer."

"And Mr. Armstrong? Was he 'reputable'?" Vik asked.

"He didn't have access to much that was of any real value, but he did know a lot of the locals."

"How did you meet him?"

"At an estate sale."

"Did you buy anything else from him?"

"Just these." She opened the drawer of a sideboard and took out six tiny three-pronged forks. "Lovely, aren't they? And sterling silver, not plate."

Marti looked at the miniatures again. "Has he ever been here?"

"When he brought the forks."

"Did he look around?"

"Of course. I wanted him to see what I was interested in, just in case he ran across something." She hesitated again. "He isn't a clever man, not smart enough even to attempt to take advantage of me. But he's useful. When old people die, the families are upset; they often have no idea of the value of their possessions. Mr. Armstrong has easy access to that market."

"Do you buy and sell, Mrs. Stazlowski?"

Again the woman hesitated. "There are things I can't bear to part with, but yes, sometimes I come across something that I think my friends might like."

"Motive?" Vik said, as they waited for the elevator.

"Maybe Armstrong had a pressing need for money."

"I don't think he would part with the frame for money."

"What, then?" she asked.

"They're about the same age. She's much too thin, but to each his own. She doesn't think much of him and he might have noticed that. What if he thought acquiring that frame was a way to improve her opinion of him?"

"Not bad," Marti said. She liked the sound of that.

7

As soon as she hung up her coat, Marti emptied the contents of the envelope Jeremiah Cheney had given her onto her desk. From the looks of it, Cheney had been thorough. The chronology began with Barnabas's birth, June 17, 1931. The schools he had attended, including teachers and friends, as well as vacations and the trip abroad with his grandparents. Marti noted that the list of friends was scant, never more than two in any given year, with no names that carried over from one year to the next. The tutor was hired midway through Barnabas's freshman year, and the list of friends stopped abruptly. There were no college days. Barnabas received a high school diploma when he was eighteen and began his theater activity when he was twenty-three. The notations in between identified places: Montana, South Dakota, Utah, Oregon, the Pacific Northwest, accompanied by the brief notation "backpacked, picked fruit, road freight trains." Barnabas telephoned every three or four months, but during this period, he never returned home.

The various playbills, which consisted of four to eight mimeographed pages stapled together, outlined Barnabas's career in amateur theater. He had belonged to amateur theater groups in Lincoln Prairie, Antioch, Arlington Heights, Highland Park, and Chicago. There was a conspicuous absence of anything comedic, and no Shakespeare. Samuel Beckett's *Waiting for Godot* seemed to be his favorite, He was cast as Vladimir in half a dozen presentations. The illustration for all of those playbills was the same, a tree and two men. "A tragicomedy," one described it as. Marti had never considered it humorous; even the illustration brought back an odd sense of sadness and isolation. She wondered why it held such a fascination for Barnabas. She checked the names of those who played Estragon, the play's only other significant role, and came up with George Jamison in three of the productions. During Barnabas's acting phase, as with his high school years, and while traveling, he seemed to have had no friends.

The only other consistency in the playbills was the fact that he had spent three summers with the theater group in Antioch, a town about twenty miles northwest of Lincoln Prairie.

"This theater group in Antioch has been active for fifty years, Jessenovik."

"So?"

"There were live shows at the Geneva, too?"

"What do you think, that we were a bunch of hicks?" he said. "Everything doesn't begin and end in Chicago."

"So I see."

When she aligned the Antioch playbills, a number of names appeared more than once. It was so long ago that she decided to find someone in charge first. Some of the actors could be as dead as Barnabas. It took Marti several calls to locate a Laura De-Lang, who, in addition to acting, had been the assistant to the producer when Cheney was performing there. Yes, she did remember Barnabas, poor man. And yes, she could see them later this evening. Marti had less luck with George Jamison. According to his wife, he was up north until Saturday or Sunday.

Barnabas's acting career lasted almost ten years and seemed to have ended abruptly. One day he was Vladimir and next he was locked up in the psych ward at Lincoln Prairie General. A week later, he was taken to Europe, where he was hospitalized from August 1964 until April 1981. There was surprisingly little in his hospital records, given the length of time he was institutionalized. The treatment of choice was Thorazine, and at each annual review, there was an order that no electrotherapy treatments be given, per the request of the family. The most frequent comment made by his doctors was "noncommunicative." Marti checked the Thorazine dosage and understood why.

There were few photos. At ten, Barnabas was a serious child, with longish light hair. The family resemblance to Jeremiah Cheney and his son, Jonathan, was evident. At twenty, his hair had darkened. At fifty, when he was released from the sanitarium, he had the posture of an old man, and his hair was completely gray. He stood with his hands clasped in front of him and did not look at the camera.

Marti passed the contents of the envelope to Vik without comment.

An hour later, he said, "Let's talk with Aunt Lindy again."

"You like that old woman, Jessenovik?"

"You know how forgetful old people are. It'll take three or four trips over there before we find out whatever she knows, which may be nothing, but then again, she probably doesn't know herself if she knows something important. And"—he tapped the manila envelope—"she seems to be the only person who's had any real contact with Cheney since he came back from Europe."

It was close to four when they parked in front of the Jesus Mercy Resale Clothing Store. The old woman was closing up.

"Can't stay here after dark," she said. "The last bus runs at six and they make half the route and go to the garage. I ain't got no time for missing one. Y'all will have to come back tomorrow."

"Why don't we drop you off," Marti suggested.

The old woman looked up at her. "What kind of car is that you're driving?"

"An unmarked vehicle."

"Oh." She sounded disappointed. "Ain't got none of them sirens or nothing?"

"Yes, ma'am," Vik said. "We've got a computer, lights that flash, the whole nine yards." He bent closer and said, "Don't tell anybody, but once you get into the back seat, you can't get out unless we open the door from the outside."

"For real?"

"Yes, ma'am."

She checked her watch, a man's watch with a chunky band and a large face. "Another five minutes and I'll miss my bus. You folks have held me up too long. Looks like I'm going to have to accept that ride. Can you make the siren go, just a little?"

"When you get in?" Vik asked. "Or when we drop you at home?"

"I was thinking more like when we were in traffic."

"You got it."

She gave them her address and Marti took the long way. She activated the siren several times as she drove.

"So, Aunt Lindy," Vik said, "you've seen Barnabas's grandfather's watch."

"Seen it back when Mr. Barnabas senior was wearing it."

"And he gave it to Barnabas junior?"

"I think it was more like Barnabas took it. From what I could tell, him and his grandpa were close. From them stories I heard, it was his grandpa's side of the family that he got his sickness from. A couple of them was right crazy, and the only reason they got away with it was because they was filthy rich."

"Did you see Barnabas with the watch since he came to live at the Merchants building?" Vik asked.

"Not that I can think of."

"Why are you so sure that he had it?"

"Can't rightly say, except that there ain't no way he would've been without it. You would have had to see him with his grandpa to appreciate it."

"Did you ever go down to where he lived?" Vik asked.

"Did once, when I first come here. I tidied up for him, did his laundry and all. He come in the next day real nice like. He could be quite mannerly when he wasn't being religious. 'Aunt Lindy,' he said, 'you're too old to be looking after me. You've got to take care of yourself now. I'm just fine by myself.' And he was right. Going up and down them stairs had like to killed me, so I didn't go down there no more."

"Did you see the watch while you were down there?"

"Sure did. It was right beside the picture of his granddaddy. That boy did love that man."

Marti hit enough traffic to activate the siren again.

"You sure you don't need them lights?" Miss Lindy asked.

"Scares folks," Marti said. "We don't want to cause an accident."

"Y'all got Armstrong in jail, ain't you?"

"Yes, ma'am," Vik said.

"I bet folks ain't too happy with that. Be a lot harder for them to pick up a TV or one of them VCRs without him. Pawnshops ain't cheap no more, and them what they got in the secondhand stores ain't worth nothing."

Neither Marti nor Vik spoke. After a pause, the old woman said, "You ain't thinking he had something to do with Mr. Barnabas being dead, do you?"

"Any reason why we should?" Marti asked.

"Not really, I don't suppose. But Mr. Armstrong sure was right interested in where old Barnabas went every Monday."

"You don't say."

"Yup. He made it a point to ask me just last Friday."

"What did you tell him?" Marti asked.

"That I watched Barnabas leave here to take the train into the city every Monday morning and he took the last train back Monday night. He did that for years. Course now, he only did it in the winter, and I can't say where he went. During the summer, it was most often Tuesday or Thursday that he took the train, and then he only went as far as Ravinia. Liked the music, Mr. Barnabas did. Always did like that music that sounded pretty but didn't make no sense, going from fast to slow and soft to loud like that, with all them drums and violins and trumpets and all."

She chuckled. "Years ago, when it was the Chicago Northwestern, folks rode them trains quite a lot. Wasn't all this driving into Chicago like there is now. Old Mr. Cheney took himself into the city two, three times a week on the train."

"Did Barnabas ever go with him?"

"You mean like on Mondays? No. When he was a youngster Barnabas did go with old Mr. Cheney, but most often it was when the old man let the boy skip school."

Marti wondered if there was something about those memories that was enough to draw Cheney back to the city.

"Where would they go? To the office?" Marti asked.

Aunt Lindy laughed again. "I can't say just what they did, but knowing Mr. Cheney, I'm sure he didn't go near no office. It wasn't just the boy playing hooky. Old Mr. Cheney was, too."

"Would they come home late?"

"Sometimes they did, and sometimes they didn't, but I never knowed them to come home before it got dark!"

Marti wasn't sure what to make of that. It certainly wasn't enough to give her a clue as to where Barnabas went when he went to Chicago.

Aunt Lindy directed them to a bungalow that couldn't hold more than three rooms and a bath. It had a sagging porch and a tiny fenced-in yard. They watched until she was inside and the lights went on.

"Looks like we've got a few things to discuss with Mr. Armstrong," Vik said as Marti pulled away from the curb. "Mrs. Stazlowski, and now this."

"I wonder what else that old woman knows."

"She's going to stretch this out as long as she can, Marti, and I bet she won't tell us anything unless it's an even exchange. We might even have to drive her down the Amschultz Expressway with the siren on and the lights flashing. At least there won't be any traffic. I hope we don't have to take her home for the rest of the winter. Not that this trip won't be worth it, just to see little Miss Future Lake County Judge's face when we spring this on Armstrong."

"I don't want to stay up half the night, Vik. Let's just give the lady attorney enough time to go home and get comfortable."

"Well now, MacAlister, we need to talk with the state's attorney real quick, see how he wants to charge Armstrong in the morning. Then there's that actress out in Antioch. And we should grab something to eat. With all that and getting caught up on reports, we should be able to get over to the county jail by eleven, say."

Marti groaned. She'd wanted to be home by then.

She got the state's attorney on the phone, explained the new developments in the Cheney case because of their interviews with Mrs. Stazlowski and Aunt Lindy.

He considered this. "Well, still circumstantial. Maybe enough to go to the grand jury with. I'd like something more, and I bet you and Jessenovik can give it to me. How about finding the watch? I think I'm still going to go with the obstruction charge and failure to report a death, along with theft of the picture frame. That links him close enough to the homicide for the time being, and the charges related to his fencing operation are well substantiated. We can always change our minds."

When she repeated that to Vik, he shrugged. He didn't like circumstantial cases, either. It felt much better when they nailed a case down beyond any possibility of doubt.

Although Laura DeLang looked to be close to Barnabas's age, she was quite attractive, medium height, with few wrinkles, and lustrous brown hair that cascaded to her shoulders. She had taken the time to freshen her makeup, but it was not overdone. She lived alone in a large house that was sparsely furnished, but with what Marti suspected were real antiques.

"Come to Mama, Gracie," she called, and a small white Pekingese with a pink bow between her ears pitter-pattered into the room and jumped into her lap.

"How is Barnabas these days?" she asked as she stroked the dog. There was a white wicker basket with a pink pillow beside the chair, and dog toys were scattered about a gleaming hardwood floor.

"Mr. Cheney died earlier this week," Marti said.

"Oh dear. I'm so sorry to hear that. I take great pains not to read the obituaries these days. It seems so many people I know are . . . passing. Is that why you're here? He wasn't harmed in any way, was he?"

"Someone killed him," Vik said. Marti could tell by his tone of voice that he didn't like Miss DeLang very much. She suspected it was because of the dog. He considered them pets, and this one seemed as pampered as a child.

"Oh dear. That is distressing news."

"How well did you know him?" Marti asked.

"How well did any of us know Barnabas? He kept quite to himself. Had very little to do with any of us. No cast parties, no going out for coffee after rehearsals, and very little to say to anyone beyond his lines. But what a marvelous actor he was. 'Temperament,' we liked to say, but, as we all found out, it was insanity"

"He played here early in the summer of 1964. Do you remember that?"

"Oh, yes. Actually it was a series of three one-act plays written by local playwrights. There was one in particular, though, a very sad piece about a couple who lost their son in World War Two and just couldn't get past his death. A lovely piece, quite moving, and all the more so with Barnabas playing the lead. It was really a standout performance, and played to standing room only. A lot of the area retirees came to see it and came back again. They still remembered the war. It seems almost prophetic now, with Vietnam happening so soon after."

"That was the third summer Barnabas was in a production here," Marti reminded her. "Was there anything different about him that summer?"

"Oh, he was quite gay, quite happy, in one of his manic phases, I suppose. Usually, he was so dour. Among ourselves, we joked and said he must be in love. Little did we know how precipitously close to the edge he was. We should have thought something, I suppose, what with him actually saying a few words other than his lines. Nothing much, but the occasional hello or good-bye. As we used to say, 'He came, he performed, and he left.' That was about it. Not that we weren't happy to have him. Anything he was in was a sure success. We staged the *Great Dionysus*—I played Greta and he was Dionysus of course. It was written by someone local, but so marvelous. I threw myself into the Rhine," she said, and paused for dramatic effect. The dog, catching the lilt in her voice, perked up and looked at her expectantly.

"That must have been something," Vik said. His lips quivered.

"Why yes, it was a memorable performance, according to the reviews."

After another ten minutes of memorable performances, all of them by Laura DeLang, Vik managed to get her back on track.

"Oh, Barnabas, yes. Such a waste, losing him like that."

"Do you know what happened?"

"Not exactly. He was playing in *Godot*, you see. A bit too dour for our audiences. I could never see the humor in it myself, or, for that matter, the foreshadowing and overshadowing and epic realities it was supposed to convey. It did get a mention in the *Chicago Tribune*, just two sentences in a theater column, but a mention nevertheless. Such an untimely, unfortunate accident, his being hospitalized when he was. He could have been right on the edge of being discovered."

"Did you ever see him with a watch?" Vik asked.

"That beautiful Swiss pocket watch?"

"Yes."

"He wore it occasionally. In that war piece that he did here, and, I understand, in *Godot*, although at the time I didn't think it appropriately in character to wear something quite that expensive."

"How was he the last time you saw him?"

"Quite manic, actually. There were those of us who thought he might be taking some kind of drugs, but we couldn't imagine what, and when he went onstage, that brooding, somber mood took over once again. That was his brilliance as an actor, you know. That massive, inexorable, overwhelming sense of loss, of utter despair that he was able to convey. How I wished for him that next summer when I was Estelle. Have you ever attended one of our productions?"

Marti admitted that she had not. Vik said nothing.

"The Geneva, of course, was *the* theater. It was such a marvelous place. I performed there years ago with the Lincoln Prairie Comedy Workshop."

"Did you perform there with Cheney?" Vik asked.

"Barnabas didn't do comedy."

"It is a great place," he said. "Too bad it isn't open anymore."

"I suppose all of those wonderful flies are still there."

"Flies?" Vik said.

"Yes. Oh—backdrops. There must be at least fifty or sixty of them hanging way up there. That's one of things I miss here. Our theater is too small and too new. Those were such wonderful days."

She launched into another lengthy description of what sounded like an ordinary play, and neither Marti nor Vik was able to interrupt her. By the time she stopped talking, Marti felt a headache coming on. When Miss DeLang did pause to catch her breath, Vik stood before she could start in on anything else, and thanked her as he headed for the door.

"But I really . . . There was this time—"

"You have been so helpful, Miss DeLang," Marti said. "I cannot thank you enough. And we will be back if we have any more questions."

Laura DeLang gave them such a sweet dimpled smile that Marti hesitated, expecting her to take a bow. Vik grabbed Marti by the arm. "We've got to go, MacAlister. We've got that appointment at ten."

"But it's only quarter to nine," Miss DeLang called. Marti looked back in time to see her standing there, with the dog in her arms, a forlorn expression on her face, as if she wanted them to stay.

"Didn't Scarlett O'Hara do something like that?" Vik said. "I've seen it in some southern movie."

"I think it was Dorothy and Toto in *The Wizard of Oz*."

"Just get in the car, MacAlister, before that woman thinks up a reason to get us back in there."

She checked the time. It *was* almost nine. Damn. "Is someone staying with Mildred?"

"Helena's there until about seven and then Steve stays until I get home. Mildred thinks I'm being too protective, but she isn't giving me an argument. I don't think she wants to be alone."

"This has to be frightening for her, even if it is just temporary."

"Is scares the hell out of me, too."

"At least you have each other. Momma always said that eventually marriage comes down to that, having each other. And both of us widows at the time."

Marti recalled a line from Browning: "Grow old along with me!" Funny how different life had seemed when Johnny was alive. It was as if they would always be young. And now he was young, forever, and she was going to be forty soon. Joanna would be leaving for college in a couple of years. Theo and Mike would be entering high school and she and Ben would start thinking about life after children. She would not grow old alone—the thought *Like Momma* jumped into her mind and just as quickly she pushed it away. Momma. She wanted her mother. She didn't want Momma to be alone.

They picked up sandwiches at an all-night gas station and headed back to the precinct. It took them well over an hour to write up their reports. By the time Vik put a call in to Armstrong's attorney, it was after eleven. Marti tried not to yawn as she walked into the interrogation room, then thought, The hell with it, and yawned twice.

"Tired, Detective MacAlister?" the freckle-faced attorney asked. "This could have waited until tomorrow."

"Afraid not," Vik said. "Now"—he turned his attention to Armstrong—"why did you want to know about Barnabas Cheney's activities last Monday night?"

"I . . . I . . ."

"Don't answer."

"Did it have anything to do with planning to go down there and steal the portrait while he was gone?"

"Don't answer," the attorney cautioned again.

"Did Cheney come home sooner than you expected? Or were you waiting for him, so he couldn't tell anyone it was gone?"

"Detective Jessenovik!"

Vik ignored her. "When were you planning to sell that frame to Mrs. Stazlowski? Or was it going to be a gift?"

"No," Armstrong said.

"You stole that frame to impress her."

Armstrong looked at Vik with a pleading expression in his eyes. "I just wanted her to see that I was a real antiques dealer—"

"Mr. Armstrong," the attorney said.

"And not just a junk man."

"At last," Vik said. "We're finally getting closer to the truth." With that, he stood up and strode from the room. Marti was right behind him.

Sharon's car was parked at the curb when Marti got home. Now what? No, she didn't mean that. She and Sharon had been best friends since grade school. She had moved to Sharon's house with her children after Johnny died. They were more than friends. They were like sisters. If only Sharon could get over her divorce and stop dating men who were losers.

Marti hesitated at the kitchen door, then went inside. She hadn't seen Sharon since the wedding. This time, instead of Sharon as maid of honor, Denise Stevens had stood up for her. Sharon hadn't said anything, but Marti was certain the decision had hurt her. She'd told Sharon that it didn't feel right, that she didn't want any reminders of her marriage to Johnny, which was true. Sharon said she understood, and Marti was sure that she did, but this was the first time Sharon had come to the new house.

Sharon sat at the kitchen table with only the light from the lamp. Her hair was still plaited in dozens of braids, but the beads were gone and the braids were short, thick, kinky, and went in all directions. She looked up but didn't smile as Marti came in. Marti sniffed as she entered the room, trying to guess what Momma had fixed for supper.

"Catfish, barbecued chicken and okra, corn, and tomatoes," Sharon said. "And Joanna actually ate some of the vegetables. It's been a long time since I had some of your momma's cooking. Lord but it's good. She fixed you a plate before she went to bed. It's wrapped in foil in the refrigerator."

Marti replaced the foil with plastic wrap and put the plate in the microwave. "Want some?"

"Girl, I've already had three helpings."

"Where's Ben?" The lights were out in the den.

"He went up about half an hour ago."

"And Lisa?"

"Upstairs bunking in with Joanna."

"Coffee?" Marti asked.

"Had some. Pop, too."

Marti came to the table with the plate and sat down. Now what? Sharon either wanted something or had a problem. She jabbed at the okra. She didn't feel hungry anymore.

"Nice place," Sharon said. "Great place, guard dog, security system, and all. Big, too. Lots of room."

"What's up?" Marti asked.

She was going to have to get at least a few hours of sleep.

"Nothing much. I just want to know if Lisa can spend the weekend."

"That's it? Sure."

"I'm going to Mexico."

"Just for the weekend?"

"It's just a little celebration." Sharon took a small box from her purse and opened it.

"Nice ring," Marti said. Just paste, but good. Marti wouldn't have been able to tell if she hadn't worked a fraud case years ago that involved fake gems. She knew she should tell Sharon that it wasn't real, but she couldn't, not tonight.

"He owns his own business, Marti. Or, as he puts it, he's a conglomerate, does all kinds of things I don't understand."

112

Marti looked at the ring. Sharon was right about that. How could she be so gullible?

"This guy is great, Marti; he really is. He's ten years older than I am. He's mature. This guy is not another loser, Marti, he isn't."

She didn't answer. They would both find out soon enough. Sharon left a few minutes later and Marti went upstairs to bed.

Momma's dining room was crowded with neighbors. Even as Marti smiled and spoke to them, she knew they weren't here anymore. Every one of them was long dead. With wide-mouthed, gapped-tooth grins, they all brought her the same news. Sharon is dead. Sharon is dead. No, Sharon was not dead. The ritual of passing plates became festive— roast turkey, fried chicken, candied yams; the laughter became louder, until those who came over to offer their condolences were shouting. Sharon is dead. Sharon is dead.

Then Marti was in the kitchen, where Johnny presided over a smoking barbecue pit. His face is all wrong, she thought. He's gotten so much older. He looks just like his father. Immaculate in full dress uniform, Johnny lifted the flame-seared meat and held it out to her, laughing until his face disappeared and there was just the badge, and the uniform, the gun, and the hat.

At once, she was back in the dining room, scooping heaping spoons of okra, corn, and tomatoes from a bowl, piling it onto her plate until Sharon's mother laughed. Always a flirt, always a tease, Sharon's mother had a man at each elbow and smiled up at each of them in turn until she became robotic, turning, looking up, laughing, with marionette jaws opening wide and snapping shut. Sharon is dead.

Marti awakened all at once. Panic seized her for a moment; then she relaxed, still by the soft snore of the man sleeping beside her. Once a cop's wife, always a cop's wife. Don't move or he would be as immediately alert as she was. But this wasn't her first husband, Johnny. Johnny was dead. This was Ben. His breath was warm against her face. His scent, pungent with musk, teased her nostrils. His hand was possessive and reassuring on her thigh. Did firemen wake up as abruptly as cops?

The dream was as vivid in her mind as an instant replay. *Sharon is dead.* She was more worried about Sharon than she realized, especially now that she didn't see her every day. She would ask Momma to have a talk with her before she went back to Arkansas. Ben stirred. His hand stroked her thigh. Drowsy, he said, "Umm," and spoke her name. Exhausted, she snuggled against him and closed her eyes.

8

Marti slept in the next morning and didn't get to work until after eight. It was Saturday and Vik had the same idea. He came in a half hour later than she did. He looked rested, and some of the lines that had creased his face with worry were gone.

"Is Mildred feeling better?"

"She's adjusting."

"You look better."

"I got a halfway decent night's sleep. And we had breakfast together." He patted his stomach. "She likes to see me eat, so she fixed potato pancakes."

Marti had fixed breakfast this morning, too. She made the best Belgian waffles of anyone in the house and everyone loved them, even Joanna. Joanna was so hard to please that Marti was always happy when she cooked something that child would eat. Now if she could just make it to a few of Joanna's basketball games. According to Ben, Joanna was at the top of her game and getting better.

Marti took the call from the state's attorney. He was going to court to ask that Armstrong's bail be revoked because of the additional theft charge. Did she have anything else? "We've got a witness who says that the Friday before Cheney was killed, Armstrong was asking where Cheney went on Mondays. And Armstrong promised one of his customers something she would like, which could have been the picture frame."

The state's attorney didn't think that was enough. "So, we wait a little longer, MacAlister. You're developing a good circumstantial case here. I'm surprised Armstrong's attorney hasn't called me. Let's see what happens after the court session. If nothing else, we should be able to get a higher bail. That might keep him in jail for a few days. He had trouble raising it the last time. Jail just doesn't agree with a lot of first-timers. He might start singing real soon."

As she hung up, it came to her. "The Supremes."

"Huh?"

"The Supremes, Vik. 'Stop in the Name of Love.' "

"Oh, Diana Ross. What about them?"

"The hairstyle, Vik. The mummy's hairstyle. I've seen a picture of them with the same cut on an album jacket. I'm sure of it."

"How can you be so sure of something you saw thirty years ago?"

"That's why it took me so long to remember."

"Well, Torres is working on that; let her check it out."

Lupe came in a little before three. "I've got to write up a report," she said, and sat down at the typewriter.

Vik looked at Marti and winked. "Does this mean you've got something for us?"

"I spent the whole morning at the library checking this out."

It took her less than eight minutes to type three pages. While she was out making copies, Vik said, "Not bad. I don't suppose we could get her to—"

"Don't even think it, Jessenovik. Just forget you ever saw that." As much as Marti might have liked to have someone transcribe her handwritten notes into something that was legible to the masses, Lupe wasn't the one. "We need her to do real cop work."

"Here," Lupe said. She distributed the notes and sat down. "I researched the Jane Doe's clothing and hairstyle. I typed everything up so I could sort things out between 1963 and 1964 and 1965."

"Have you narrowed it down to three years?"

"Two actually. Things began changing in '65. I just wanted you to see why I think she died in '63 or '64."

"And it only took you half a day," Marti said. "Rookie luck."

Lupe flashed her a grin. "Just about everything she had on—belt, blouse, flats—are consistent with styles in 1963 that carried over to 1964, except for the slacks. Culottes and pedal pushers were more popular in '63. The pants were out there in '63, but they're more consistent with what was being worn in '64."

"I think that fits in with my idea about the hairstyle. I know I've seen an album jacket with the Supremes wearing their hair short and straight, but longer in front."

"Vidal Sassoon," Lupe said. "The chunky, sculpted bob, 1963, but you know how it is with hairstyles—unless it's really far-out, if it looks good on you, you might stick with it for a while, until something else that looks just as good comes along."

"And this is why you think she died in one of those years," Vik said.

"Actually, it's because of her underwear, especially her bra."

Marti glanced at Vik just in time to see him stare at Lupe's breasts. He caught her looking and she tried not to smile as a red flush crept up his neck, then reached his ears.

"There was a big change in bra construction in 1965. They modified the fabric so you couldn't see those bra strap and underwire lines. They came up with the 'no bra' bra. Her bra is definitely pre-1965."

"When did they stop wearing girdles?" Marti asked.

"They were definitely in decline by 1968, but they didn't have panty hose yet, still needed garters and garter belts."

"We didn't have panty hose in the sixties? It seems like I've been wearing them forever."

"I can't even imagine putting on a garter belt or a girdle," Lupe said.

Vik got up and gave the rest of his coffee to the spider plant and fixed another cup.

"She only wore a size five," Lupe said. "She didn't have anything to hold in."

"Was she that small?" Marti didn't have enough experience with mummies to know how much the process caused shrinkage.

"Her bra size was a thirty-two A."

"Did they give us some idea of height?"

"She was five four. She was small."

Marti scanned Lupe's notes. "Not bad," she said. "I think this rates lunch."

"Not at the Spicy Tamale," Vik said. They compromised on a restaurant with Mexican and American cuisine. Before they left, Marti called to confirm that their other actor, the one who had played opposite Cheney in *Godot,* would not be home until tomorrow. After lunch, the three of them spent the afternoon at the *News-Times,* scanning microfiche from 1963 and 1964, without coming up with so much of a mention of anything that they thought could relate to the disappearance of their mummified Jane Doe. They did come up with a short list of burglaries and thefts involving jewelry, just in case one or all of the rings had been stolen. That done, they called it a day.

Marti arrived home after everyone had left for Joanna's basketball game. She checked to see that it was a home game and headed over to the high school gym. The game was in progress when she got there. As she watched from the entrance to the gym, Joanna made a basket. Home bleachers were on the far side of the gym. A coach told her once that they did that so that the away team could make a quick getaway if they won. The visitors were down by four now. Marti heard Momma before she had time to scan the bleachers.

"Go on, girl. Strip that ball. You got it, go, go, go." There she was, on her feet, arms raised, fists clenched, cheering as Joanna sprinted down the court and got the basket.

Marti waited until the quarter was over before making her way across the court.

"Hey, Ma, up here," Theo called. He and Mike were sitting on the highest bench with the boys from next door, Patrick and Peter. There hadn't been any kids living nearby in their old neighborhood. It had been just the two of them for so long that Marti was glad they had made new friends.

Ben flashed her a huge grin and Momma moved so she could sit beside him. They all clapped and yelled as the teams came back out on the court. Joanna was the tallest player on her team. The other team had two players who were taller. By halftime, the game was tied.

"You made it," Ben said. "Does this mean both cases are solved?"

"No. It just means it's Saturday night and we're temporarily out of leads."

"I'll take that."

A few minutes later he said, "Uh-oh."

"What?"

"Look. Over there."

"Where?"

"The bleachers behind the hoop, fifth row," Ben said. "Center of the bench. I can't point."

"There's Chris!"

He grabbed her arm. "Don't wave."

"Ben."

"Watch, Marti. Just watch for a minute."

As she did, it became obvious that Chris was with the young lady sitting beside him. "Uh-oh," Marti agreed as the girl stood up, then bent over to kiss Chris on the cheek. She was petite, perky, skinny enough to be a candidate for anorexia, and white. "I guess that explains Joanna's mood." Thank God it wasn't something she had done, or not done, as was more often the case. "What a relief, but poor Joanna."

"Don't say it," Ben said. "Don't even think it."

He was right. Joanna wouldn't have anything to do with them if she thought they felt sorry for her. The girl sat on Chris's lap just as the team came out from the locker room. Marti looked at Joanna in time to see her look to the stands and look away. Marti felt like drop-kicking Chris.

"That little . . . I could snatch him up out of that seat and beat the hell out of him. Carrying on like that at Joanna's game. It's a damn good thing I'm not assigned to a squad or I'd hassle the hell out of him every time I saw him driving down the street."

"It's okay, Officer Mom," Ben said. "It's just a boyfriend. She can handle it."

Momma was on her feet again. "You go, girl. Take it right to the hoop, yes Lord."

"He was her first boyfriend, Ben. Her only boyfriend. If Johnny'd ever done something like that to me, I'd have whipped up on both of them."

"After all the time I spent with that boy," Ben said. "And he's still as big an idiot as he was the first time he came to the house. Look at them."

Now they were kissing. From the looks of it, if she got her tongue any farther down his throat, she'd choke him. "I can't believe they allow that kind of behavior in a high school gym. No wonder teenage pregnancy is on the rise. All they have to do is hide behind the bleachers. I'm going to talk to the principal about this."

"Marti . . . I'll be damned."

Now the two of them were standing up, holding hands, and Joanna was shooting a basket right below them. She nailed it.

"Way to go, Joanna," Marti yelled. The score was close, the game was almost over, and the crowd came to its feet.

"Yes," Momma yelled as Joanna stripped the ball. "Go, girl, go on. No! Get the open man. Yes!"

Joanna passed it to a teammate, who scored.

"Now get the rebound! Yes! Get 'em, Joanna," Momma yelled. "Kick butt." No one was more ecstatic when Joanna's team won the game by three points.

The boys were having a sleep-over. Ben took them in the van to pick up pizza. Marti, Momma and Joanna drove home.

"Girl," Momma said, "you are something else. You're playing as good as those girls on those college teams. Marti, you've got to get that little spin move under the basket on tape, that and that fake she did when that other girl got the basket. You need to work on them, girl. You got some moves."

Momma did most of the talking. As soon as they got home, Joanna went upstairs to shower.

"Did I miss something?" Momma said as soon as they were alone. "I could have swore that girl scored eighteen points and had seven assists and nine rebounds. The way she's acting, you'd think they lost and it was her fault."

"She did lose," Marti said. "At least I think she thinks so." She explained about Chris.

"Well, if that boy ain't got no better sense than that, he's got who he deserves."

"I agree, but I don't think Joanna feels that way yet."

"At least she's got enough sense not to let it take her mind off her game. No boy is worth that. Did you see how she handled that ball? That girl is good, really good."

Marti poured a gallon of cider into a pot and added mulling spices. They would be taking Momma to the airport tomorrow. This was the first game Momma had ever seen Joanna play, and it probably would be the last. She thought of her cousins in Arkansas again. Some nerve, taking advantage of Momma.

The door opened and the boys came in, laughing and talking.

"Joanna was so cool," Peter said. "We're going to have to shoot some hoops." He was wearing a leather cap, casual shirt, and knitted vest. Her boys, younger, still insisted on jeans.

"We stopped at the video store and got the *Star Wars* trilogy," Ben said. "Remember that? I think I'll watch it with them if they look at it again tomorrow."

Joanna didn't come downstairs for pizza, so Marti went to her. The upstairs rooms were still somewhere between just moved in and settled. Joanna had decided not to bring anything with her but her furniture and clothes. They had bought bed linens right away, but she hadn't decided what colors she wanted, so there was no bedspread, quilt, or curtains, just vertical blinds, which were closed. The carpet was beige, but they agreed she could change it. Joanna was standing in front of the mirror. She had shampooed her hair and was trying to comb it.

"Come on, let me."

Marti sat on the bed and Joanna sat cross-legged on the floor. She parted her hair into four sections and began combing from the back. "Not easy being fifteen sometimes, is it?"

"How would you know? You always had Daddy. Now you've got Ben."

"No, Joanna, I always had me. First me, then Johnny, then Ben."

Joanna didn't speak right away; then she said, "I don't get it."

"Yes, you do. You played your game, watched those two come in, and played your game. You have yourself. You haven't lost who you are or what you are. You've lost Chris. You'll be okay."

"I know I'll be okay, Ma." She sounded close to tears. "But I don't want to be okay. I hate all of this strong-woman bullsh— especially when it has to be me."

"I know," Marti said. "I used to resent that, too. It seemed like it was an excuse to dump on me sometimes. Even your father would say that: 'You're a strong woman, Marti MacAlister. I got me a strong black woman here.'"

That used to please her, or at least she thought so at the time. It wasn't until Johnny died and everyone expected her to be strong all of the time that it became annoying.

She let go of Joanna's hair, put the comb down, and sat on the floor beside her. "It's okay. It's just me and you. I'm not always strong, Joanna. You don't have to be strong right now, either."

She took Joanna in her arms and rocked her while she cried.

9

arti woke up early Sunday morning. The whole house was quiet. Ben was still asleep. She debated waking him up, but getting up without feeling as if she hadn't had enough sleep and walking through the house while everyone else was sleeping promised a treat she hadn't had time for since they'd moved in. She looked in on Joanna first and wondered if the girl would ever stop stepping out of her clothes and leaving them where they fell. The cat, Goblin, peered out from the closet. She had made a bed on Joanna's sweats.

The boys still shared a room, even though they each could have had a room of their own. Bigfoot, the family dog, looked up from the foot of Theo's bed when she opened the door and gave her a swish of his tail. The room was big enough so that they didn't have to stack the bunk beds, and it was easy to see that two very distinct personalities lived here. Mike wasn't as sloppy as Joanna, but he came close. Theo was compulsively neat. The door at the end of the hall farthest from her bedroom was closed. The guest room. Momma must still be asleep, too.

She walked down a half level, where there were two rooms, empty except for unpacked boxes. They hadn't decided what to do with them. If she waited long enough, the rooms would probably become what they were supposed to be on their own. Theo had put a terrarium by the window, and Mike had set up a card table. A chess game was in progress. Neither of the boys had the patience to play longer than an hour.

The living room was empty. They had combined furniture from

both houses in the den, bought a new dining room set at Leaths, but they hadn't had time to think about what to do here. The fireplace was made of fieldstone. Maybe she would begin by hanging a picture above it. A seascape maybe. She would know the right one when she saw it. If she ever had time to go looking.

Momma was in the kitchen rinsing blueberries. "I thought that with so many children here this morning, company and all, I'd make some muffins." She was still wearing her bathrobe.

"Are you okay?" Momma always got dressed as soon as she got out of bed. "Are you sick?" If she was, she could stay for a few more days.

"Sit down, baby."

Momma hadn't called her that in a long time. "What's wrong?"

"Well, sister . . ."

That was something else she hadn't heard in a while. How bad was this?

"Your aunt Sadie is in the hospital. She had another stroke."

"You need to get an earlier flight."

"No, baby, it's not that. Actually, I wanted to stay awhile longer."

"You did? You do? Then why are you so sad?"

Tears welled in Momma's eyes.

"Please don't cry. I'll cry, too." Marti felt the tears coming.

"I have missed you so much, sister. I have missed you and the children so much."

"Oh, Momma. We missed you, too."

"But you've got Ben now. You're beginning a new life together. I'm not part of that."

"Don't you feel like you're a part of it? Ben's already calling you Momma Mac."

"Oh, I know, he is such a sweet man. But I'm old and I've got arthritis, and I'm hoping to get older and be like your aunt Sadie someday."

"And I'll take care of you when that time comes, not some other member of the family." Maybe she shouldn't have said that.

Momma patted her hand. "What I really wanted to do, sister, is stay on for another week. Spend a little more time with the children. Go to another one of Joanna's games. She reminds me so much of you. Except for her eating habits. There's nothing I can do for old Sadie right now, and her children are at the hospital with her. If I go back now, they won't bother to come. She needs them more than she needs me."

Marti took Momma's hands in hers. "I don't want you to leave at all. But right now, I'm just as selfish as Aunt Sadie's family. I need you, too. I can't keep up with all of this and do my job. Ben is a good man, but I'm just scared to death that things will really fall apart when you're gone."

"Then I should go, so that you'll see that they won't."

"No, you should stay. Spend time with your grandkids. Go shopping with the church sisters. Have a life. The thing is, I need help, and I don't want you to go from helping Aunt Sadie to helping me. You should have a life of your own."

"Baby, it's just that you are just married. You two need time to yourselves. You're both too busy as it is."

"Stay the week. Please stay another week. There's an apartment over the garage. You don't have to leave at all."

Ben was awake when she went upstairs. She could hear him singing in the shower. He had a nice baritone and sang in the choir. While he was in there, she got dressed, made the bed, and sorted through the clothes she had draped over the chair. Ben was much neater than she was.

"Uh-oh," Ben said from the doorway. "Lady present." He dropped his towel.

"Full frontal nudity is not allowed after the lady is dressed for work."

He grinned. While he toweled off, laid out his suit, and put on a shirt and tie, she told him about Momma.

"She's staying another week? That's great! Wait until the kids find out." He sat on the edge of the bed and unrolled his socks. "When I was a kid," he said, "growing up on the south side of Chicago while you grew up on the west side, I lived on this little street four blocks long over by Racine near Seventy-first. This time of year, everybody would still have their Christmas decorations up. It was one of those neighborhoods that we don't seem to have anymore. My parents owned the same three-flat that they're living in now—and need to sell. One of my aunts lived on the first floor with her kids, my grandparents lived three houses down, and everybody on our block knew everybody else. I miss that, don't you?"

She nodded.

"If I could wish one thing for our kids, that would be it."

"You want Momma to stay, the same as I do."

"Sure do. Have you got time to go to church with us?"

"I think so. But Ben . . ."

"What?"

"Momma's just going to be here for another week. Things could get pretty damned crazy around here when she leaves."

Ben laughed. "Could get? You're working two cases; I'm going back to work tomorrow. How about still are crazy, and bound to get crazier with a cop and a fireman/paramedic living in the same house?"

Vik raised his eyebrows when she came in at noon, but he didn't say anything. For the first time since she'd come back from Wisconsin, she felt good.

"George Jamison called," Vik said.

"Who?"

"Jamison. The actor. Barnabas Cheney, the—"

"Okay. I remember. He's back from his trip."

"You got it. I've got an address in Highland Park where he'll be rehearsing all afternoon."

"Great." When she went to pour a cup of coffee, there wasn't any. No wonder he was in such a lousy mood. "Where's Cowboy? Don't tell me those two screwed up their usual Saturday-night busts, too."

"Looks like they might have redeemed themselves. They flushed out a nest of old farts partying with a couple of minors and they're still charging them."

Damn. A few more days on the hot seat might have done them some good. "You could have made some coffee, Jessenovik, instead of just sitting around."

"I was hoping Torres would show up. What did you do, tell her we've got Sundays off?"

She got out the filters and measured in the coffee. "She's got a christening to go to over at St. James the Less. She's the godmother."

Vik didn't have an answer for that.

Heavy traffic on Route 41 was compounded by an accident before they reached the turnoff for Highland Park. It was close to three by the time they found the address. It turned out to be a small theater, seating perhaps ninety, and was located above an Italian restaurant. The stage was the space in front of the seats, which were arranged in a semicircle on a grade.

The lights had been dimmed. A man sat on a stool with only the gunmetal gray wall behind him and a spotlight. He looked to be at least Barnabas Cheney's age. Half a dozen actors were watching. Marti stood with Vik just inside the doorway.

"Why too have verdant pastures turned to barren fields with bitter crops of ashes?" He spoke with the deep and vibrant resonance of a young man.

As he went back and forth, from virgin forests and lush pastures to pollution and urban blight, he took her with him, his voice almost mesmerizing. He spoke with such passion and persuasiveness that she could see what he was saying as clearly as if a motion picture were being projected on the wall. She became so caught up listening to him that when he stopped speaking, the silence was so abrupt that she looked about to see where she was. Then the silence was broken by applause and 'bravos' from the actors.

He repeated the soliloquy two more times, and even knowing what he was going to say next didn't lessen its effect on her. The spell his voice cast wasn't even broken when he paused, shook his head, then repeated a sentence several times, varying the

127

inflections and intonations. Twice he laughed when he didn't get it right. The final run-through, without interruptions, was as powerful as the one she had walked in on. When he got off the stool, he became a short, skinny man with bowed legs. One arm was shorter than the other. Marti thought the incongruity between voice and stature had made him the perfect choice for *Godot.*

He smiled as he came toward her. It was as enchanting as his voice, and for a moment she marveled at what a genuine stage presence could do. As he spoke or smiled, he was transformed.

"Are you the detectives from Lincoln Prairie?

Marti introduced herself and Vik.

"And you found some old playbills with my name on them?"

"Yours and Barnabas Cheney's," she said.

"Oh, Barnabas. *Waiting for Godot.* He was a marvelous Vladimir. We even staged a two-week run in Chicago. In a theater. Small, mind you, but with a marquee."

Marti wondered what he did, or had done, for a living. The voice would be wasted on anything but acting. "Is there someplace where we can talk?"

"I'm afraid space is at a premium. But since everyone else is rehearsing, let's go in here."

He led the way to a long, narrow room with clothing hung on hooks and racks and a table with odd things, like a telephone from the forties and a statue of a dog—props, Marti assumed.

There was a kitchen table by the window, with cheese, crackers, a jar of peanut butter, and a coffeemaker.

"Help yourself," Jamison said.

Marti's stomach grumbled and she reached for the cheese and a couple of crackers.

When they had coffee, and Jamison tea with honey, he said, "Now, why have you come to see me about Barnabas?" Even when he spoke quietly, his voice was so melodious that Marti almost forgot to answer.

"Barnabas is dead," she said.

"I'm sorry to hear that." His voice became wary. When neither

Marti nor Vik spoke, he said, "I take it, since you are here, that he did not die of natural causes."

"No," Marti said, and shook her head.

"Then I'm sorry to hear that. He was a marvelous actor. Assuming that he came to some harm, I take it you have not arrested the person responsible."

"Not yet."

"I'm not sure how I can help you. I haven't seen him in over thirty years."

Marti didn't know, either, but if Armstrong didn't do it, and it wasn't some opportunistic stranger, the answer had to be somewhere in Cheney's past.

"We're having a great deal of difficulty locating anyone who knew him. When we saw that you had appeared with him three times in the same play . . . Why do they call *Waiting for Godot* a tragicomedy? I thought it was sad."

"Oh, there is some humor in Didi and Gogo standing around waiting for God. With Barnabas as Didi, there was always an urgency, a tension in Vladimir's inner struggle. What part of himself would gain the upper hand? It was all the more intense because Barnabas himself was never too far from madness. You know that, of course. His family seemed to go to great lengths to act as if he were not insane."

"How was his behavior insane?" Marti asked.

Jamison thought for a minute, then smiled. "I don't know if Barnabas was capable of pretense, but he never pretended to be anyone other than who he was. Very moody, wild mood swings. One minute something could be quite funny and the next he was angry because you were laughing. Those were rare times, though. Toward the end, nothing was ever funny, and the intensity with which he played Didi had them bolted to their seats, their attention riveted on the stage. You should have seen the reviews we received when we were playing in Chicago."

According to Jeremiah's chronology, that was when Barnabas's career ended.

"What happened in Chicago?"

"Nothing in particular. You mean because he was institutionalized right after we closed? We returned to Lincoln Prairie, didn't see each other because we had no reason to. Barnabas was living in a property that his family owned somewhere on Geneva Street. I only heard about his being sent abroad because he went quite insane in a very public manner, striding up and down Geneva Street insisting that the Communists and the Ku Klux Klan were in the process of overthrowing the government and there was a conspiracy to control the militia." He laughed. "If one has to go, better with a very loud cry than a soft, whining whimper."

"Do you know what could have triggered it?" Marti asked. "During that period of time, you probably saw him more than anyone else."

"Idleness, perhaps. The acting channeled the madness. We were both between parts, with no immediate prospects. The madness had no stage to contain it, so he took to the streets."

Marti thought back to her conversation with Laura DeLang.

"Did Barnabas have a girlfriend that summer?"

"Barnabas seemed to have a problem with women. Offstage, he was quite a chameleon. Hours of brooding silence followed by hours of raving diatribes. As for women, it was much the same. They were either like his sainted mother or whores, no in between. Even before women's lib, the ladies did not like that." He took a breath, as if he was about to say something else, but he did not.

"We heard he had a love interest during that time," Marti prompted.

"Oh no. He had a friend who happened to be female, but it was not what you were implying. They shared an interest in the theater, that's all. It's interesting how rumor and innuendo can totally obscure the truth."

What did that mean? "Was someone implying there was more to their relationship than friendship?"

130

"No. No." He looked at her for a moment, then said, "But of course now that he's dead, I'm sure that there are those who will insist it was a romance. It was, but only with the theater."

"Why? Was Barnabas gay?"

"No, that he was not. But he was very . . . mercurial that summer. He went from euphoria to depression in minutes. Usually, he was more consistently depressed. I think that's how this talk of romance began. We in the theater community pay homage to our eccentrics because they give so much more to their roles, but that was why he had no immediate acting prospects. Vladimir was a safe role for Barnabas, if he was near the edge, but everyone took a step back as the mood swings became more extreme. Nobody wanted to be the one who sent him totally over the edge. Of course, it happened anyway, but at least it wasn't one of us who triggered it."

The talk with Jamison gave Marti something to think about. Who was the girl? What had happened between her and Cheney? What, in fact, had triggered Cheney's complete descent into madness? She had thought of it as a slow, general decline until now.

"Funny, there's no mention of a woman in the information Jonathan Cheney gave us. No mention of any friends at all for a long time before that summer."

"Maybe the family didn't know."

"I doubt that. They knew about everything else. My guess is that they had someone keeping an eye on him."

She called the Cheney's Gold Coast attorney right away. "Could you give me the appraised value of the silver picture frame?"

"Jeremiah must have given you that information when you spoke on the phone."

He had. That wasn't why she was calling. "I can't read my notes. Is it five hundred, five thousand, or fifty thousand?"

"Five thousand," he said.

"And that is the appraised value?"

The lawyer cleared his throat. "It was never appraised. The

value was in the portrait, not the frame. Its value to the family, to Barnabas, was not calculable. However, we believe it was painted by a well-known French portrait painter but not signed. There is no provenance, but again, that is not what makes it valuable to the family."

That was more than she had expected. It gave them more to use to go after Armstrong. "But if it were auctioned?"

"It could possibly bring in a considerable sum."

"Possibly considerably more than five thousand dollars." Was Armstrong smart enough to know that? Mrs. Stazlowski maybe, but had she seen it?

"Possibly considerably more," the lawyer agreed. "But that is not guaranteed."

"There was one other question," Marti said. "It's about the young woman Barnabas was involved with here the summer he was institutionalized."

There was a sharp intake of breath on the other end of the line. "I'm afraid that question far exceeds whatever Jeremiah agreed to allow me to tell you."

Then it was true. "Talk to him," she advised.

"I'm not sure when I can. He's in the hospital right now, undergoing a chemotherapy treatment."

"Right away," Marti said. "This is urgent."

The attorney called back ten minutes later.

"I have her name and address, but no idea if it is current," he advised her. "And there was never any indication that this was anything more than platonic. Is there anything else?"

"Not now. I'll call if there is."

"Yes, I'm sure you will." He hung up without saying good-bye.

"For something that was so innocent, so platonic, Vik, everyone sure is reluctant to talk about it."

When Marti checked, there was no current listing for a Justine Harvey. Vik agreed that they should check out the address anyway.

Miss Harvey had lived on the far southeast side of town, not far from the navy base. The house was still standing, and occupied, although it, and the neighborhood, had seen better days. It was dark outside when they got there. Lights were on in the house, upstairs and down. When they knocked, a young boy answered the door. "Ain't nobody home but my grandma," he told them. "Momma's done gone to the store." As he spoke, a car pulled up behind theirs and a young woman got out. She was wearing a heavy parka and had skin the color of coffee with cream. When she began taking bags out of the backseat, Vik helped her. She invited them inside.

The interior had seen better days, too. The hardwood floors were bare and scarred and the stove in the kitchen had legs. The sink had come with house. But the place was clean and starched white curtains hung at the windows. They sat at a Formica table that had cigarette burns.

"I'm Danielle Evans," the woman said when they showed her their shields. "I could tell right away you were the police. Can I get you some coffee, or pop?" the woman offered. She put a bag of cookies on the table.

Vik looked at Marti. He was more aware of black hospitality than he had been a few years ago and didn't want to offend.

"No thank you," she said. "We just had supper. We're looking for a woman named Justine Harvey. She would have lived here in the sixties."

"That's a long time ago. Before I was born. Let me go upstairs and ask Momma. She bought this place somewhere around then. I'd take you up, but we just brought her home from the hospital yesterday."

While she was gone, the young boy entertained them with card tricks.

"Timothy, are you messing with those cards again?" the woman said when she returned. The boy just grinned at her. "Go find yourself something to do." She gave him a light tap on the backside and he ran from the room, laughing. "Well now, Momma says she bought the house from Wilhelmina Harvey in 1965. She says the woman told her she was moving back to Tennessee. She doesn't remember where. Sorry we couldn't be of more help."

As they were leaving, Marti noticed a picture of Jesus knocking on the door that looked just like the one that had hung in her house when she was growing up.

Marti sat in the car for a few minutes, noting that this was a predominantly black neighborhood.

"Well," Vik said.

"Did many blacks live in this part of the town in the sixties?" she asked.

"As far as I can remember, yes. Way back, in the forties and fifties maybe, I think there were more Germans and Poles, but by the sixties, I think that had changed."

Harvey didn't sound German or Polish. "Be right back."

This time, she asked if the Harveys were black, and Mrs. Evans confirmed it. The mother volunteered the additional information that they went to church at Second Baptist when the Reverend Cleotis Jones was pastor.

"I'll bet the only reason this is so hush-hush is because she was black," Marti said as she turned the key in the ignition. "But I think it's worth looking into. If they were more involved than anyone is letting on, and the family interfered or intervened somehow, that could be what sent Cheney over the edge."

Back at the precinct, it took a few phone calls, but Marti was able to locate the Reverend Cleotis Jones, now retired and living in Arkansas.

"Why yes," he said. "Wilhelmina was a founding member of our church. She passed away just a few years ago."

"What about her daughter?" Marti asked.

"Justine or Della?"

"Justine."

"Well, she's right there in Lincoln Prairie. Her name is Justine Kerr now. If I'm not mistaken, she lives on . . . let me see now . . . it's either Virginia or Maryland, but I can't remember which. Just a minute." He put his hand over the phone and spoke with someone. "Mrs. Jones says she lives on Virginia."

134

Marti thanked them both and hung up. This time she found the name and address in the phone book. She called first. After some hesitation, Justine Kerr said she would come to the precinct in about an hour.

When a uniform brought Kerr to the office, Vik excused himself. She was a midsized kind of person, medium height, slightly plump, with graying hair worn in cornrows and a round pleasant face now creased with worry lines. Her apprehension showed in her eyes.

"I read about Barnabas in the paper," she said as Marti motioned her to a chair. "I'm sorry for whatever happened to him, but I didn't have anything to do with it."

Her face was vaguely familiar and Marti wondered where she had seen her before.

"Right now, I'm more interested in what happened between the two of you in 1964."

Justine Kerr squeezed her hands together so tightly that they showed white at the knuckles. She looked down for several minutes, then said, "We were just friends, really. In those days, what else could there have been between us?"

"Did you want there to be more between you? Did either of you want that?"

Justine shook her head. "No. I wasn't interested in him in that way. He was a nice man, attractive but moody. He was always very moody, unless he was acting, or talking about something involving the theater; then, he was magic. And Lord, when he was on the stage . . ."

Marti thought of George Jamison and understood.

"He went to the movies a lot. I did, too. We talked, that's all. We talked. He didn't take me to the movies or anything like that. We didn't date. We just liked the same movies. And he knew so much about them, not just about the actors but also about whoever wrote them and how they really made them, how they were filmed on sets. He asked once or twice if I'd like to go to dinner, but my family would have had fits if I'd ever gone out with a white man."

Marti got the impression that she would have liked to have dated Barnabas, whether he was moody or not.

"Even now, when I teach a book that's been adapted to the stage or screen, I think of Barnabas."

At that, Marti placed her. Mrs. Kerr taught at the high school. She wasn't one of Joanna's teachers, but that was where Marti had seen her.

"He was so alive, so intelligent, and so damned good as an actor. He was the most fascinating man I've ever met." She smiled. "You know, I just got married nine years ago. But there was never anyone like Barnabas. Lord knows, my husband is not, though he is involved in community theater. But nobody ever measured up. Barnabas was so good. He was so damned good."

Marti still was not convinced that was all there was to their relationship, but if that was what precipitated Barnabas's breakdown, it didn't seem important enough now to force the issue.

It snowed Sunday night. By the time Marti left for work Monday morning, another six inches was on the ground. It was still dark as she backed out of the driveway. Smoke curled from the chimney and snow covered the roof and windowsills. Tree branches were outlined in a icy, white glaze, and fir trees were weighted down with snow. A postcard-perfect picture except for the guard dog who stood alert and eager behind the chain-link fence. She looked at the windows above the garage and thought of Momma, already up and preparing stewed fruit and hot cereal for the children. Momma needed a place of her own, a life of her own. Instead, she would return to Arkansas in a week.

The roads were so bad that she moved along at a crawl. There were a surprising number of people on the road. Twice she braked for for fender benders just ahead of her. She still had to remind herself to hold her foot on the antilock brakes without pumping. She was so intent on watching the cars ahead of her that she didn't notice the ones beside her. A sudden loud blast from a horn startled her and she turned in time to see a car swerving toward her. She ran up on the sidewalk to keep from getting side-swiped, but she didn't hit anything. Grateful, she waved at the driver who had leaned on his horn. If he hadn't, she would have been hit. There were swirls in the road where the car that almost hit her had fishtailed. It was far ahead of her now, moving too fast for these road conditions. The brake lights came on as the car swerved again. All she could tell was that it was a dark-colored older-model vehicle. Then she thought, Again? Or perhaps it was just a coincidence.

Even though she'd left half an hour early, she made it to the precinct just in time for roll call. Vik arrived just as she did and they walked into the building together. As soon as they reached the office, Marti pulled out the Cheney file. Where did Cheney's relationship with Justine Kerr fit in? Or did it? Could it possibly have anything to do with his death? They shared an interest in the theater, in the movies, so much so that the man Justine married was also involved in community theater. She reached for Cheney's file and opened it.

"Where exactly is three forty-six North Geneva, Vik?"

"Why?"

"It's where Cheney lived the summer he was hospitalized."

Vik thought for a minute. "It's somewhere in the block where the Geneva Theater is."

"The same building?"

"Not necessarily near the theater. The building takes up an entire block, and there are fire walls between each storefront and apartments or rooms for rent above them. I know the Chinese restaurant is three twenty, and that's right next to the theater, which is right next to the shoe-repair place on the corner, so three forty-six would have to be farther north."

"Did the Cheneys own that, like they own the Merchants building? Is that why Barnabas was living there?"

"Who knows?" Vik leaned back and clasped his hands behind his head. "The Cheneys weren't townies; they were Lake Foresters. I don't know who would have known exactly what they owned. We just knew that most of downtown was theirs." He thought for a minute, then said, "One of my neighbors is a retired alderman. He would know. I'll give him a call." When he hung up, he said, "Jack says they owned that entire block where the Rexall drugstore was; that would be the southwest corner of Geneva and Jefferson. They owned the block where the Geneva is, and the block were the Merchants building is. He doesn't think they owned the property where the Woolworth was or those that the college owns now, where the Globe department store used to be."

As he spoke, Marti visualized the places he was talking about. "The Rialto was at the south end of the block where the Rexall was. That means they owned both theaters." That could be a coincidence, which to her was reason enough to look into it.

"Yeah, it's the Palace now. But they're four blocks apart."

"What about the homicide at the Rialto?"

"That one was an open-and-shut case. Too bad in a way. It was one of Curly Smith's last cases, but not one of his biggest. I would have liked to have seen him go out with a case that everyone would remember."

Now that she knew the Cheneys had owned both theaters, she was more interested in whether or not there were any similarities between that victim and the mummy found at the Geneva, or between that homicide and Barnabas's death. "A homicide at the Rialto, and now a mummy at the Geneva. It sounds like the theater district was a hot place."

"Curly kept things under control when it came to serious crime."

Marti had never met Curly Smith, but she did know that even though he'd retired before Vik came on the force, he'd had a lot of influence and played a large part in Vik making detective as soon as he did. Vik's dad retired as a beat cop. He didn't have Curly's clout. When Vik spoke of them, it was obvious that he held Curly in the highest esteem.

Vik chuckled. "Curly was one hell of a detective. One hell of a guy. If I had been ten years older, or he had been ten years younger, we would have worked together."

This was as good a mood as he had been in since the day before she told him she was getting married.

"My dad worked that downtown beat in the fifties, handled the routine stuff. The Rialto had a side door that opened on Gardner Avenue. One kid would pay to get in; then he'd open the side door for his friends. My dad would watch these kids sneak in through the side door. He would grab the last one and wait for his friends to come outside looking for him. Then he'd make a big deal of taking down their names, march them around to the box office, and make everyone who had money pay. He'd pay if they couldn't. If the kids got obnoxious, he called their parents. If they behaved themselves, he just threatened to."

He leaned back and chuckled again. "The Geneva had the best balcony. You could throw popcorn down and see who it hit. They kept the balcony closed at the Rialto."

"Where the homicide was. What went down?"

"Lovers' quarrel. James Farland worked there as a janitor. He had a fight with his girlfriend, choked her to death, then hid her in a closet, panicked, and ran. The manager found the body the next day."

"Did they have live shows at the Rialto?"

"No, just movies."

"Murder at the Rialto and a mummy at the Geneva. Some things never change."

"Jeez, Marti, where's your sense of history? Jack Benny played the Geneva."

"My sense of history is just fine. Historically, we've found two bodies in the theater district. The Cheneys owned both properties. Now Barnabas Cheney is dead."

Marti picked up the phone and dialed Records. She requested the files on the homicide at the Rialto Theater, now the Palace. Because it had happened so long ago, the files were archived. It could take a few hours.

"I told you that was Curly's case," Vik said. He spoke quietly, but there was an edge to his voice that made it seem like a growl.

"So?"

"So cancel the request."

"Why?"

"Because it was Curly's case."

"Your friend and mentor."

"Right."

"He was still just a cop, Vik."

"Curly always got his man."

"And? Nobody's perfect. Besides, Farland is out now, remember?"

Marti leaned back and watched as he filled his cup with yesterday's coffee, then banged the pot down with almost enough force to crack the glass. She waited until he had torn the wrapper from a candy bar and shoved half of it into his mouth. When he finished chewing, she said. "We have to go over the case. There could be a connection."

"I know. I know. What that has to do with Curly's handling of the case is what I don't know."

She hadn't even seen the files yet, and he was already defensive.

"Vik, maybe these cases are totally unrelated. Or maybe this James Farland killed *both* women. Maybe the woman we identified who died thirty years ago will lead us to the dead woman we haven't identified. I don't know. But we sure as hell have to start somewhere, and from where I sit, we begin with the files on the Farland case. Just because it happened to be Curly's case, that's just too bad."

Vik got up and walked out, slamming the door. She guessed she had that "Nobody's perfect" part wrong. Apparently, according to Vik, Curly *was* perfect.

"Well, well," Slim said. As soon as he walked into the room, the scent of Obsession for Men became overwhelming.

"I see you bathed again—in perfume."

Cowboy was right behind him. His five-gallon hat was wet with snow. "If it isn't the little woman," he said. "In early today, ain't she, Slim?"

Cowboy took off his sheepskin coat and hung it in the closet. Slim tossed him his black leather trench coat.

"Might be that time of the month," Cowboy said.

Slim sauntered over to the calendar.

"No. Not for another week."

Marti wanted to ignore them and ride out their sarcasm, but maybe she had done that long enough.

"Then her old man must be on duty."

"Sure didn't take her long to seek out a little protection once she caught that intruder in her house."

That one was definitely below the belt.

Cowboy began measuring coffee. "They were already engaged."

"I bet that would have been a long engagement if she hadn't found herself suddenly in need of a man. That tough act only goes so far, then it's reality time. Time for a man. Happens to the best of them."

"Detective MacAlister does not like being referred to in the third person," Marti said. She got up, walked toward Slim until they were toe-to-toe, and kept walking, forcing him to back up until he was against the wall. "Detective MacAlister is also a black belt in karate and an expert marksman. Detective MacAlister does not require a man's assistance to subdue anyone." Slim was only a couple of inches taller than she was. She put both hands on his shoulders. "Now that we're up close and personal, is there anything else you'd like to say?"

He raised his hands. "No, ma'am, Officer Mac. Not me."

He said it jokingly, but she hoped he had gotten the point.

Vik was in the elevator before he remembered he needed his coat. No way was he going back to get it. He punched the button to the basement instead. He remembered the Farland case because it was one of Curly's last, but also because it happened so close to Curly's retirement. His father retired with nothing more than a farewell dinner among friends. Curly had left with a letter of commendation from the mayor and the city council. His friends in the department threw a big party for Curly, and his family and friends, with champagne and Chivas Regal toasts and Curly had called him to the microphone. There, in front of everybody, he called him "son."

Marti didn't say anything to to Vik when he came back, even though he had been gone for almost half an hour and didn't even have a can of Mello Yello or a candy bar. Everyone was quiet when he came in. Vik looked from her to Slim to Cowboy but said nothing. In silence, Marti waited for the reports on the Farland case. By the time they came, just before noon, Slim and Cowboy looked as if they were wondering what was going on between her and Vik.

"This could be serious, man," Slim said to Cowboy on their way out. "It's too early for menopause, isn't it?"

"Let's just hope she's not pregnant."

Marti spent all of twenty minutes going over the Farland case, then passed the file to Vik. He took just as long. When he shoved everything back into the folder and handed it back, he said, "Circumstantial, like Curly said. He did a hell of a good job getting a conviction."

On the surface, Marti agreed. She hated circumstantial cases. There were always a few nagging doubts that couldn't be tied up. She put the report to one side.

"So," she said. "Farland is married, he's got a woman on the side, this Dawn Taborn. She goes to the movie. He works there. It is assumed that this is a rendezvous, romantic assignation, whatever. It is also assumed that they argue about something, since there are no witnesses. She's found dead in the basement the following morning. He's found five days later holed up in a one-car garage behind a friend's house in Chicago."

"Farland was working at the Rialto nights as a janitor. He had access to the basement. He killed her in a fit of passion, hid the body in a closet, panicked, and ran. A classic case. Logical as well as circumstantial. That's one of the reasons Curly got a conviction."

She decided against reminding him that Curly was the arresting officer, not the prosecuting attorney.

"According to Justine Kerr, Jeremiah Cheney was quite a movie buff, Vik."

"Look, if Cheney were involved in it in any way, Curly would have found out about it."

"They owned half the town then," Marti reminded him.

143

"That wouldn't have made any difference to Curly. If anything, he would have preferred nailing a Cheney."

She wanted to remind him that cops weren't above taking a bribe then any more than they were now. If this were anyone but Curly, she would have. The Farland case was so old . . . but, he could have been responsible for their Jane Doe's death, too. There weren't any leads in Curly's file. If he had missed it, too bad.

"Farland is out of jail now, Vik. He's out on parole."

"So?"

"I don't think I want to pay Farland a visit just yet, but Isaac is staying at the same place." She thought about that. She had been there several times without knowing that there was anything special about Farland beyond what she read in the paper. She could spot an ex-con as fast as an ex-con could spot a cop, and, where Isaac was staying, there were several who had done serious time. "Maybe I'll just stop by again today and see how Isaac is doing."

One of Marti's church sisters was in charge of the transitional housing facility, but she wasn't there when Marti arrived.

"I know my way around," she told the resident at the front desk. "And I'm sure I know where to find Isaac."

Isaac, still known as Isaac the Wino, had spent thirty days in detox and was now in rehab. He was one of Marti's snitches. She knew better than to expect these programs to work miracles, but Isaac had already stayed sober a lot longer than she'd expected him to. The place was a converted fire station. Thirty men shared a dorm, rows of beds each with a foot locker and dresser to hold their belongings. Marti went to the kitchen first. Of all things, Isaac liked to cook and, thanks to lessons from her church sister, he was getting good at it. Today the kitchen was empty, but she could smell a pot of chili simmering on the stove.

When she went to the rec room, Isaac was playing solitaire. He had looked at least ten years older than thirty-seven when he first arrived here, and had been thin to the point of emaciation. Now that he had put on a few pounds he was looking better. Not only that but he also bathed regularly and brushed his teeth, so she didn't have to make it a point to sit upwind of him and keep her distance. The residents were expected to hold jobs, but Isaac had a few medical problems that hadn't been resolved. He was alone except for a man who sat with his back to the wall reading a newspaper.

"Whatcha up to?" Marti asked as she pulled up a chair. She positioned herself so that the other man was in her line of vision. "Want to play a couple of hands of spades?"

As Isaac flipped the cards over, she noted that his hands no longer had tremors. She hoped he liked being sober enough to stay that way.

"How's it going?"

"Fine, just fine." He raked in the cards, shuffled them, and held them out to her for the cut. "Gotcha" he said, and shuffled the cards again. There was still a sadness about him. A few months ago, he had lost his best friend.

"Dare is somewhere watching you, Isaac, and happy as hell."

"Yes, ma'am. I sure know you're right. Ain't easy, though. But I'm trying."

"Not just for him," she said. "For yourself."

"Yes, ma'am."

While Isaac dealt the cards, Marti looked at the man with the newspaper, clearly James Farland. He was stocky and bald and had spent a lot of time lifting weights. He looked up from the newspaper every ten seconds. She beat Isaac the first two games but lost the third. By then, Farland had finished with the newspaper and left.

"He don't go nowhere," Isaac said in a quiet voice. 'Fraid to leave this place. 'Fraid to walk to the store. Got to be inside all the time. Got to be somewhere with his back to a wall. Watching, always watching." He shook his head. "Been in jail almost as long as I been alive. Shame what it does to a man."

What *had* prison life done to him? Marti wondered. A lot of men went in because they had killed in a sudden rage and came out able to kill without getting angry. Others came out with enough anger to kill everybody. She'd met enough ex-cons to know that *rehabilitation* was often just a word, and the definition was "not getting caught."

James Farland went to the dormitory window and stood to the side so that he could look out without being seen. He'd expected the cops to come and arrest him long before this, what with Cheney dead. Instead, this one comes again and plays cards. They must not have enough to arrest him yet. No matter, even if she left without him this time, she'd be back, her or some other cop. It didn't matter none to him. Wasn't nothing out here for him no more. Didn't matter much where he was. He'd taken care of most of what needed tending to. Wasn't much else now that mattered. Not much that mattered at all. He had known all along Isaac was her snitch, hadn't given him nothing to tell her.

Lupe was there when Marti got back to the office. Marti gave her the Farland case notes. Lupe looked up after a few minutes and said, "There's nothing here."

"You've got it," Marti agreed. "If you ever complete a report or take field notes as scanty as those, you're history."

"That was then; this is now," Vik said. "Curly was one hell of a cop."

"I think I've already heard that one, Jessenovik."

He scowled at her. Lupe looked from one of them to the other but said nothing. Marti brought her up to speed.

"You think there might be a link between Farland's girlfriend and our Jane Doe?" Lupe said.

"Could be," Marti said.

"Do you think Farland might have killed both of them?"

"We won't know that unless we can find a link between the two women, or something that links both of them to him."

"If this mummy had anything to do with Farland," Vik said, "Curly would have figured it out."

146

"I don't know him," Lupe said. She looked at Marti. "Do you think this could all be linked to Cheney, too?"

Marti shrugged.

"Well, the timing is little off. Cheney was killed sometime between Monday night and Tuesday morning. The mummy was discovered while those politicians were touring the Geneva on Tuesday. We got the anonymous call on Cheney Wednesday morning. If Cheney was linked to both deaths, finding the mummy should have been what made someone decide to kill him."

Vik rubbed his hands together. "Even a beat cop can figure that out."

"Unless," Lupe said, "it was in the paper that they were going to have that tour. Whoever knew where the body was must have been getting a little worried that sooner or later it would be found."

"And," Vik said, "Farland is out on parole. And he is not in a secured facility."

"If he killed Cheney—" Lupe began.

"There are a lot of ifs here," Vik said. "Too many, if you ask me. I think we've got Cheney's killer now in Armstrong. Or he's back out on bail. I think everything else is speculation. Dumb speculation."

"Either that," Lupe said, "or Farland was convicted in error."

"And Cheney did it?" Marti said.

Lupe pointed to the file. "We'll never know nothing if that's all we've got."

Marti wanted to see how far Lupe would go with this. She was also enjoying Vik's attempts at indifference. A slow flush was creeping up his neck. "You've got a point there, Torres," she said.

"Farland's out on parole. Why don't you have a talk with him?"

"Because we don't know enough yet," Marti said. "I've seen him a few times. Saw him today. He's at the same place as Isaac."

"We've got to be careful with Farland," Vik said. "He ran to ground when he killed Taborn. We don't want him to run again when we're ready to nail him for the Jane Doe homicide."

"Because running might prove he's guilty?"

"No," Marti said. "All that would prove is that he's scared."

"So, Jessenovik," Lupe said. "You admit that Farland might have killed both women, but you think it has nothing to do with Cheney's death and that Armstrong is the one who offed him."

Caught between admitting Curly might have made a mistake and denying that any of the deaths could be linked, Vik said nothing.

Lupe scanned the autopsy reports on both females again. "Look at the differences in the way the pathologists wrote the reports on these women. How you can you tell if there are any similarities? The language is so different."

"We know that the Taborn girl was manually strangled," Marti said. "Someone applied pressure to the arteries of Jane Doe's neck. We'd better have Dr. Pickus do a comparison of the autopsy photos."

Marti called Dr. Pickus's pager number.

"You're serious about this," Vik said.

"What else have we got?"

"What have we got," he countered. "Two theaters owned by the Cheneys, three totally unrelated homicides, one of which was solved a long time ago by one of the best—no, by *the* best cop who ever wore a badge for this department."

Marti didn't reply. Curly. That was what all of this came down to. Vik would not admit that Curly could have been wrong.

While Marti and Lupe worked at putting together a list of people to interview, Vik stared out the window and alternately drummed his fingers on his desk and snapped pencils in half. Farland's family was the easiest to locate. His parents were still living, as were his wife and daughter. They would be the last people Marti talked with, other than Farland himself. Dawn Taborn was another matter. Because the notes on her were so scanty, Marti didn't know where to begin. She called the *News-Times* and asked them to retrieve and fax the obituary and all newspaper articles relevant to James Farland and Dawn Taborn and was told she wouldn't get them until the following day because they didn't have the personnel available to handle the request. She called the school board. It would take three days to locate and retrieve their records on Taborn. She went through Curly's scant notes and the autopsy reports on both women again. At ten after eight, they called it a night.

Marti was not in a good mood when she sat down at her desk the next morning. It was Tuesday, seven days since they had found Cheney, and they still had not made an arrest. Vik didn't seem happy, either. Cheney had gotten off of the train at 12:00 A.M. Tuesday morning. Within the next six to eight hours, he was dead. From 12:00 A.M. this morning, until 5:30 A.M., two teams from the Gangs Unit moved about the area undercover, observing and calling in anything suspicious. It was so cold that one drunk sleeping in a doorway would have died of hypothermia if they hadn't found him. That, an underage hooker who couldn't go home until she turned fifty dollars in tricks, and a runaway teenager were all they came up with. None of them had been in the vicinity the week before. Marti and Vik met with both teams in front of the Merchants building at 5:30 A.M. and from then until 7:45, when people with jobs or business at the County Building, public-aid office, or the Social Security building began converging on the area, they questioned every deliveryman, pedestrian, store owner, bartender, and street person within a three-block radius.

They paid particular attention to any location that had a phone. There was not a lot of activity. In two hours and fifteen minutes, they listened to a confession from an eyewitness to a fender bender who had denied seeing anything initially. They refused to accept a plastic bag filled with evidence collected to convince the dog warden that a blind man was not cleaning up after his Seeing Eye dog. They referred three complaints of people urinating in doorways of local businesses to the community policing unit. They did not glean one useful bit of information.

When the lieutenant sent for them, Vik didn't seem any more pleased to go to his office than Marti was.

"So," Dirkowitz said, "what have we got on the Cheney case?"

Marti checked out the view from the window. Let Vik handle this, since it involved his buddy Curly.

"It's been a week; that doesn't bode well for an arrest, unless you know something you're not telling me. The family would like to have closure on this. They have 'advised' me of this several times. They have also 'advised' the mayor, our congressman, two senators, and the governor. Is there any chance my phone will stop ringing anytime soon?"

Neither of them answered.

"Well?"

Vik cleared his throat. "We're not where we want to be on these cases, sir."

"How so?"

While Marti admired the way the watery gray sky and the placid gray lake seemed to meld, Vik explained that Armstrong was their only suspect in the Cheney homicide and they had not ID'd their mummified Jane Doe. He hesitated, then acknowledged that since both women were found in theaters owned by the Cheney family at the time of their deaths, there was the remote possibility that there could be a connection.

"I take you do have a suspect."

"A possible suspect, sir."

"Jessenovik, wasn't Farland one of Curly Smith's last cases before he retired?"

"It sure was," Vik said. "Circumstantial, but he pulled it off."

"Damn." The lieutenant shook his head. "My old man always said one of Curly's cases would come back to haunt us. I sure as hell hope this isn't it."

Marti decided that the white specks wheeling and diving in the distance must be seagulls. It was incredible how many second- and third-generation cops were on the force here. The lieutenant's father and Curly had served at about the same time.

"MacAlister." Dirkowitz picked up the grenade he kept on his desk, a reminder of his brother, who had died in Vietnam.

"Yes, sir."

"Enjoying the view?"

"Yes, sir."

"Do you agree that the jury is still out on this one?"

"Cheney's death might not have anything to do with what happened thirty-four years ago, sir, but then again, maybe it does. I'd like to charge Armstrong and be done with it, but until we have sufficient evidence to support that, it doesn't seem like the prudent thing to do."

"I agree." He dropped the grenade, signaling that the meeting was over.

Slim and Cowboy were there when they got back to the office. Marti was not happy to see either of them. She wanted to say something about the way Slim's cologne was clogging up her sinuses but decided to leave well enough alone, since neither of them was bothering her. Another half hour of silence convinced her that someone was going to have to step into the breach, and she was the logical choice, since everyone else's ego was in the way.

"What's this I hear about the toe sucker in the nursing home?"

Cowboy chuckled. "The night nurse said one little old lady was convinced that there was an alien invasion and another one thought someone was siphoning her thoughts out through her feet."

"We told him . . ." Slim began. He started laughing. "The old guy was senile. We told him we were going to tell his mother if he didn't cut it out."

Cowboy laughed, too. "What the hell could we do, haul him off to jail? The old geezer's ninety-four."

"He believed us," Slim said. "Pleaded with us not to tell his parents on him."

Cowboy was almost doubled over, he was laughing so hard. "And the nurse said he's been a model patient for two days now."

Marti didn't think it was that funny.

Vik said, "It's a damned shame when two grown men, officers of the law, have to resort to meaningless threats to coerce the senile into behaving like mature adults."

For some reason, she thought that was funny as hell.

After Vik called the *News-Times* and alienated whoever was pulling the morgue files on the Farland case, and Slim and Cowboy left for a court appearance, Marti snagged the last chocolate-covered doughnut. "Okay, Jessenovik, where to begin?"

"Good question," Vik said "We've got a missing watch, an unidentified caller, and a dangling suspect in the Cheney case. We've got a remotely possible connection between Dawn Taborn and the mummified Miss Jane Doe. Or—or maybe and/or—we've got a possible connection with Cheney, since his family owned both theaters where the bodies were found."

"Think he saw something?"

"If he did, he was to damned crazy to tell anyone."

"Suppose *he* killed them?"

"Now let's just get this straight, MacAlister. Curly was a damned fine cop."

"Who kept lousy notes and never interviewed anyone associated with the victim, Dawn Taborn, not even her family."

"You are not going to malign Curly Smith!"

"Don't point your finger at me, Matthew Jessenovik! I am getting sick and tired of the testosterone levels in this office!"

Vik ran his fingers through his hair.

"And damn it, Jessenovik, I'm not going anywhere with you if your hair is standing on end."

"So?" He leaned back his chair. "Son of a bitch," he said. "Son of a bitch."

Something in his tone of voice made her bite back a reply. A few minutes later, he said, "Curly and my dad were best friends. Dad looked up to him, and so do I. He gave me the first gun I carried when I came on the force. One of his, just like I was his kid or something. I carried that gun until I had to switch to the automatic."

"I respect that, Vik," Marti said. "But I'm your partner."

Vik looked out the window for what seemed like a long time, then said, "You're a good cop, MacAlister, a damned good cop. And I respect that." His hand went to his head. This time, he patted his hair.

Marti relaxed. For the time being at least, they were back on track. She went through her notes again and then leafed through the Cheney file. "If he did kill those girls, then Farland took the fall for him."

"No, Marti, you're looking at this all wrong. Farland killed the Taborn girl. That much we know. The questions here are, Who killed the Jane Doe? And who killed Cheney?"

Vik walked over to her desk and picked up the Farland file. "We can send this one back," he said. "We'd better stay focused on who killed Cheney and who killed the Jane Doe. This case has already been solved."

Marti gripped the Cheney folder so tightly, the skin under her fingernails turned pink. Back to square one. What the hell was it with Vik and Curly Smith?

"Let's talk with the Stazlowski woman again," he said.

"Why?"

"Because the best reason Armstrong had for taking that frame was to sell it to her, or give it to her to impress her. He doesn't have anyone to back up his alibi, either. Let's talk to him again about what he was doing Monday night; let's talk with his neighbors again."

Marti wondered if this was intended to divert her attention away from Curly and the Farland case. "Mrs. Stazlowski stated that she didn't know what he wanted to show her."

"She wanted to get rid of us. She would have said anything."

"My impression was that she didn't know."

"Well, I—"

"Okay, Vik. Okay. As for Armstrong, I don't want to talk with him again until I can ask him about more than his alibi. Now, Cheney got off the train about midnight. The uniforms who canvassed Armstrong's neighbors didn't come up with anything that would make or break his alibi—that he was watching TV Monday night."

Marti sat with her chin in her hands. What was she going to do? They had two murder investigations—maybe one big one—to solve and Vik was in denial about one of them. He had to know that this was not the way to proceed. They didn't have forever. There was a killer out there.

"Okay," she said. "We canvass Armstrong's neighbors again, and we see Mrs. Stazlowski again."

Vik looked at her, eyebrows raised, as if he thought she was being sarcastic. She was just hoping that if they moved fast, he would run out of ways to avoid looking at the Farland case. If these three homicides were connected, she didn't know how. If the girls' deaths were connected but not related to Cheney's death, she needed to find that out, too. And if Curly was right about Farland, she needed to know before Vik became so defensive they couldn't work together. Taking time to humor Vik was time that diverted them from finding a killer, but the faster he ran out of reasons to shield Curly from scrutiny, the sooner they could get back to doing their job.

Mrs. Stazlowski was not pleased to see them. The fine lines around her eyes and mouth had not been covered with makeup, and without eye shadow and mascara, her eyes seemed washed-out. Her blond hair hung to her shoulders in untidy disarray and her turquoise kimono was wrinkled.

"Now what do you want?" she asked. She brushed at her hair and put her hands to her face, then sighed and held open the door. "That miserable little man," she said. "If I had known he would cause me this much trouble, I would never have gone near him. What can I tell you so that you will never come here again?"

Marti tried to catch Vik's eye, but he avoided looking at her. When the woman looked at her, she waited for Vik to speak. After a moment's silence, he cleared his throat.

"Did Mr. Armstrong ever indicate exactly what it was that he was going to show you?"

"No, he did not."

"Was there anything in this room that he paid particular attention to or commented on?"

"No, there was not."

"Did you ever indicate to him that there was anything in particular that you were interested in?"

"No, I did not."

"Did he have any reason to come here, other than to persuade you to buy something?"

"No, he did not."

Vik seemed to have run out of things to ask, which made sense, since they had no good reason for being here in the first place. In the small pause before he could speak again, Mrs. Stazlowski caught the implications of his last question.

"Are you implying that there was anything improper between me and that . . . that junk collector? Between me and someone who wouldn't know something valuable if it had a price tag on it?"

"Why no, no, ma'am, of course not."

Mrs. Stazlowski became even less attractive as her eyes narrowed and her chin jutted out. "Will there be anything else, Officer?"

"No. That's all for now. Thank you for your time."

As they went out the door, she said, "And unless you have something a lot more important to say to me than this, I do not expect to see either of you again."

"Ma'am," Vik said, "this is a homicide investigation."

"Well, unless you think I killed whoever it was, don't bother me." She slammed the door before they could turn away.

Marti watched as Vik stomped down the hallway ahead of her. There was no need to tell him that they had just alienated someone whose help they might need later on. She could also tell by the set of his shoulders that there was no sense in trying to dissuade him from canvassing Armstrong's neighborhood again.

The temperature was hovering around five above zero, with a windchill factor of ten below. She had dressed warmly, but not warmly enough for a two-hour canvass. By the time they went door-to-door in a two-block radius and Vik asked questions about anything that might have happened that involved Armstrong from the time Cheney left the train station early Tuesday morning until the time Armstrong showed up at his store on Wednesday, Marti's feet felt like blocks of ice and her fingers were stiff, even though she was wearing gloves and keeping her hands in her pockets. Most of her face was protected by her scarf, but even so, her eyebrows felt like they were getting frostbitten. The only satisfaction she had was that Vik looked equally uncomfortable. There were times when the lengths a man would go to avoid admitting he was wrong were mind-boggling. Could testosterone alone be responsible for the extent of his pigheadedness?

Back at the precinct, she pulled her chair over and hogged the heat duct. She all but dared Vik to say something. Instead, he got a cup of coffee and kept his coat on. Neither of them attempted to write any notes. Marti was holding her cup with both hands and her fingers hurt. The hot coffee didn't get anywhere near the bone-deep chill that kept causing spasmodic shivers. . . . If she got sick now . . . Damn, this foolishness had to stop soon.

"Hey, guys!" Cowboy breezed into the room. "Cold as a mother out there, ain't it?" Slim was right behind him.

"Oops," Slim said. "Looks like you two have been out playing detective. I sure hope you caught somebody. Anybody who goes out in this looking for anything deserves something."

"That's one good thing about being a vice cop this time of year," Cowboy said. "Business goes indoors, or in cars, at least. The johns would freeze there little whizzers off."

"Yes," Marti agreed. "I've noticed that that is a very significant part of the male anatomy, although frequently overrated." She waited for some marriage-related remark, since she had left herself open for it, but for once they had enough sense to keep their mouths shut.

By the time Lupe came off shift and joined them, the faxes had arrived from the *News-Times*. Marti made copies and distributed them.

"I've got the obituary," she said. "Vik, you and Lupe split up the rest any way you want to."

Vik hadn't touched his copies. He looked as if something smelled bad. Something did, Marti agreed. His attitude.

The obituary indicated that Dawn Taborn had gone home to her Heavenly Father on July 26, 1964. She was nineteen years old. Survivors included her son, Jamiel, and one brother. Her parents, an aunt, and an uncle had preceded her in death. No age was given for her child, but Marti guessed he would be somewhere between thirty-four and thirty-six now. Jamiel. Was he named that as some variation of James? Was James Farland his father?

Dawn was buried from Second Baptist Church, with the Reverend Cleotis Jones officiating. Reverend Jones again, from the same church Justine Kerr and her family attended. How close were the two women in age? Had they known each other? Did Farland attend Second Baptist, too? Was that the connection? And, during that summer of 1964, did another young female member of the congregation go missing?

Marti thought for a minute. She didn't know much about Second Baptist. It was an old wood-framed white church, on Jefferson Avenue. As its name implied, it was the second Baptist church built in Lincoln Prairie. The members had split off from First Baptist, which had just built a new church and had a larger congregation. Many of First Baptist's members were professionals. Most of Second Baptist's were not.

She got on the phone again. This time, the Reverend Cleotis Jones suggested that she speak with his wife. Mrs. Jones had a weak, thready voice and didn't sound like she was in the best of health.

"Oh, yes," she said, "Dawn. That poor child, an orphan herself and leaving an orphan to mourn her."

"Was her son's father dead also?"

"He died in a car accident before the child knew she was pregnant."

So much for the Jamiel/James coincidence.

"Do you know where her brother is now, or her son?"

"Her brother died in Vietnam. As for the boy, he went into foster care. I believe I heard that the foster parents adopted him, but I can't swear to it."

"Do you know exactly who that family was?"

"Nobody from Lincoln Prairie. The boy went someplace in Chicago."

"Was his last name Taborn?"

"As far as I know."

After all this time, it could be difficult, if not impossible, to track him down. Maybe Marti wouldn't want to. How much had he been told about his mother?

"How old was he when she died?"

"Not quite two years. I think his birthday was sometime close to Thanksgiving. Or maybe it was Christmas."

"Did James Farland attend your church, too?"

"Why yes. Terrible thing, wasn't it? A surprise to the entire congregation. They were such an upstanding family, real church-goers. My husband went to see James every third Sunday right up to the time he retired and we came back here. They still keep in touch. James is out of jail now, praise God. I never could believe he would do something like that—and not just harm Dawn but any of it. He was a devoted family man."

"Were Justine Kerr and Dawn friends?"

"Well, I can't rightly say. Both families were active members. Now let me think. Justine sang in the choir, and Dawn did not. I think, of the two, Dawn was more active in the church."

Just like James Farland.

"Beyond that, I'm afraid I don't really know. Oh, yes, and Dawn was our youth representative at the National Baptist Convention that year. Dawn was—she thought a lot of herself. She was much more mature than Justine. I'm not sure how close they were in age. Now that I think of it, I can't recall Dawn dating anyone in the congregation. Justine, on the other hand, went through at least half of the boys in the choir."

"Mrs. Jones, did any member of your congregation, any young woman close to Justine's and Dawn's age, go missing that summer?"

" 'Go missing'?" She was silent for a moment. "Missing? No. Some of our young people went off to college, but nobody went missing. We knew where all of them were."

"Are there any church records that we could look at that go back that far?"

"Why of course. You just give the Reverend Kendra Jones a call, the assistant pastor. She'll be glad to help any way she can. She's our granddaughter."

Marti glanced out the window. It was already dark. Snowflakes whisked by in a vertical direction. That assignment would go to Lupe.

After she hung up, Marti wondered if Aunt Lindy went to Second Baptist. She wondered how many black churches there were in Lincoln Prairie in the sixties. She would have to ask Slim about that. His father, now deceased, had been a minister. Thinking of Aunt Lindy made her decide to see her again as soon as she had time. She should know something about Barnabas Cheney's social life or the lack of it back then. She probably knew about Justine Kerr, as well.

Vik was close to smiling by the time she was finished telling him about the connection between Farland and Dawn. He didn't actually say, I told you Curly always got his man, but his smugness was annoying. She thought of what the minister's wife had told her: that everyone was surprised, not just by Farland's conviction for killing Dawn but by the assumed relationship between the two. Mrs. Jones also contradicted what Curly had implied, that Dawn was promiscuous. He must have talked to someone in order to reach that conclusion, but who? She didn't expect him to tell her, but she thought somebody should ask.

"Vik, why don't you give Curly a call? He must have talked to someone about Dawn. He had some pretty definite ideas about her character."

"I suppose Mrs. Jones disagreed with what Curly said about her."

"Something like that."

"Sure."

She watched his face in profile as he talked with his old mentor. Once he'd asked the question, he didn't say much more than "um-hum." Several times, his eyebrows knitted together, and by the end of the conversation, he was drumming his fingers on the desktop. He didn't speak right away after he hung up.

"What did he say?" Marti asked.

"Oh, just that he asked around, discreetly, and, umm, found several young men who had slept with her."

"Did he say anything about her baby's father?"

"No. At least he didn't identify anyone as being the child's father. He did know that the kid was born out of wedlock."

Marti was almost willing to bet that was all he knew. Back then, that was enough to gain a girl a reputation. Even if the father had died before they had a chance to marry, the requirements for getting pregnant were sufficient. Curly had reached the same conclusion others had, but without checking the facts.

Vik's face was inscrutable, but she could tell by the set of his shoulders that something was wrong. More than likely, he was angry with her again because she dared to even question the great Curly. Whatever the outcome, she would be glad when these cases were solved. Why couldn't the man have kept decent records? If he had, she and Vik might not be at odds over this.

Lupe made a fresh pot of coffee. "This stuff from the newspaper is worthless. Nothing on Barnabas Cheney at all. There are a few mentions of the family, a charity event, and the possible sale of the building where the Geneva is. That was August seventh. Barnabas was shipped off to Europe August second. Farland's trial began on the tenth. Dawn's death and the trial got no big headlines and few write-ups. There were no photographs. The trial lasted three days, and the judge sentenced him to thirty to life. I don't see anything in the newspaper that conflicts with anything in Smith's reports. I'll go get a copy of the trial transcripts tomorrow."

"Good," Marti said. "We'll meet here when you get off first shift, then decide where to go from there."

Vik had nothing to add. Worse, it was as if he had locked the doors and shuttered the windows. She needed his input, relied on his hunches, and depended on his judgment. Here, though, she was clearly on her own.

Marti glanced at her watch. It was after eight and she had a lot of unanswered questions. She called Justine Kerr, who reluctantly agreed to meet with her during fourth and fifth periods tomorrow at the high school and suggested she bring a sack lunch. She would stop by and see Aunt Lindy in the morning.

The desk sergeant called just as they were about to leave. Armstrong's attorney and a gentleman wanted to see them.

"Now what?" Vik said. He snatched his coat, ignoring the hanger that fell to the floor as he strode out of the office ahead of her.

The attorney was pacing back and forth in the narrow confines of the interview room. The man with her was middle-aged and Hispanic.

"Well, Detectives, I expected you to keep me waiting." She stopped pacing but didn't sit down. Marti and Vik didn't sit, either. "I understand you remain concerned about my client's whereabouts last Monday evening. This is Mr. Hernandez." She indicated the man. "Mr. Hernandez, would you tell us what you were doing the night of January fifth?"

"I go to see Mr. Armstrong."

"And what time was this?"

"It was after midnight."

162

"Why so late?"

"I work second shift. I don't get off work until eleven."

"And why did you go to see Mr. Armstrong?"

"He fixed my VCR."

"Can you tell us what time you arrived and when you left?"

"It was maybe twelve o'clock. Mr. Armstrong and I have a beer and watch a video. I leave maybe two, two-thirty."

"When did you have occasion to see Mr. Armstrong again?"

"Three-thirty."

"Why?"

"My television wasn't working. I live right next door. I can hear that he is still up."

"And what time did you leave his apartment?"

"Maybe five. I waited while he fixed it for me."

She turned to them. "Do you need anything else, Detectives?"

Vik shook his head. Marti said nothing. According to Armstrong's earlier statement, he had been alone the entire evening. Let the lawyers sort it out. She waited until the attorney and Hernandez were out of earshot, then she looked at Vik and said, "Stupid. It was stupid to go back there and canvass when we didn't have another scrap of evidence. Do you really think that man picked up his VCR at midnight? Do you think he went back at three-thirty because his television wasn't working? What do we do now? Lean on Mr. Hernandez until he admits he was buying stolen goods and it was twelve noon? You'd better hope Armstrong didn't do this, Jessenovik. He didn't have an alibi until we called his attention to it, and now we've got to release him."

She left him standing there and headed for her car. No way was Matthew Jessenovik going to talk her into anything else that was stupid just to keep his illusions or delusions or whatever about Curly Smith intact. She was still angry as she pulled into her driveway. All this, and she had missed Joanna's basketball game, too.

Mildred was asleep when Vik got home. He was glad. After Stephen left, he thought about warming up something to eat, but he didn't feel like being bothered. Instead, he sat in the kitchen and opened up the newspaper. Dishes were stacked in the sink. Mildred must have gotten tired early. Maybe she had a bad day. She wouldn't complain, not Mildred. Sometimes he wished she would. Then there were times like last night, when she was still awake when he got home, but too depressed to say anything, when he wished she would smile and pretend. Poor Mildred. How did she put up with him?

Just for tonight, he wished for life before MS. He wished he could talk to her about Curly. Mildred had known Curly almost as long as he had. She knew what a great guy he was, remembered how Curly took him fishing when his dad was on duty, remembered the camping trip the three of them went on every year to the UP, the Upper Peninsula, God's country. Just them and the night and owls and maybe a wolf somewhere nearby, and the pesky raccoons. There were always skunks. Whenever they came to camp, they got whatever they wanted. He smiled, remembering the one who came one year with two babies in tow. Nobody had moved from their sleeping bags. Nobody had gone out of their tents. Momma skunk came back every night. They left food out for her so she would eat and go away.

Those were good times. Curly showed him how to shoot a rifle, then a handgun. He still had a fly ball he'd caught one time when he went to a Cub's game with Curly. During the winter, it was the Blackhawks, every chance they got. Those were good days. He had always wanted to be a cop like Curly, a detective, not a beat cop like his dad. And he was. And, those files be damned, Curly was a good cop. Maybe those files, instead of being as worthless as Marti thought, proved it. There was nothing in them that could incriminate anyone but Farland. It was like Curly had said on the phone, up to Vik to maintain the tradition of solid police work, up to him to keep everyone's honor intact, up to him to be like Curly.

Evan Armstrong turned off all of the downstairs lights, went upstairs, and turned off all of the lights except for a small lamp that he put on the floor in his bedroom. He reached into his pocket, took out the beautiful watch, then sat on the floor. His lawyer said everything was okay now. They couldn't bother him anymore. It was safe to keep the watch here instead of hiding it at his sister's house. He couldn't trust her with it, even if she didn't know where it was. If she found it, she would try to sell it, and then he'd get caught again.

He opened the jar of silver polish and rubbed a soft flannel cloth on the white cream. He had cleaned the watch half a dozen times already, but it was so beautiful. He rubbed a finger over the initials on the back—J.S.C. Maybe there was some way to get them off, or disguise them. That was it. A good engraver ought to be able to make that look like something else. Then he could wear it. He'd put on a suit and go over to see Mrs. Stazlowski again. This time, she would see that he wasn't just a junk dealer. And he wasn't. He had majored in art history. It was just that his degree was like having one in anthropology: Nobody would hire him, and he didn't want to spend the rest of his life getting a master's and a Ph.D.

The watch was heavy in his hand. The links of the chain were too big. The scrollwork called for something delicate. Real Swiss movement, almost a hundred years old. He'd love to look inside, see how it was made. Maybe when he got the initials disguised, he could take it to a watchmaker, or someone who repaired them.

This was much too beautiful, too precious for someone like Cheney to appreciate, even if he hadn't been crazy. Rich people had too many beautiful things to appreciate any of them. Too bad this and the picture frame were all that Cheney had kept. He had lost the frame, but not this. This was his to keep forever. Nobody could come here and search ever again. Nobody could take this away from him. Nobody. Not ever.

For one of the few times since
she had known him, Marti was glad to see Slim when he and
Cowboy ambled in Wednesday morning. Vik was going through
Curly's file on the Farland case. Marti didn't know why he wanted
to see it again. He was also going through the lab reports that had
just come in on the Jane Doe, which provided nothing of value at
this point. Marti hoped this meant he was thinking like a cop
again, but she suspected that he might have asked for Curly's file
to reinforce his own conviction that Curly had been an exemplary
police officer and perhaps to try to convince Lupe of this.

"Hey, Slim," she said, "what do you know about black churches
in Lincoln Prairie in the sixties?"

"The sixties? Hell, I wasn't born until 1965. My father was assistant pastor at First Baptist."

"What about Second Baptist?"

"What about it? The congregation split in '55 into First Baptist,
Second Baptist. No Third Baptist, so far. My father founded
Greater Faith in 1970. I don't know if that meant he thought
there was less faith at the other two churches or what."

"But there were other churches."

"To hear the conversation around my table, those were the only
churches of any consequence around here." He sauntered over to
her desk and gave her a dimpled Cupid's bow smile. "Why are
you asking?"

"I was just looking at this Farland case and talking with a few
people. Second Baptist was pretty popular back then."

"It would have had the larger congregation," Slim said. "The real split was that First Baptist had a few members who were a bit more . . . seditty, stuck-up college-educated folk, professionals. They had an associate pastor who had a degree in whatever ministers get a degree in and was more . . . intellectual, and that's where they wanted to go. My father went with Second Baptist. He was one of those hellfire-and-damnation preachers. Church sisters had to faint and half the congregation get the Holy Ghost for him to have preached a good sermon."

And this environment had produced a vice cop who was either exceptionally lazy or exceptionally tolerant and found human foibles as humorous as they were criminal.

"So, sins like adultery and fornication were taken seriously at Second Baptist."

"Definitely. Enough to put your membership in serious doubt if you strayed. Not to mention becoming the butt of at least half a dozen sermons, with a few marginal references throughout the year."

"Did you know the Reverend Cleotis Jones?"

Slim raised his hands above his head and swaggered about the room. " 'And God said,' " he began, imitating a preacher. " 'And God said . . . Can I get an amen? . . . God said . . . "I am going to *raise* up a people . . ." ' That man ruled his congregation. There was no question of who God was, and there was no question as to who stood at His right hand and literally interpreted every word from His mouth, as well as a few random thoughts from His mind. You did it the reverend's or no way. That's why my daddy and some of the others left."

The Reverend Cleotis Jones had seemed like such a mild-mannered person on the phone. Maybe in retirement he had gained more acceptance of the follies of man, or maybe he had felt compelled, like some parents, to be hard on his "children." "And if you committed adultery as a member of the Reverend Cleotis Jones's congregation?"

"You did not go to that church anymore. That man would put you out in a minute."

Yet that man, who, according to Slim, went beyond upright, had stood by Farland all these years. Dawn Taborn had also been a member of that congregation. They were alleged—proven in a court of law—to have been sexually involved with each other, yet Jones said nothing against them, and neither did his wife.

If Farland had killed Taborn, was it really the result of a lovers' quarrel? Or was it something else? Could it have been an unacknowledged sexual interest, which, for a member of Jones's church, would have been as big a sin, maybe even worse? Maybe Curly hadn't been able to investigate this case adequately. Maybe he hadn't understood enough about the culture of the people involved to probe deeply for the truth. Maybe he'd hung his hat on the most obvious conclusion, and while there was some truth in it, the real truth was unknown. This had happened in the sixties. The cultures were more segregated then. Perhaps, because he didn't understand the subtleties of the church community, Curly went with what he could understand—overt rather than repressed promiscuity. Based on what she was finding out, his conclusion that Farland killed Dawn, although faultily reached, could be accurate.

Marti arrived at Lincoln Prairie High while the students were changing classes. The noise hit her as soon as she opened the door. Four years ago, there were adult hall monitors. Now two uniformed officers were stationed at the school. One of things that had pleased her when she'd first come to this town was being able to send her children to public schools without too much concern about drugs or gangs. That was no longer true; nor was it true that she could insulate them from those dangers by sending them to a private school. Drugs were everywhere. It was only a question of which were available and at what cost. It was up to her to provide the environment that would make drug and gang activity unlikely. Just being a law-enforcement officer was not enough, never had been. Sometimes being a cop's kid could be just as bad as being a preacher's kid. The problem, like the noise, seemed overwhelming.

Justine Kerr was much more at ease in the temporarily vacated

168

school office than she had been at the precinct. "Pop or coffee?" she asked as she put a lunch sack on the desk.

"Coffee will be fine. Black." Marti had grabbed a sandwich out of the machine in the precinct basement. Everyone used to refer to them as "mayo on cardboard," but since they'd changed food services, the bread was soft, and so far nobody had found mold growing on the cheese.

"Here we go." Kerr put two Styrofoam cups on the desk but ignored the chair behind it and sat down closer to Marti. "I still don't think I can help you, but Barnabas seemed like such a gentle man—driven, even manic, but there was this gentleness that came through. And when it came to acting, he was good, really good."

"You liked him."

Justine busied herself with her lunch sack and avoided looking at Marti. Marti waited.

Justine took a deep breath. "Yes," she said.

"Why is it so difficult to say that?" Marti asked.

Justine didn't answer and wouldn't look at her.

"Because he was a white man?"

"I didn't like him *that* way."

"In what way did you like him?"

"As a friend. As someone who shared an interest I had in theater."

"Did you ever act?"

She shook her head. "Back then, there wasn't anyplace around here where I could have. Even going to a play around here, I was stared at."

"Did you go to see Barnabas's plays?"

"A few times."

"But there was nothing between you?"

"No. Just friendship."

Marti wasn't so sure she believed that. There was just the slightest tremor when Justine spoke, and she still wouldn't look at Marti.

"You waited a long time to get married."

"Because I learned something. There was more to a relationship than sexual attraction." She took out a bowl with a sealed cover. Salad. She popped the lid off, and the salad dressing smelled good.

Marti wondered what Barnabas had looked like as a young man. His nephew, Jonathan, Jeremiah's son, was quite handsome. She was certain there had been an attraction, at least on Justine's part. But her church, her parents, her upbringing, these would have forbidden any acknowledgment. Even now, Justine was uncomfortable. Marti unwrapped her ham and cheese sandwich and checked to make sure that the ham wasn't dried out. She would have eaten it anyway, since things like that didn't bother her anymore, but it was nice to drizzle the mustard and mayo on soft cheddar and fresh meat.

"Have you been teaching here long?"

"Almost twenty years. I started at the junior high level."

Sharon had taught high school English for a few years. She changed jobs with almost as much frequency as she changed men and was teaching at the elementary level now. Marti wondered if the two women knew each other, but she didn't ask.

"My daughter is a student here."

"I know. Joanna. She's in the International Studies Program."

It was the equivalent of a gifted students' program, and Marti was pleased that Mrs. Kerr identified Joanna as a scholar and not as an athlete. She didn't think Joanna took herself seriously enough as a student, or put in enough effort. For her, a B to C average was good enough.

"Did you know Dawn Taborn?"

Kerr seemed surprised by the question.

"She was a few years younger than I was. But yes, I knew her."

"Were you close friends?"

"We weren't friends at all. Dawn was very active in the church, but our interests were different."

"Do you still attend Second Baptist?"

"No, my husband's family are members of First Baptist. We go there."

"The Reverend Cleotis Jones sounds like an interesting man. Do you remember him?"

"Everyone remembers that man," Kerr said. "He was much too literal. If the Bible said God made the world in six days and rested on the seventh, then, by God, they were calendar days, even though there was no such thing as a calendar then." She picked through the lettuce and speared a tomato wedge. "A closed mind. No room at all for any other interpretation."

"Do you know what happened to Dawn's son?"

"Her son? I have no idea. Her parents were both dead. I think that's why church was so important to her. An aunt raised her and her brother, but she died just before Dawn graduated from high school. She really didn't have anyone. You know how church sisters are, real good about taking you under their wing. I'm sure she needed that."

"Do you think that's why she got involved with James Farland?"

"You don't believe that, do you? Nobody who knew Dawn, even slightly, like me, could think that of her."

"And James Farland?"

"He was as literal, as narrow-minded, as Reverend Jones. You know those types. Sometimes it's total conviction. Sometimes they sin mightily in their hearts."

Marti thought of Dawn's son and wondered what had become of him. Did he know who his real mother was? Or had his foster parents raised him as their own without telling him about his birth mother? This happened in the early sixties. Times were different then. Somewhere around that time, Marti could remember walking past the house three doors from where she and Momma lived and seeing a neighbor child sitting on the front step, sobbing. When Marti asked what was wrong, the child, who was seven or eight, said, "Momma's just my grandmother. Nona is my mother. I don't want Nona to be my mother. I want her to keep being my sister." The grandmother had raised the child as her own. Nona had come north for the summer. She didn't stay long, and Marti couldn't remember her ever coming to visit her child again. The little girl played hopscotch and jumped rope, acting as if Nona didn't exist at all.

"Do you recall any other young woman, maybe someone Dawn's age or closer to your age, who went missing about that time?"

"Missing?"

"Perhaps she left to go to college and nobody heard from her again. Maybe she moved back south and didn't keep in touch. It doesn't have to be anything unusual, just someone who went away and was never heard from again."

Someone must have noticed when their Jane Doe disappeared.

Kerr finished her salad while she thought about it. Marti had already finished off her sandwich and was swallowing the last of the now-tepid coffee, which wasn't strong enough for her liking.

"I know what you mean," Kerr said. "That happens a lot. You lose touch, then one day they come into your mind and you wonder what's become of them. But no, nobody like that comes to mind now."

"If someone does—"

"Of course I'll let you know."

When Marti returned to the precinct, she spent the better part of an hour typing notes on her interview with Justine Kerr as well as on her conversations with Mrs. Jones and Slim. If nothing else, no matter what the outcome, the victim in the Farland case was finally going to have a voice.

"So," Vik said when she got up from the typewriter and stretched, "find out anything new?"

She hesitated. Did he really want to know? Was he making conversation? Was he snooping for his friend Curly? There wasn't much being said on this end of the line when the two of them talked last night.

"I'm beginning to understand more about Dawn and about Farland."

"And?"

"I'm beginning to think he might have killed her, and I don't think we're going to get any closer to the mummy by looking at the Farland case. So far, nobody I've talked with remembers anyone going missing or even leaving home and not coming back."

"Good. Now we can forget about Dawn Taborn and get back to business."

"Not yet," Marti said. "I think Dawn deserves a little more closure than she was given. Part of the problem was that there were no relatives to interview. Another was that the church she belonged to was not easily accessible to outsiders. The fact remains that by inference at least, she acquired a bad reputation. She deserves better than that if it wasn't true."

Lupe zipped in a little after one and dropped a copy of the Farland trial transcript on her desk. "Gotta run. Got a hot one in the lockup. Caught him in the act of selling rock cocaine within twenty feet of a school." She left before Marti could say anything.

Marti read through the trial transcripts twice. The second time she underlined, highlighted, and made notes. There was no mention of anything remotely related to Miranda-Escobedo because the Supreme Court rulings in Escobedo v. Illinois and Miranda v. Arizona weren't handed down until 1966. But the rights that were verbalized in the Miranda warning didn't come into existence with those rulings; they were just required to be spoken aloud. As far as Farland's case was concerned, it was as if instead of these rights having existed ever since the Constitution was written, someone had amended the Constitution to include them. It was as if he did not have these rights when he was arrested and tried. Was Farland even aware of those rights? They certainly had been violated. For the first time, she was aware of what a difference being required to say them aloud had made for everyone, law breaker and law enforcer, as well as for the innocent. The other thing that surprised her was the way Farland's attorney had handled the case. For all intents and purposes, he'd offered no defense at all. He was in private practice, appointed by the court. It was a pro bono case and Daniel Randell had given minimal service for his zero-dollar retainer.

As far as Marti could determine, Randell had filed the appropriate papers, entered the right motions at the right time, cross-examined witnesses called by the prosecution, and called a few witnesses of his own. The Reverend Cleotis Jones was a noticeable exception. The problem was what Farland's attorney had *not* done. She wasn't sure about legal briefs and such, but she had never reviewed a case before with such scant efforts by the defendant's attorney. Usually, there was enough paperwork to choke the legal system, enough objections to keep the judge awake, and at least a few attempts to get the prosecutor off balance. This trial went as smoothly as a performance by the Lincoln Prairie Symphony Orchestra, and the grand finale was Farland's conviction. Even Farland's mother, a witness for the defense, played a part. By the time the prosecutor got finished with the poor woman, she was as much as admitting that her son had done it, the way she was begging for his life.

She tossed the transcripts to Vik. After he read them, he said, "Jeez, I might have to take back some of what I said about Curly. I think he would have gotten this one without as much circumstantial evidence as he had."

"I'd like to have an excuse to talk with Farland's attorney," Marti said. "Just to see if he has any justification for such a minimal defense. Even if justice was served, everyone deserves better than this."

"Marti, this is dead, done, over with. You can say what you want about Curly's files, but the man didn't have to do any more than he did. Farland was guilty. The lawyer must have known it, too. This was the sixties, Marti. There were lawyers who did the best they could with what they had and allowed justice to be served."

"And?" There were still lawyers like that.

"And Farland was guilty, plain and simple, and everyone knew it."

"Vik, this is the poorest excuse for a trial that I've ever come across. Technically, everything was done that should have been, so I don't know if there was collusion or any other cause for appeal, but when you read this transcript, you see that everyone went into this believing the man was guilty. *Everyone.* By the time the trial was ending and his mother was called to the stand, it sounds like she thought so, too. What did these guys do, go out for a drink the night before the trial began, agree on the verdict, and go through the motions for the next three days?"

"Give it a rest, Marti. You're just determined to blame the whole damned legal system because one guilty man got caught and convicted before we got into the rights of the accused. You know he was guilty. You're just angry because Curly was right."

She didn't answer. It wasn't what had happened that bothered her; it was the way it had happened. If Vik thought it was okay, maybe she had been wrong about him all this time. Maybe he wasn't the cop she thought he was. Maybe he wasn't the person she thought he was, either. Until now, she had liked working with him. Marti took a deep breath, a step back. Until now. How important was this Farland case to their relationship?

Farland was guilty, at least as far as she could tell, and that did mean that Curly had been right, whether she liked his methods or not. There was nothing, not even the defendant's testimony, to contradict him, because Farland never testified. There was no confession, but no vehement denials, either, just this lethargic farce by the defense and the prosecution. The accused had had nothing to say for himself, and given the circumstantial evidence, that was probably the most damning thing of all. Farland had not defended himself. The question in Marti's mind was, If Farland was innocent, why didn't he say so? Why didn't he vigorously deny the charges? Why didn't he take the witness stand? Everyone involved must have asked themselves those questions.

The only reason she could think of for Farland's acceptance of guilt and all that went with it lay somewhere within his relationship with the Reverend Cleotis Jones, his involvement with his church, and perhaps his connection with Dawn. What if he did have an affair with her but didn't kill her? According to the Bible, the wages of sin are death. Did something happen between them that made Farland equate her death and his imprisonment with biblical justice? Marti went back to the typewriter. She committed her thoughts to paper, added that to *her* file on the Farland case, not because it made any difference now, but because even though she had two homicides pending and she had given this as much time as she could, Curly's files did not begin to tell what had happened.

By the time Lupe came in, Marti was back to work on the Cheney and Jane Doe cases, and getting nowhere. There were no leads. Vik had been sitting there with a satisfied expression on his face ever since she'd put the Farland file to one side. She gave Lupe the Farland trial transcripts to go over and was not surprised when Lupe gave a low whistle. "They might as well have just plea-bargained this one and saved the state the time and cost of a trial."

Now that Lupe mentioned it, that was what it sounded like, a plea bargain that everyone was in on but the defendant. Or *had* Farland been in on it? What had his attorney said to him? There were no notes on that. There were too many questions, even if Farland was guilty.

"I think we need to put this mummy case into some kind of historical perspective," Marti said. There were so many cultural nuances about the *People vs. Farland* case that the system had not understood. What were the implications for Jane Doe? She filled them in on what she had learned about Farland and Dawn in terms of their church and their religion. "Now that I've had time to give some thought to Dawn Taborn's background, it's got me thinking. Nobody I've spoken with about the Farland case knows of anyone going missing during that time frame. But look at Dawn—orphaned, the aunt who raised her dead. She dies and leaves a little boy and nobody has clue as to what happened to him. That could be what we're dealing with here. For some reason, the right people aren't aware that she's missing."

"That doesn't sound possible," Vik said.

"No, it's not that difficult to lose track of people. I think we've got to broaden our focus, look beyond Lincoln Prairie. I also think we've got to take a good look at the possibilities in Lincoln Prairie. According to Slim, there were three major black churches here then, not too many small ones. And black churches were a major influence in the community then. We've got to tap into that. Maybe the older members, people Jones's age, will remember something."

"And," Lupe said, "we've got to remember what this place was like then. Vik was here. You were in Chicago. I wasn't born."

"The Geneva was open for business," Marti said. "People were in and out all the time. It's hard not to think of it the way it is now, closed, empty." Lupe was right. She could only see things as they were now, not as they must have been then. "When our Jane Doe went in there and was left in that hidey-hole, movies were still being shown. She could have worked there."

"There was still an occasional live show then, too," Vik said. "She could have been passing through with one of those, if there was one that summer."

"And nobody found her," Marti said. "Which has to mean that not too many people knew that closet was there."

"Maybe nobody but the killer," Vik said.

"Did Farland work at the Geneva, too?" Lupe asked.

Vik was thoughtful. "The Cheneys owned both places. It's a long shot, but maybe they still have employment records. And somebody must know if any live shows played there that summer, just in case this is someone who was passing through."

"What about Cheney?" Lupe said. "Is Armstrong still our primary suspect?"

Neither Marti nor Vik answered.

"Did I miss something?" Lupe asked.

"Armstrong has kind of taken himself out of the running," Marti said. "At least temporarily. He's produced an alibi that might hold up unless we change the time of death, or get enough on him to put his alibi on the witness stand and break him down."

"Are we back to the stranger theory?" Lupe asked. "Someone setting Cheney up as a mark?"

"Technically, that's the best we've got right now," Marti agreed. "But I'd put my money on Armstrong before I'd bet on a random act of violence."

The idea that she could have three homicides on her hands,

one a man named Cheney, and two women who had been found dead in theaters owned by the Cheney family, without some connection seemed unlikely, but until she found something to link them, she had to accept the possibility they were unrelated.

Vik left the room while Marti and Torres were talking. He went to the main section of the building, which was closed now, found the guard, and got himself admitted to Records. The old stuff was stored in boxes in the back, but because they had asked for Curly's file, two boxes were on a table. He found a few of Curly's other cases and flipped through them. Then he went back to the office. Nobody was there, so he made a phone call.

"Curly. Hi, it's me, Vik."

He smiled when Curly called out to Clara, "Hey, it's Gus's boy. Come say hello."

"Vik, is that you? It's been so long since I've seen you." Clara was soft-spoken, just as he remembered. It had been a long time.

"We have horses now, Vik. Remember when you were little and Curly took you to that carnival? I still have that picture of you on that pony. It's right on my dresser."

Vik could here Curly talking, but he couldn't make out what he was saying.

"And fishing, Vik. There's a lake not five miles up the road. Curly caught some sunfish last year. You two should go fishing again. You always had such a good time together. Curly misses you. I do, too."

Curly interrupted Clara just like he always did. "Vik, that woman is always yapping," he said. "There's no stopping her once she gets started."

Same old Curly, Vik thought. Same old Clara. He did miss them. He and Mildred had talked about driving up to McHenry County to see them. It wasn't that far away. They just never seemed to have the time.

"What's up, kid? You calling just to say hello?"

"I just wanted you to know that we've more or less dropped the Farland case as a point of inquiry," Vik said.

"What did I tell you? We nailed 'em for life in those days. No such thing as getting a conviction reversed."

"We pulled the trial transcripts, too."

"Not bad, huh, the way we wrapped that one up. That's the way things were done back then. It was a hell of a lot easier to send them up than it is now. Nobody ever looked twice at that case, until now. We had damned few capital cases back then. People knew they couldn't get away with murder."

As Vik hung up, part of him thought of the increase in the crime rates and agreed with Curly. But part of him became uneasy.

It was dark when Ed Logan left the church after dinner. The others got into the van that would take them to another church, where they could spend the night, but he didn't like being that close to people. He walked instead. He liked winter. The cold kept the streets empty and people stayed in their houses. He used to stay inside, too. Down in grandma's basement. He couldn't do that no more.

"Hey, Frankie!"

He stopped. The door was open in a house just ahead. Light came from the doorway and the windows. A girl was standing there. A boy was running down the middle of the street. Ed backed into the shadows of a van parked in a driveway and squatted down out of sight. When the girl didn't call again, and the boy didn't answer, he eased up by the headlights and looked in the direction of the house. The door was closed now. He could still see the boy walking, not straight ahead, but zigzagging from one side of the street to the other.

He thought of Dancing Man again. Had he done something to him? Hurt him? He didn't want to hurt him. He didn't want to hurt anyone. Had Dancing Man been dancing in the snow that time when he had seen him? Ed's feet got cold while he was watching. Could it have been winter, like now? He headed away from the church where the mats were set up, back to Dancing Man's house. Maybe, if he went there, now, while it was dark, maybe he would remember.

13

Marti was wide awake by the second time the phone rang. She picked up the receiver before it could ring again. It was her private line. "MacAlister."

Not another body. "Where was he found?" She got up and began getting dressed while she talked. "Have we got an ID on the victim?" She listened, then said, "Get the second shift's beat cop over there right away. He knows most of the street people who hang around that area. Have you called Jessenovik?" She reached for a pair of wool slacks. "Thanks. It'll take me fifteen minutes, tops."

She checked the clock. It was 3:20 A.M. Ben was on duty at the fire station on the south side, where the body had been found. She put on extra socks and a heavy sweater over a turtleneck. With luck, she'd be inside somewhere before the cold made insulation meaningless. She stopped in the kitchen long enough to put some of Momma's peach cobbler in a bowl for Ben, since he was on call and had missed out. He'd be at the crime scene and she could give it to him then. She left a note on the message board for Momma.

The body had been found behind a Dumpster in the parking lot across the street from the Merchants Hall. The parking lot had been plowed and snow was piled against the only building that abutted it. The Dumpster was about five feet from the building. Whoever found the victim had gone out of their way to look for him. It was an open area and the wind was blowing hard and cold. Marti shivered as she got out of the car. She wrapped her scarf across her face, turned up her collar, and pulled on a second pair of gloves, an insulated pair that Theo or Mike had left in her car.

A fire department ambulance was parked nearby, along with three squad cars and a vehicle from the coroner's office. Vik's car wasn't there yet. She spotted Ben standing by the ambulance with another paramedic and waved to him. The cobbler would have to wait till she talked to the ME.

Dr. Cyprian was the ME examining the victim. Even before she got within twelve feet of the body, she recognized him because of his beard. It was one of the vagrants who hung around here, the one who had seen Cheney. It took a moment to recall his name, but not long enough for her to have to check her notes. Logan, Edward Logan. Why hadn't he gone to a shelter? What was he doing here? How long had he been here?

"Got anything for me, Dr. Cyprian?" Her breath blew like smoke.

His breath did, too. "Look for a hammer."

"Is that all?"

"This one is messy. Blood and brain matter must have gotten spattered on whoever did it."

Marti was impressed. Two direct answers from the inscrutable Dr. Cyprian. Another wedding gift? Leaning forward, she could see the damage to the back of the head, and there was a lot of blood on the ground. Did she dare push for more? A compromise perhaps. "Anything else?"

"I think he's been here for a while, four or five hours, maybe longer. I'm going to post him when I get back, while it's easiest to confirm the effects of the weather."

Wow! Three out of three. Not bad. She wanted to ask him why he was being so cooperative but didn't want to call attention to it. "Thank you, Doctor, thank you very much." In India, women had dowries. Did this sudden verbal largesse have anything to do with that? Whatever it was, she was not going to nitpick, but why was he being so cooperative? Maybe he was resigning. "Dr. Cyprian, you're not leaving us anytime soon, are you?"

"Why no, I'm certainly not going anyplace else. Why would I leave the place that has given me my first opportunity to examine a mummy close up? It far exceeds the meager training I received in my forensic anthropology class."

So that was it, maybe. She walked over to the uniforms and nodded to an officer from the second shift who was in civvies. "Who got here first?"

"I did," the young uniform said. She recognized him as a rookie. Just her luck. She was willing to bet that either the crime scene was contaminated or some crucial bit of evidence had been overlooked.

"Are you the beat cop or did someone call it in?"

"It was just a routine check, ma'am. They'll go anyplace where they can get out of the cold. The count was down at the shelters tonight, so I was doing a little extra checking around."

"What did you do when you found him?"

"Checked for a pulse, any sign of breathing. The guy was obviously dead, so I left the same way I came, called it in, requested backup and an ambulance. I began checking to see if there were any possible suspects in the vicinity, but I didn't attempt to enter any buildings until I had backup. We didn't find anyone hanging around."

She was impressed. So far, she was batting 2 and 0. Of course, Vik hadn't shown up yet. She would probably manage to strike out once he got here. "Did you see any vomit around here anywhere?"

"Vomit?"

"Doctor Cyprian says this one was messy."

"Oh, no, ma'am, nothing like that."

"Did you recognize him?" she asked.

"No."

The beat cop spoke up. "I did. Ed Logan, remember him?" Marti nodded.

"Damned shame. He didn't have anything worth stealing, and I don't know of him ever bothering anyone."

"Yeah," Marti agreed. "Damned shame." She patted his shoulder. "Sorry. We'll get whoever did it." She walked over to Ben. "I hope you've got some coffee. It's colder than a witch's tit out here."

Ben laughed out loud. "This is Officer MacAlister," he said to the guy standing beside him. "My wife. Marti, do you remember my trainee, Allan? He survived. He's a licensed paramedic now."

Allan pushed straight dark hair beneath his cap and gave her a shy smile.

Marti held out her hand. "Congratulations."

Ben got a thermos out of the ambulance. Steam rose as he poured coffee into the plastic cup.

"So, have you got everything under control over there?" He laughed again.

"What is so funny?"

"Not funny," he said. "More like amazing."

"Oh?"

"This is only the second time I've ever watched you be the homicide detective in charge."

She didn't know if that was good or bad and didn't ask. Suddenly, she felt like she was walking on eggs again. Maybe it wasn't such a good idea, a female cop married to a male noncop. It sure felt right when she was away from the job. Was Ben uncomfortable? He didn't seem to be. Embarrassed? Her stomach began its nerves and stress dance again. It seemed like it had been at least a couple of days since that had happened. Maybe a few days at a time was all she would get.

"What did you find when you got here?" she asked.

"That cop," Ben said. He pointed to the rookie and chuckled, a deep, happy rumble that usually made her feel happy, too. "He showed me where to walk to get to the body, and told me I'd better walk out the same way. Said that the homicide cop was a real itch about having the crime scene messed with. I thought he was talking about Vik until he said, 'I don't want *her* ticked off with me.'"

"Did he say that?" Her stomach felt like it was tying itself in little knots.

"I cleaned it up a little, but you've got the gist."

"That's great." She was pleased that the beat cops felt that way about her, and especially a rookie, but she was suddenly reluctant to seem pleased. What was wrong with her? This wasn't a little-girl job or a sexy-lady job, either. It was woman's work, and if Ben couldn't handle that . . .

Ben came over and gave her a kiss on the forehead, then the cheek, then her nose.

"You're getting close," she said. "What's that for?"

"You are something else, lady." He took a step back, folded his arms, and looked her up and down. "You are really something else."

Her stomach began untangling itself. "What can you tell me about the victim?"

"I'd look for a hammer *and* check out the marks on his neck."

She gave him a peck on the cheek.

"That's it? The tip of the day and that's all I get?"

Marti tried not to laugh. She couldn't say, For now, not with Allan standing right there grinning at the two of them.

Vik drove up a few minutes later. As Marti watched, he talked with the same people she had, then walked over. "Cyprian is finishing up," he said, giving a nod in Ben's direction.

"I'll get out my camera," Marti said.

When she came back, Vik had the nesting thermos cup filled with coffee and all three men were laughing. Maybe Vik was adjusting to Ben after all.

"Momma made a peach cobbler." Marti handed the foil-covered bowl to Ben and then saw that Cyprian was heading for the coroner's station wagon. "Let's go, Jessenovik."

She gave Ben's hand a squeeze. "We'll release the body for transport as soon as we can."

"Yes, ma'am," Ben said with a low chuckle. As she walked away, he said, "There goes the little woman." She wasn't offended.

As Marti walked toward the body, she began the process of distancing herself from someone she recognized and could remember alive. It was easier when the only context she knew the victim

184

in was as the deceased. Knowing them alive first gave everything a more personal dimension, even when it was a man she had spoken with twice and only briefly. For a few minutes, she wondered about family and relationships and what had been left unsaid and undone forever. When she reached him, she took off both pairs of heavy gloves and slipped on some leather driving gloves that she hoped would at least protect her hands from frostbite. She took as many photographs as she needed and then she squatted beside the body, trying to avoid the blood, and moved his head to a more natural position, one where the blows didn't show. Everyone was some mother's child, and there were times when, just for a moment, she was a mother, too. She looked up, to see Ben standing at the perimeters of the crime scene, watching her. He wasn't laughing now.

Marti and Vik went from the cold street to the cold morgue, warming themselves in an outer office while Cyprian prepared for the autopsy. It was 5:00 A.M. While they were waiting, one of the assistants brought out the personal effects in plastic evidence bags.

"I'll be damned," Marti said. "What do you want to bet that this is Cheney's grandfather's watch." The attendant turned the bag so that she could see the initials on the back. The initials J.S.C. were inscribed in elaborate scrollwork. "He was holding this in his hand. His hand was beneath him, with the weight of his body on it."

There was also a key. "How interesting," Marti said.

"It was in his coat pocket, but there's a hole in the pocket, too." He took the coat out of the evidence bag to show her.

"Gee," Vik said. "I wonder what the key fits? Check it for prints and arrange to have a copy made right away."

The autopsy took longer than she expected. Ed Logan was not a healthy man. In addition to miscellaneous problems like rotting teeth, pyorrhea, and a few ailments associated with malnutrition, Cyprian found damage caused by at least one minor heart attack and arteries so clogged that Logan wouldn't have lasted a year without surgery. He, too, noted the marks on the sides of the neck. When Marti asked him to comment, he pointed out the head injuries and the direction of the blows.

"So you're saying he was hit once on the top of the skull," Marti said, "as if he was facing his attacker, and then on the back of the head, as if he was trying to get away."

"That is correct."

"And the first blow didn't take him down," Vik added.

"No, it did not."

"And the neck?" Vik asked.

"The evidence we have seems to suggested that Mr. Logan was hit from the front, by someone taller than he was, but without enough force to render him unconscious. It then appears that he turned away, and the perpetrator grabbed him by the neck, thumbs forward, and put pressure on the arteries, rendering him unconscious. The injuries suggest that he was then hit from above, while facedown, with much more force than the initial blow. At this point, the perpetrator hit him repeatedly."

"But the first blow struck was a single blow to the head?" Marti asked.

"That is correct, based on the position of the body when I first examined it and the fact that the body was not moved. There was no pattern with the blood to indicate otherwise. When he fell facedown and was struck again, he did not move again from the place where he lay."

Marti took a closer look at the neck injuries. "Are these similar to the injuries to the mummy's neck?"

"I was wondering when you would notice that. I will send photos off to Dr. Pickus. She has not yet sent a report on the comparison of the mummy's injuries to those of the victim in the Farland case. She is still consulting on that with Dr. Gless."

"Is this type of neck injury common enough to be typical?" Vik asked. "Or is this something only someone like a martial arts expert would know?"

"I am also hoping that Dr. Pickus can answer that. I don't consider the injury atypical or unusual, but it is not one that I commonly see, either."

Marti found it interesting that the injuries to the neck were not the perp's method of choice, which seemed to be a whack from a hammer. Rather, strangulation was what he resorted to when the intended method didn't work. Sooner or later, that method could tell them a lot about who he was. One other thing that concerned her was the fury with which Logan had been attacked. If this killer was one who had killed before, he was becoming more violent.

As soon as they were outside and the first blast of cold air hit them, Vik said, "See, we wasted all this time checking out Curly's case, and the killer he convicted is out on the street, killing again. I'm having James Farland brought in."

"Farland! He just got out of prison. We have no proof, and we certainly have not connected him with the mummy."

"But we will. You even believe he did it."

"I think that in all probability Farland killed Dawn Taborn, but without premeditation. Since we haven't even identified the mummy yet, we certainly can't say he did that. We don't know what in the hell is going on, or why."

"That's right, MacAlister. This puts us right back at square one. We don't know who did what. But we do know one thing: None of this began to happen until after Farland was paroled and after that tour of the Geneva was in the *News-Times* for a week. If these deaths are connected, the only suspect we have is Farland."

They were both yelling. A man walked past them in the predawn light and Marti looked back, to see him standing there, in spite of the cold, watching them.

"Logan must have seen Farland go into the Merchants building," Vik said.

"Logan was sleeping in a church basement that night," Marti retorted.

"Then Logan must be the one who made the phone call."

"Logan? Use the phone? Call the police? That's stretching what we *know* about Logan a bit far. Plus, the call was made from Milwaukee, not from here."

"What about the marks on the necks, MacAlister? On each neck, including Dawn Taborn's? Pickus can't even confirm it. *That's* stretching it. What we do have are *two* victims, Dawn Taborn and Edward Logan, with similar marks on their necks."

"And how in the hell did Logan get the watch and the key?"

"Somebody was trying to set him up, that's how. Now ask me who."

Vik walked ahead of her, stomping a trail in the hard-packed snow. He didn't speak again, and neither did she. After roll call, the lieutenant asked Vik to come to his office—alone.

Vik sat across from Dirkowitz and waited. Dirkowitz sat silent and toyed with the hand grenade for a few minutes. The lieutenant must have noticed that he and Marti were angry with each other during roll call.

"Jessenovik, both you and MacAlister have sent for Curly's files on the Farland case. What's the reason for that?"

"We've dropped that as a possible lead."

"I see. Why did you think it might be related?"

"I think we discussed that, sir. The Cheney family owned the buildings where both women's bodies were found."

"And Curly was a close friend of your father's and your friend, as well."

"Yes, sir." He thought of the fishing trips and pony ride that Clara had mentioned. As soon as Mildred was up to it, they were going to visit them.

"Look, Vik, we've got three unsolved homicides on our hands, two of them recent. If for some reason you're too close to the case, or if Mildred's not doing well and you're under too much stress, you need to tell someone, take some time off, whatever. I need two functioning cops on these cases, or least one who isn't being interfered with by one who's not functioning. If for any reason you cannot handle this, you will have to let me know. Understand?"

"Yes, sir."

"Good. This is neither a reflection on your ability as a police officer nor anything but genuine concern for your wife. We run a comparatively small shop here, Jessenovik. I need your expertise and your professionalism. In return, I have to give some consideration to your family. My wife is expecting my first kid. I can understand your concern." He dropped the hand grenade on the desk, and Vik was dismissed.

Vik did not go back to the office. He went outside and began to walk instead. The case of the *People* vs. *Farland* had not been strong. If Farland hadn't known that going in, he sure as hell had found it out during thirty-odd years in jail, and Curly was the prime architect of that paper house of circumstantial evidence. He had looked at a few of Curly's other cases and hadn't found much there, either, but this had been a capital case. Who *had* Curly interviewed? What kind of an investigation had he conducted? It wasn't enough to assume guilt because a man ran. Thirty-four years ago, being black and in the wrong place at the wrong time *was* reason enough to run. Curly might believe that the innocent don't run, but Curly and Dad had disagreed on that one, and he had to go along with his dad. He could remember several incidents in school where that had been the case, and the kids would have been considered guilty as accused if someone hadn't stepped forward and told the truth. If *he* hadn't stepped forward in one instance.

He stopped, looked to see where he was, realized he had circled the block at least twice and was walking past new construction on the library again, and decided to turn back. It was too damned cold to be walking around. His feet felt like blocks of ice. He wasn't going to back off on these cases. He wasn't going to stay home. He wasn't going to let Curly get hung in effigy for a case he got a little careless with. Hell, the man had been three months away from retirement back then. He *was* going to get whoever killed Cheney and the mummified Jane Doe, and Logan. If he and Marti didn't agree on who that was—James Farland—he would have to convince her, and, in the process, prove to everyone's satisfaction that Curly had been right. Logic and objectivity worked every time. There was no substitute for solid police investigative procedures. They would go by the book.

Marti didn't look up when the door opened. Slim and Cowboy had left for court and there was no sudden odor of Obsession for Men, so she knew it was Vik. Had she behaved this compulsively when she was convinced that Johnny had been killed in the line of duty, when everyone else had tried to say he had eaten his gun? She must have been just as determined then to preserve Johnny's record until she proved how he'd died, but they had been husband and wife; Curly and Vik hadn't even been partners. Curly might have been like a father to Vik, but Vik's mother was dead then, not his dad. Vik's dad had been a cop, too, so the fact that Vik needed a department role model couldn't be the reason for this hero worship. What was it with these two? Curly wasn't even Polish. Maybe this was the extreme in male bonding. Did Vik have the objectivity to handle a case that brought him this close to his friend? It was up to him to decide that.

She waited until he fixed a cup of coffee, went through his in basket, and read through his reports. Then she said, "We need to talk about these cases. The body count is at three, with no perp in sight. If we're totally at loggerheads on this, then we can work independently, as long as we debrief with Lupe every afternoon." She didn't want to do it that way. They had always worked their cases together. If they stopped now, she felt that something irretrievable would be lost. She didn't say so, just tried not to hold her breath while she waited for Vik to say something.

After a few minutes, Vik took out a legal-sized pad. "Victim number three, an indigent who has Cheney's watch and a key. Did they send over a copy of that key yet?"

She exhaled slowly. They were still a team. "They delivered it fifteen minutes ago."

"Are you thinking what I'm thinking about whose door that might fit?"

"Cheney's," Marti said. Thank God he was back to being a cop.

He would probably never tell her what the lieutenant had said, or where he'd been for the last forty-five minutes, but at least he sounded more like himself.

"Damn," Vik said. "There can't be a connection. If there was, Curly would have found it."

"He didn't know there was a second woman dead," Marti said.

Vik came close to smiling. "No, he didn't. You're right. And that means that there must not have been any local fuss about anyone being missing. He would have made the connection right away."

"What are you saying?" she asked. Vik gave her a blank look that told her he was still more concerned with justifying Curly's actions and and convincing himself the killings were unconnected than he was with finding the truth.

"Damn it, Marti." He reached for his files and a few reports that had just come in. "Okay, let's walk through this again." He sounded tired. She knew she was. And they still had the whole day ahead of them.

14

By 9:30, Marti knew she was going to have to keep moving to stay awake. It wasn't anywhere near lunchtime yet and she'd already had two cups of Cowboy's coffee and a can of Mello Yello. Vik had spiked a cup of coffee with a couple of teaspoons of instant. They had spent two and a half hours questioning every street person they could round up and had come away empty. Logan had showed up for yesterday's evening meal at a nearby Catholic church. He never arrived at the Lutheran church that was providing shelter for the night. Nobody had seen him with anybody, and, as usual, he hadn't spoken to anyone. Nobody had ever seen him with any kind of watch. There was no mention of the key. Marti and Vik didn't ask about it and nobody volunteered anything.

Everything in the immediate vicinity was more commercial than residential. Two teams had scoured the area, questioning shopkeepers, bartenders, deliverymen, and anyone else they could find. They, too, came up empty. As usual, nobody knew anything, and given the time of night when the murder had happened and the near-zero temperatures, that didn't surprise her. They arranged to meet the beat cop from the second shift an hour before he went on duty. They agreed to meet at the Unitarian church where Logan had slept the night Cheney was killed. Marti wanted to check the security there for herself.

Vik yawned. There was something boyish about the way he rubbed his eyes. "Say, Marti, do you know what's going on with

with Cyprian? Is he getting ready to call it quits around here or something?"

"I asked him and he said no. The only thing I can think of is that it has something to do with his remark about this being a wedding gift."

"That puts marriage in a whole new light. He said more during Logan's postmortem than he's said during his last five. I'm glad he's not going anywhere. He didn't say anything about when this little honeymoon will be over, did he?"

"Not yet, but I think we'll know." The muscles in her shoulders and neck were kinking up. She stretched, then arched and hunched her back a few times. "What do you say we go over to the Merchants building and see if this key fits anything."

"Good idea." He lurched to his feet and got his coat. "We can stop in and say hi to Aunt Lindy."

The key in Ed Logan's pocket slipped easily into the lock on the front door to the lower levels of the Merchants building.

"Why am I not surprised?" Marti asked.

Vik didn't say anything. He didn't seem pleased.

"One less loose end," she said

That didn't have a positive effect, either.

"How did he get it?" Vik groused.

"Some people want all of the answers."

Armstrong's place wasn't open yet. Aunt Lindy seemed glad to see them. "Didn't know I would miss that boy so. I didn't never hardly see him unless the weather was warm. Funny how folks grow on you, ain't it? Even them odd ones. You two sure do look tired today. It's that fellow they found across the street this morning, ain't it? Why don't you come on out back?"

She walked toward the back of the store as she spoke. Marti nodded to Vik and they followed her. The room had a stove, sink, small refrigerator, and a wooden table and chairs. Marti counted seven pictures of Jesus on the walls, all different. There was also a washing machine and a dryer, and an ironing board was set up.

Marti could see that the old woman was sorting through several plastic and paper bags filled with clothing, which presumably she was going to launder.

"Just sit yourselves down right here. I've got some coffee and I made these honey pecan rolls before I left the house this morning." A plate with several dozen rolls covered with plastic wrap was on the table.

"Here we are." She put thick institutional-type mugs on the table and poured coffee from an old metal pot with a glass bubble in the center of the lid where you could watch the coffee perk. "A couple of my church sisters will be over later. They come once or twice a week to get what they need for whatever families they're working with."

Marti thought of Momma. She was going into Chicago to have lunch and see a play with a church group today and had bought herself a new hat for the occasion.

"Can you remember back when Barnabas was living in the Geneva building?"

"Child, I can remember when Barnabas was a boy and played in that old theater. Smart, Barnabas was. He could remember whole speeches, whole plays. I'd come to town to pick up some things for myself and bring him along and drop him off at the Geneva and come back and just stand there and listen. That boy could act for real. Didn't surprise me none when he played at that theater in Chicago. 'Barnabas is in the theater,' his folks would say, happy that the boy was doing something that they could brag on, but they wasn't bragging about the right thing. That boy was good, made me forget who he was when he was up there."

"Did he ever go to the Rialto?" Marti asked. The coffee was hot and weak, but the rolls were good.

"Boy didn't like the Rialto near as much. That place didn't have that orchestra pit and all them hiding places children like. Only time he went to the Rialto was if he wanted to watch a movie."

"When he was a teenager, did he date?"

"Shu, girl. Barnabas was talking to himself by then. They'll tell you he was right in the head until he got to acting for a while, but

194 ·

the truth is, Barnabas wasn't never right in the head. They just didn't want to deal with it. Time Barnabas was a teenager, he was walking around talking to himself and answering back. Made the hair rise on the backs of my arms the way he laughed."

"No girlfriends," Marti said. She popped the last of the roll into her mouth, savoring the honey and cinnamon.

"Have another," Miss Lindy said. She helped herself to another and passed the plate. "Got plenty more than enough for them two what's coming by later." Honey dripped as the old woman pulled her roll apart. "It wasn't that Barnabas didn't like girls, mind you. He did a whole lot of looking and had them pictures and magazines and did them things by himself, but he didn't do no courting."

"Now how do you know all that?" Marti suppressed a grin.

"Girl, I changed the linens on his bed. I know a lot about what he did there, a lot about what all of them did."

"Did he ever have any problems with girls?"

"A coupla times. It sounded to me like he just wanted to talk to them and didn't know how."

"What makes you say that?"

"Lord, child," and she gave Marti a gap-toothed smile that made her look more like a wizened child than an old woman, "I can can remember his poppa just fussing at him. 'Why would you tell her something like that, Barnabas? "I like your buttocks." Why would you say something like that?' Or 'Barnabas, you can't just touch a woman's breasts.' Then there was the time he exposed himself in the Rialto, and the time he fell off the ladder and broke his arm looking in some woman's window. He wasn't but thirteen then."

Cheney's behavior had been inappropriate. It sounded as if he'd had a few problems. "Did he have any preferences?" Marti asked. "Did he have a thing for Marilyn Monroe types, or women who wore spike heels?"

"Funny you should ask that. Now mind you, this ain't nothing the family ever discussed, or is ever likely to. But everyone, even the maid he climbed the window to spy on, was colored."

Colored girls. That was what connected Cheney, Dawn Taborn, and the Jane Doe. "You're kidding me," Marti said.

"No, ma'am, I sure ain't. Even when Barnabas was a little boy, he would run his little hand up my momma's dress. Tried it once with me. I told him if he did it again, he'd come away with a nub where his hand used to be. We was good friends from then on, and he never did try nothing else. Momma said she'd walk him to the store and he'd be just lookin' at the colored what worked around there. Didn't seem to have much interest at all in his own people, but he sure enough did like us. Of course you know about the lawsuit."

No, they didn't. If there had been one, it had never made it to court, or there would have been a record of it. "I've heard rumors," Marti ventured. Vik opened his mouth to say something and she kicked his ankle.

"That girl's folks were smart. Got them a settlement. It wasn't the first time Barnabas got caught, though. It happened a coupla times before, but to folks too scared to threaten anything. They worked for families in that town. Didn't want to be losing their jobs."

Who was the girl? Marti wondered. If the family didn't work in Lake Forest, it must have been someone who lived here. Was it their Jane Doe? Or could it have been Justine?

"There's no way you'd know any of the names of these families?"

"There was a number of them, the Jacksons, the Mitchells, the Harveys, the Atkins."

"Wilhelmina Harvey?" Marti asked. Could Aunt Lindy be talking about Justine?

"Them's the folks. They was church folks. Had two daughters. I'm not sure which one got herself mixed up with Barnabas, and I can't say as to how. Wasn't no Harvey working in Lake Forest. I'd have to think about the other girls." She gnawed on her lip for a minute. "There was this girl what worked as a laundress a couple houses down. Folks she worked for are dead now, though. House has changed hands half a dozen times. Then there was that dumb

196

Bailey child. She helped in the kitchen, could whip up anything without measuring a thing, but not a bit of common sense. She's the one what fell going down the back steps—there wasn't but two steps mind you—and she broke her leg. Then there was the time she put her hand through a window her mother had just washed. And the grease. Child was cooking and they say she picked up a jar filled with hot grease, burned her hand holding it, then poured it over the back of her other hand trying to put the jar down. She's the one that shoulda threatened to sue 'em when Barnabas caught her in the back hallway and almost ripped her dress off. It might have given her a chance to learn a different kind of work."

"Anyone else?"

"Nope, but there sure enough was others." She stood up and smoothed her dress. "I got to be showing you something he gave me a long time ago. I thought about it the last time you was here and forgot just as fast." She left the room and returned a few minutes later with her palm outstretched.

"Gave me this ring he did. Told me that made us best friends. I never did wear it, though. I wanted him to know that I appreciated him giving it to me, but I was afraid he would think it meant something it didn't if I put it on."

Marti looked down at the ring. Silver with a blue sapphire. Bingo. "Did he buy this?"

"Course not. To them folks, something like this was just a trinket."

Marti was thinking of the ring they'd recovered from the mummy. From the sour expression on Vik's face, so was he. Not that he was bothered a bit because Cheney could have killed the Jane Doe; proving that Cheney killed her would make at least one case go away. It was the similarities in the neck wounds that could tie the mummy to Dawn Taborn and the Farland case. If that meant Curly had caught the wrong man, what was the big deal for Vik? Everyone made mistakes, even when they weren't as sloppy as Curly had been.

"Did he just take this from his mother?" Marti asked.

"More than likely."

"And you weren't worried that someone would say that you stole it?"

"Course not. They knowed I wouldn't never take nothing from them, just like they knowed Barnabas would. His momma liked sapphires like some women like diamonds. She said it was because she was born in September and this was her birthstone. She had lots of jewelry with sapphires—bought it, folks gave it to her. Loved sapphires, she did. And they was really rich. Most wealthy white people count every penny and squeeze every nickel and dare you walk off with a dime, but those folks had been rich for so long that they wasn't scared they was going to lose it. They was always real generous with me, all of them. I got some sapphire earrings that his momma just took off one day and gave to me."

Marti weighed the ring in her hand for a moment before giving it back. Had Barnabas given the Jane Doe a ring? And, if so, how important was that?

The bell over the front door tinkled and Aunt Lindy pocketed the ring and rushed out of the room.

"Hello, dear," Aunt Lindy called. "Come right in. Nobody else from the church come with you today? Are you in a hurry?"

Marti couldn't hear the reply.

"Good. I've got some folks in the kitchen I'd like you to meet, and some honey pecan rolls."

She bustled into the room with a woman who didn't look to be more than sixty-five.

"Now, dear, guess what? These are police officers. You did know we have a colored one now who's a detective?"

Marti had a hunch that Aunt Lindy had forgotten the woman's name.

"What church are you from?" Marti asked.

"Greater Faith," the woman said. "One of our former pastors, God rest his soul, had a son who's a police officer."

"Yes, I know him," Marti said.

"You know Amos?"

Amos? The woman had to mean Slim. But Amos—was that his real name? He only had the initials A.B. on his ID. Should she go for the *B*?

"Yes, that's him," Marti said, "Amos—"

"Amos Bennett Ross." The woman dimpled when she smiled. She must like Obsession for Men.

Vik made a rude noise as he stifled a laugh.

The woman went on as if she hadn't heard. "He was named for Amos Bennett, the first colored man to settle in these parts, a freeman, too. Came here from Connecticut in 1833. A.B. is the third man in his family to carry that name. His brother S.D. is named for Samuel Dent."

Marti waited, certain the woman would tell her who that was. The only Dent she could think of was Richard Dent, who had played for the Bears.

"Samuel Dent was a colored soldier, ex-slave from Alabama, settled in Lake Forest after the Civil War."

"Lake Forest," Vik said.

"Yes, sir. You just take yourself down there and go to the Lake Forest Cemetery and you'll find his grave. Folks there liked him a lot."

"We coming up on Black History month again, ain't we?" Aunt Lindy said. "Sister, I know the children got to learn, but I sure hope you ain't planning to have your Sunday school class put us through the local history pageant again. Not four years in a row. Maybe one of 'em could just read Martin Luther King's speech like they do for his birthday. That sure is a nice speech. I could listen to it two or three times."

Aunt Lindy got ready to pour more coffee and the church sister jumped up.

"Now see here, Sister Lindy, you just set yourself down and let me take care of that." The woman emptied the pot, rinsed it out, measured enough coffee to make something a lot stronger than Aunt Lindy's brew, and set the coffeepot on the stove. "You always

waiting on folks, Sister Lindy. It's time we were waiting on you."
She adjusted the flame, then sat down. "Won't take but a few
minutes. Lord but those rolls look good."

They were, Marti agreed, but Momma's were better.

"You ladies wouldn't happen to remember something that happened at the Rialto back in '64, would you?"

They exchanged glances.

"James Farland," the church sister said at about the same time
that Aunt Lindy said, "Dawn Taborn."

"Did you know them?"

"No," the woman volunteered. "They attended Second Baptist.
My family remained members at First Baptist until we joined
Greater Faith."

"Then you remember when the churches split," Marti said.

"Why, you have gotten to know this community," the woman
said. "Your church wasn't founded until 1976."

Marti smiled and nodded. Word did get around.

"Can you think of anyone around that time who either came
into the community and didn't stay long or who left to go to college or move someplace else and never returned?"

The two women looked at each other, then at her and shook
their heads.

Armstrong's place was still closed when they left. The hands on
the cardboard clock in the window pointed to nine o'clock. It was
almost noon.

"I think we need to talk with Curly," Marti said. As much as she
hated having to meet the man, he might be able to tell them
something that could lead to the mummy. She was certain that,
like Vik, he would be too defensive to admit anything less than
perfection in the Farland case. After they saw Curly, she would
have to talk with Justine again.

Curly lived in a log house. They seemed to be becoming popular,
at least in this part of the Midwest, and she had seen them here

and there as she drove through Lake County and the surrounding northwestern ones. So far, nobody had built one in Lincoln Prairie, and it wasn't something you could put in a subdivision. Besides, Curly owned a lot of land. She could see horses in the distance, not too far from a barn. The house was surrounded by at least an acre of trees.

"I remember the house that was here before the cabin," Vik said. "A big old farmhouse. The land belonged to Curly's grandfather, who farmed it, grew alfalfa, I think, then to his father, who sold off some of it. Now it's his. A log cabin's not something I'd want, but it sure suits old Curly."

Right, Marti thought as she parked on the side of the unpaved road. Curly in the land of Lincoln—truth, justice, and the American way. Vik's near hero worship was beginning to get on her nerves. She had never been inside a log cabin, and she didn't know if Curly's was the norm or not. She expected to see the logs exposed inside, too; instead, the walls were ordinary, but the entire first floor was open and the fireplace took up all of the side wall. Rustic, she decided as she looked about. Everything was Early American. There was a rack with five rifles on the wall, along with the head of a black bear and an antlered elk. She looked for a coonskin cap but didn't see one. Marti decided to let Vik do the talking.

"Where's Clara?" Vik asked.

"She's down with the flu," Curly said.

"Sorry to hear it."

"She'll be sorry she didn't get to see you. She's asleep up in the loft. The last time she got the flu, it went into pneumonia and she ended up in the hospital for five days. How's Mildred?"

"She's having another bout with the MS, but she'll get the best of it, same as always."

Curly looked at him for a moment, then reached out and patted his shoulder. "I'm glad she has you to look after her."

Curly's concern was genuine. He obviously really did love his wife, and Marti could see he thought a lot of Vik and Mildred, too.

201

There was no question of how Vik felt toward him. She would have to remember that.

A fat calico cat strolled into the room. It sat near the fireplace, flicked its tail a few times, then moved away and curled up on the braided rug. Another cat, gray and white, groomed itself on the windowsill. Well-behaved cats, she decided. There wasn't a single cat hair on the furniture that she could see, and no throw covers to protect it. Marti sat in a chair comfortable enough to fall asleep in, with a view of the kitchen, a kitchen that she liked, with a cooking island, copper-bottomed pots hanging from a circular rack. She turned her attention back to Curly, waiting for Vik to speak.

After they talked a little more about Mildred's health, Vik's kids and grandkids, and the joys of country living, Vik said, "We took another look at the Farland case."

"The man was guilty as sin."

"That was obvious," Vik agreed. "The thing is, we've got another body—black female, found in the Geneva. She was killed at about the same time as the Taborn girl and was close to the same age."

"You mean the mummy they talked about in the newspaper? How did they find out that much about a mummy so fast?"

"We brought in someone from Chicago with experience in forensic anthropology."

Curly whistled. "Damn. That was fast. I would have expected it to take a couple of months, at least, even longer."

"Not anymore," Vik said.

Marti could see from the expression on Curly's face that he was not pleased with this reminder of how much things had changed since he'd retired. Vik seemed aware of it, too.

"We're thinking that maybe Farland's girlfriend can lead us to the mummy. Who knows, maybe Farland killed them both." Vik said it as casually as he might mention that the sun was shining, but the effect on Curly was immediate. His face got red.

"There wasn't any way for you know there was a body at the

Geneva, too," Vik said. "Farland had an obvious motive, and opportunity."

Curly rubbed his jaw. "You're right. Farland worked at both theaters, as I recall, but the night the girl died, he was at the Rialto. Besides, they're four blocks apart."

"We have another victim, a Barnabas Cheney," Vik said. "His people owned both of those theaters."

Curly shook his head. "I remember Barnabas. He was one hell of an actor. Crazy as hell, but harmless and friendly, at least to me. He talked to me every time he saw me. But Farland? He was a quiet one, too quiet. Of course, we got him to talk." He rubbed his hands together. That was something Vik did, too. "Farland just wasn't too bright. Grade school dropout. Slow-witted, but not stupid. You know how those quiet types are, lightning-quick tempers when they get mad. You got to watch out for those quiet ones. They're sneaky as hell."

Marti had a fleeting thought of Johnny.

"Sneaky," Curly said again.

She thought of Theo. How dare he say that.

"And a liar," Curly said. "Once he started talking, the man lied so much that I just let him keep going and wrote it all down. He told so many lies, his lawyer didn't even put him on the witness stand. They were all a bunch of liars. His own mother couldn't keep her story straight when we got her up there."

Marti could understand how intimidating the whole process could have been. Farland had no priors. He had never been in court before. She was beginning to wonder if Farland had spoken under duress.

"There wasn't nothing smart about him, though," Curly went on. "And he sure as hell wasn't clever. Good thing for us. We didn't have any trouble at all figuring out it was him. Dumb as he was, it would be a shame if he got away with killing another one. It makes sense that it must have been him. Too bad nobody was reported missing, at least not around the time when he must have killed the other girl."

"We're looking for something in your case that might lead us to our Jane Doe," Vik said. "Do you remember talking with anyone who knew Dawn Taborn?"

"There wasn't any need to. The case was open-and-shut, even if it was circumstantial. It was a bench trial, but there wouldn't have been a juror in the state who would have believed Farland was innocent. The man convicted himself."

"There's also nothing in the case file about her background," Marti said. "Family, work, school—nothing."

Curly gave Vik a look that Marti couldn't interpret. Vik's shrug was almost imperceptible. His eyebrows almost met across the bridge of his nose, signaling his annoyance.

"No need for it. She was dead. He was gone. He hadn't shown up for either job or gone home since the night she was murdered. We found him, locked him up, end of story." He gave Vik a slow smile and a wink. "When I was cop, we got our man. This was before the system got so screwed up that today we can know someone is guilty and not be able to give the court the evidence that will convict him. Farland was guilty. That was enough. It cut down on a hell of a lot of paperwork, too."

Marti glanced at Vik just in time to see him give Curly a quick nod in agreement.

"Back then," Curly said, "all we wanted to do for the victim, and the family, was get the guy who did it behind bars. That girl was fooling around with a married man. We left her reputation intact, left her family in peace. We didn't drag her name through the mud." He laughed. "According to the family, you would have thought she was a nun instead of a . . . well . . . Her parents were so grateful that after the trial was over, they thanked me."

Marti stared at him, incredulous. He was making most of this up. What kind of an investigation had he conducted? There was no family, except for a little boy, whom Curly apparently didn't even know existed. Nobody she talked with had suggested that Taborn's reputation was anything like what Curly was implying. Had he made those assumptions without checking them out just because the woman was black? Or was it because Farland was married? Or was it just convenient? Curly's notes were accurate about one thing: There had not been an investigation.

Vik was quiet on the drive back, which surprised her. She hoped his silence meant that he was beginning to see that his hero might not be quite the cop he thought him to be, that Curly Smith was just as human as the rest of them. Part of her was glad that Curly wasn't everything Vik thought he was. Part of her was angry because Curly had let Vik down.

15

When Marti returned to the precinct, an interoffice envelope from the Board of Education was on her desk. Not only were Dawn Taborn's records inside but also a copy of the yearbook for the year she graduated, with a request that it be returned. Vik's eyebrows knitted in a furious scowl as he looked at it.

"Know what, Jessenovik?"

"What?"

"I'm tired as hell."

"Me too."

Marti pushed the yearbook to one side and slouched in her chair until her head was resting against the back. "I'm going to have to talk with Justine Kerr again."

"Looks that way. When?"

"After school."

Vik yawned and rubbed his eyes. "We need to talk with Farland, too. Let's bring him in. You think we can charge him with offing the Jane Doe?"

"We don't even know who she is."

"Yeah, well, he didn't give them any arguments when they charged him with the Taborn homicide."

Marti wondered about that. "If he killed both of them, what about Cheney? Hell, what about Logan?"

Vik clasped his hands behind his head. "Damned if I know."

"We need a motive."

"Have you got the energy to come up with one?"

"Give me a few minutes." But before she could propose anything, a uniform stuck his head in the door.

"This came in on the fax."

"Thanks," she said. He stood on the other side of her desk and held out several pieces of paper. She had to sit up to reach them. "Feast or famine."

This time, it was the employment records for three downtown theaters for all of 1963, 1964, and 1965. "This could be useful." She passed them over to Vik.

"A job for Lupe," he said.

"My thought, too. Have they stopped making No-Doz, Jessenovik?"

"I think so. When Lupe gets here, let's have her put in a call to a couple of drugstores."

"We don't have drugstores anymore, Vik, just pharmacies attached to department stores and supermarkets."

"Oh."

Vik tilted his chair back and closed his eyes. After that, neither of them moved for a while.

The uniform from the second shift who worked the beat where Logan had been killed came in at 3:15.

"Got anything for me?" Marti asked.

"I heard about the watch," he said. "I still don't believe Ed did anything wrong. I checked at the church again. He was there the night Cheney died."

"So what do you think happened?" Marti asked.

"Damned if I know."

"Why wasn't he at the shelter last night?"

"I've talked to everyone I could find, and the last time anyone saw him was at a church on Eureka. He ate and left. He should have ended up over at that Lutheran church on Wicker, but he never got there."

"Was there anything unusual about his behavior?"

The uniform looked at her for a moment. "There's something unusual about most of my street charges' behavior. There was nothing more unusual. Ed went off center maybe every four to six months. He wasn't due again until March or April."

Vik swung his feet off of his desk. "Son, how long have you been working that beat?"

"Three years."

"I thought so. Is this a permanent thing, or do you guys rotate?"

"It's a good fit. They'll probably leave it alone."

"And if they don't?"

He shrugged. "Then I guess I'll work a different beat. But a lot would be the same. Most places you go, you deal with people living on the street."

"I'd like to take a look at the place where Logan was staying the night Cheney died."

"Sure. Can you meet me there about six?"

"We'll be there," Marti said. "And keep asking questions about Logan. Let me know if you come up with anything."

After the door closed Vik waited long enough for the uniform to be out of earshot. "He's a social worker. Does he know that? A social worker, not a cop."

Marti didn't have the energy to touch that. "We're finally getting somewhere, Jessenovik."

"Huh?"

"I think we've got a real connection between Cheney and all of these women, Taborn, Doe, and Justine."

"Because they were black?"

"Right. We got lucky with the ring, although I haven't figured out what to do with that yet."

"And we struck out on getting any information from Aunt Lindy on any missing young women, we can't prove Farland offed Cheney, and we've struck out on Logan, so far anyway."

"Why would Farland off Cheney?"

"How the hell do I know, MacAlister?"

"Who had a motive to kill Cheney?"

"Anyone could see the man was crazy. He didn't even have enough sense to wear boots in the wintertime."

"There's the frame and the watch, Jessenovik."

"Armstrong. I think the man's a voyeur, but given the right circumstances, anyone could become a killer, and he did want to impress that Stazlowski woman."

"Maybe we didn't pay enough attention to him, Vik. Maybe we didn't ask the right questions." Damn, she was tired. They needed to know who the mummy was, how she fit, if she fit.

"I think we're going to have to put a little more effort into this, MacAlister. I don't think we're going to get any more breaks."

"Me neither." She got another cup of coffee, took one over to Vik, and gave him the employment listings faxed in by Jonathan Cheney. She took the envelope from the Board of Education.

There was nothing unusual in the school records. "Damn," she said. "Not one mention of Farland in here, or Cheney, or any guys at all. Just days late and days absent and grades. She did get good grades, talked to the school counselor about colleges, never followed up. No disciplinary actions."

"Ordinary, everyday people die all the time."

She began thumbing through the yearbook, then thought about the index. "Dawn eleven, Justine zero."

"What are we keeping score for now?"

"Yearbook appearances."

"Justine was a few years older."

"I know that."

"Wake up, MacAlister."

"Speak for yourself."

She used Post-it stickers to mark the pages where Dawn appeared, paged through the entire book, looked at just those pages with a photo of Dawn, then sat back and waited. It came to her after a few minutes. She looked again. In every photo where Dawn appeared in proximity to a boy, it was always a white male.

"Vik?"

"What?"

"I think we might have something here."

She explained.

"It doesn't mean anything, Marti. That was the sixties. Things like that didn't happen. Hell, I'm Polish, never even thought about dating anyone who wasn't."

"Never looked at a pretty black girl?"

He reddened. "Marti, men always look."

"Well, we know that Dawn was smart, confident enough to give a speech at a Baptist youth convention, stayed away from the young men at her church, and belonged to a congregation with a very strict code of conduct. From the looks of this, there might have been a reason why she didn't date. Or maybe she did, and nobody knew, for obvious reasons. Farland was black, older than she was, married, and had a child. If they did argue, and he did kill her, I think it was much more likely because of something he saw her doing that he disapproved of, rather than something they did together."

Vik leaned back in his chair and said nothing. His hand started up to his hair.

"Don't," Marti said. "The day is young; we may have to go somewhere."

He slapped the palm of his hand down on his desk. "Curly was a good cop."

She had lost count of how many times he had said that.

"Curly was a small-town cop. If he suspected she was seeing someone white, he would never have acknowledged it. Or maybe he did, in his own way. Maybe that's why he said she was promiscuous."

Vik didn't say anything.

"Vik, I am not trying to take anything away from Curly or his record as a cop. All I'm saying is that this happened at a particular time and within a specific social context, one vastly different from life as we know it now. That's all I am saying. Can you accept that?"

His wiry eyebrows came close enough to get tangled. He cracked his knuckles, then broke a few pencils. "Okay," he said. It came out clipped and curt. His expression didn't change.

"Good. I'm going to surprise Justine Kerr, but first I'm going to get a couple of candy bars. Want one?"

"Milk, too," he said. "Whole milk. Mildred says milk extends the effect of the sugar and that I should never have them both at the same time."

While Marti was gone, Vik went over to her desk. Not a cop's desk at all. A woman's desk, a mother's desk. Pictures of the kids, and now the fireman. A Popsicle-stick pencil holder from Theo—cute kid. A ceramic mug with MA printed on it from Joanna. And what was that? A little statue of a teddy bear dressed like a fireman? He sat back down, leaned back, and closed his eyes. Marti's husband had been a cop, a narc, but he'd found time to be a husband and a father. And she lost him; it wasn't the other way around. It made a difference—who went and who was left behind. It made a big difference. Women were better at the emotional stuff.

His dad had never gotten over Vik's mother's death. Three times a year, he had a Mass said for her and they all went to church—her birthday, their wedding anniversary, and the anniversary of the day she died. Although his dad never drank in public, except for a few beers at a pub or a ball game, there were many nights when he went to his room with a pint of Wild Irish Rose. Everyone called his mother Roslatka, her nickname since childhood. Some nights, when his dad shut himself up in his room, Vik had a hockey game or it was parents' night at school, or something was going on at church. Curly always seemed to know about that. Curly always called, and most times, Curly filled in. No way would he let Curly down now.

Justine Kerr lived in a brick ranch on the far northwest side of town. The street was long and narrow and bordered by mud-splattered piles of plowed snow. The house sat back on a wooded lot. Lights placed at intervals along the driveway led up to the walk.

Justine opened the door without checking to see who it was. Marti guessed that meant her husband was home.

"Oh, no," Justine said.

"I need to talk to you."

211

"Then you'll have to talk here."

"Fine." It was too cold to play word games. "I think there was more between you and Barnabas than what you told me."

"And if there was?"

"Was there?" Did Justine's family initiate legal action against Cheney?

Justine hesitated.

"You liked him."

"Yes, I liked him. He was . . . special. . . . He was . . . nice. He was a very nice man."

"Were you intimate?"

"God no. I couldn't do that."

"Did you want to?"

"You are getting damned personal, Detective. I don't think I have to answer that."

Marti decided to back off, even if she was getting cold. "Justine, I need to know if he made any advances toward you, and how you handled that, and what he did then. This is crucial to my investigation."

"He was a nice man," she said again. "And a brilliant actor."

"And?"

"And . . . he couldn't . . . sex, I mean. He tried, but he couldn't."

"How did that make him feel?"

Tears filled Justine's eyes. "He cried," she said. "He cried."

"Was that the summer that he—"

"Yes," Justine interrupted. "Yes. That kind, decent man. I asked him for something that he couldn't give me. I . . ."

"Justine?"

A man came up behind her. "Is everything okay?"

"Yes, of course. She just needs directions."

The man looked at her for a moment. His eyes were were a deep blue. His expression was intense. Dark brown hair curled at his neck. He was tall, athletic, and Caucasian. He had what some people would call "presence." Marti could almost envision him on the stage. "Thank you," she said, and walked away. Justine had

212

obviously cared deeply for Barnabas. It seemed unlikely that she would have allowed her parents to pursue a lawsuit.

The beat cop was standing in a doorway at the rear of the Lutheran church when Marti pulled into the parking lot at 6:15. Earlier in the day, the sun had tried to make a brief appearance but hadn't quite succeeded. Instead, the temperature had kept dropping. Now it was hovering just above zero. Marti was hoping that it wouldn't snow.

"There's the social worker," Vik said as he exited the car.

They followed the uniform down a flight of stairs to the basement of the church. "The guy who runs the place should be here anytime now. I thought you would want to talk with him. Meanwhile, have a look around."

Marti scanned the layout. One large room, no windows. A door across from where she was standing, a door at the other end of the room. She checked the nearest door first. It led to the rest rooms and a flight of stairs that went to the sanctuary. The other door, which was at the front of the building, led to the church and to the doors that would take her outside. The beat cop came up behind her.

"This area has to be accessible because of the fire laws, but there are at least four people here, usually six, and these exits are watched. They don't want anything of value in the church to disappear."

"Nobody could leave without being noticed?"

"No way. There are women here, sometimes children. It has to be a safe place; nobody wanders around."

An older man with shiny bald spot that was encroaching on what was left of his hair, came over to them. "I'm so sorry to hear about Ed. We've got someone willing to donate a casket, and the minister here will conduct a service. That is, if you don't locate his family." He looked at Marti.

"We haven't been able to track down any next of kin. Maybe when it hits the newspapers. Were you here a week ago Monday?"

"Yes. I usually leave once everyone settles down for the night, but we were shorthanded, so I stayed."

"And Ed Logan was here all night."

"Yes, he slept right over there." He pointed to the corner at the front of the building—the one farthest from the exit. "He always slept there. Actually, he sat up, with his eyes closed. I don't know if he was sleeping or not. He was paranoid, and being around people made him nervous. But he never bothered anyone."

"How well did you know him?"

"I didn't. He was always quiet, respectful. He took his hat off as soon as he came through the door. I can't remember what his voice sounded like. He'd listen when you talked to him, nod maybe, and every so often, he had this smile, but he never said anything."

"Did he have any friends?"

"Not that I know of. All of the regulars knew him, but I can't ever remember seeing him talk to anyone. He seemed like such a nice man." He turned to the beat cop. "Whatever we can do, Joe. Just let me know."

When she asked him about the watch, he said he had never seen Logan with one. She did not mention the key. They were withholding that.

As they walked to the car, Vik said, "Do you know who that man is?"

"Your great-aunt Hezekiah's second cousin."

"No, MacAlister, he was a vice president at one of the biggest companies around here. And now look at him. He retired and became a social worker."

When Marti and Vik got back to the precinct, Lupe had spread a checkered tablecloth on Marti's desk and brought a platter of homemade tamales and burritos. The hot, spicy aroma filled the room.

"Sometimes, when the weather is miserable and cold like this, my nieces and nephews and I have a picnic," Lupe said. "No beer—

we're on duty—but try this." She poured lemonade from a gallon thermos jug. "Come on, Jessenovik. All that sauerkraut and horse-radish has made you sour. This warms the body *and* the soul."

"When do you find time to cook?" Marti asked.

"It's my day off. Guess what else I've been doing?"

"Laundry?" Marti said. She had a hunch that was what she needed to do.

"No."

"I give up," Vik said.

"See," Lupe said. "There is a word for people like you—*sour-puss*. Here, have a tamale."

Vik accepted the food.

"What have you been up to?" Marti asked.

"I talked with that lady reverend you told me to see. She didn't have much to say, but she knew a lot about this place years ago. She even knew about the Cheneys."

"Oh?"

"It sounds like Barnabas Cheney was pretty busy at the family business."

"What business?" Vik asked.

"The theaters. Not just onstage. He'd let you in free if he liked you. And if you were black, and female, he might like you enough to let you in free a lot."

"And this woman could remember that."

"She was just a kid, but she got in free with her aunt. She said that looking back, she thinks her aunt wanted to see the movies for free, but she took her niece along as sort of . . . to keep Cheney from getting too friendly."

"How old was he?"

"Early twenties."

"It's easy to malign the dead," Vik said.

Marti wondered where that came from, but she didn't ask. "I had another talk with Justine Kerr. It seems that Cheney might have had a problem with . . ." She looked at Vik, then said, "In-timacy."

"What kind of a problem?" Lupe asked. She looked at Vik, too, then said, "Coitus interruptus?"

"It sounded more like never erect."

Vik's face got red.

"How about that," Lupe said. "How did he react? Did he get mad? Would he have killed because of it?"

"He cried," Marti said.

"Damn. Demented killers don't cry. Now I'll have to rethink this."

"Let's eat while you're thinking," Vik said.

Marti reached for a paper plate and helped herself to a couple of tamales.

"So," Lupe said as she polished off a burrito, "James Farland killed both women, and Cheney's death is a separate issue that has nothing to do with that."

"We don't have a motive for Farland to have killed the Jane Doe."

"True," Lupe conceded. "But, then again, if we knew who she was, maybe we would."

"Or," Marti said, "Cheney could have killed both women, and someone killed him to get revenge."

"James Farland," Vik said.

Marti told her about Aunt Lindy's ring.

"So, if the Jane Doe had a ring that he gave her, we know Cheney knew her. We know that he had a thing for black women and a thing that he couldn't get up."

"And we know that he cried," Marti agreed.

"I like that in a man," Lupe said. "But only when I don't want him to be a cold-blooded killer."

Vik said nothing. Lupe looked at him, probably expecting an argument. Instead, he walked out of the room.

"What's wrong with him?" Lupe said. "He's not himself at all. Is his wife that sick?"

"I don't know," Marti said. "When I ask about Mildred, he says she's doing okay, but her sister is still there with her days, and his son goes over in the evening and stays until he gets home. I don't know what's wrong."

That wasn't true, but she could not say anything to Lupe about Curly.

Vik took the stairs down to the basement. What if Cheney had killed either or both of the women? That was what he was beginning to suspect. If that was true, that could be why Curly's notes were so scant. He couldn't believe that Curly would give in to the pressure of a wealthy family. He would not have accepted a bribe. Never, not Curly. Damn. Whose bright idea was it to go into that theater anyway? They'd been mentioning it in the paper for weeks, but why now? If they hadn't found that mummy, none of this would be happening. If Farland killed Cheney and it came out that Curly had overlooked a few pertinent facts in the Taborn homicide . . . If Farland killed Cheney, he must have had some reason to believe that Cheney killed the women. He must have seen something, or known about something . . . but if so, why hadn't he told anyone? Or had he told someone? Did he tell Curly? If he did, maybe Curly was next.

Vik went to a pay phone.

"Curly, it's Vik. I was thinking. Now that Farland is out, maybe you should keep an eye out for him."

"What makes you think that?"

"Nothing. You know how it is when someone you sent up gets out."

"Yes, I do know, and thanks. I'll watch my back. Where is he, anyway?"

Vik lied. "I haven't a clue." He had already said too much, but Curly was his friend, his father's friend. They went way back. He owed him.

Marti was wavering. The more she thought about what Lupe had said, the more she was inclined to think that Cheney had killed both women and that Farland had killed him. That did not explain the similarity of the marks on the women's necks to the marks on Ed Logan's neck, but the answer to that could depend on how someone had learned the chokehold, or whatever it was. She called the medical examiner's office in Chicago, and left a message for Dr. Pickus. She called Janet Petrosky instead and asked her to hold Logan's body until Dr. Pickus could come up and take a look at it.

Next, she called Laura DeLang, on the off chance that someone might have seen Cheney with a black woman and not made the connection that they were a twosome or that Cheney wanted it to be that way.

"Miss DeLang, could you answer a couple of questions for me?"

"Why of course, but I'm off to a shoot in half an hour. It's just an industrial film, but it's work, so you'll have to talk fast."

"You mentioned that Barnabas Cheney seemed to have a love interest. Was there ever anyone in the audience or backstage who could possibly have been the young woman he liked?"

After a few moments silence, Miss DeLang said no.

"Did any friends ever accompany him to the theater and watch the performance?"

"I'm afraid he always came alone, at least as far as I know."

Disappointed, Marti thanked her. She tried George Jamison's number but was told he was at a rehearsal.

Next, she tackled the employment lists faxed by Jonathan Cheney. Fifty-five people were listed in alphabetical order, along with their addresses at the time of employment and their Social Security numbers. Only eight had been full-time employees. Dates of employment were listed in three columns, one each for 1963, 1964, and 1965. She used Hi-Liter markers to identify them by the number of years they worked. James Farland had worked part-time all of 1963 and up until the time of his arrest. Marti passed the list to Lupe. "Make a copy and run all of the names through the computer. I'll take anything I can get."

"Fifty-five people," Lupe said. "Are you going to interview all of them?"

"Maybe. A little research should narrow it down."

218

"What are you looking for?"

"I don't know. Maybe our mummy, maybe someone who knew her, maybe someone who had dealings with Cheney. We'll see."

"I'll get started as soon as I clean off your desk."

"And Lupe, one more thing."

"What?"

"When you get down to color-coding lists, your investigation is in deep trouble."

Lupe flashed her a grin. "I'll remember that."

While Lupe was gone, Marti called a friend with access to census-related information, hoping to find some pattern in the list. As late as it was, within two hours, she knew who was deceased, who was African-American—none were Hispanic—and that none of the addresses was current. When she eliminated everyone who had moved out of state, seventeen names remained. Three of those were black females. She looked at the list again and put an asterisk beside the names of the black females, including those who were deceased or had moved out of state. Now she had eleven. Five were dead. Six were living. Three lived out of state.

She made a copy of the list and passed it to Vik. "Why don't you try to find out how they died? Start with the black females." He grunted but seemed agreeable.

When Lupe came back a few minutes later, Marti cross-referenced anyone with a police record. Only one of the eleven black women did—for prostitution. She was still in the area, but she was fifty-eight now. Marti wondered if she was still turning tricks. Then she wondered if Cheney had frequented prostitutes. Men with sexual inadequacies or fetishes often did.

It was getting late. The sky had been dark for hours now and snowflakes the size of her palm were drifting down when she looked out the window. Joanna had a game tonight. She would miss it, and so would Ben, but Momma, Theo, Mike, and Peter and Patrick, the boys from next door, would be there. She hoped having them there would be a buffer for Joanna if Chris and his new girlfriend showed up.

"Here you go, Torres." She explained where she was and gave Lupe the names of the three women who lived out of state. As easy as picking up the phone and calling six women sounded, it wasn't. She got the hooker's—or ex-hooker's—phone number. The other two women who lived in Illinois weren't listed. Then she figured these two women had married. After a number of false starts, she located relatives in the area. Lupe got a listing for one woman who was already married when she worked at the theater, but she had even more trouble locating the other two.

"Nothing unusual about the way the women died, except for one," Vik said. "She was mugged three years ago in a parking lot at a mall in Chicago, but they got the perps."

"I've located all three of mine but haven't spoken with them yet," Marti said.

"Sorry, guys," Lupe said. "I'm odd man out. There's one of mine I cannot track down. There's nothing. It's as if she doesn't exist."

Marti felt a familiar adrenaline rush and looked at Vik. She could see that he felt it, too. "What's the name?" she asked.

"Missouri New."

"Great name," Vik said. "One that people are likely to remember."

"You don't think . . ." Lupe said. "This isn't our Jane Doe?"

"Hard to say right now."

Lupe looked disappointed.

"Look, kid," Vik said, "this is what we wanted, someone we can't account for. Even if it doesn't pan out, it was well worth the time."

"Okay, amigo," Lupe said.

Even though Vik was pleased with the find, Marti could see the conflict in his eyes. Vik the cop was eager to find Missouri New. Vik, Curly's friend, didn't want to know any more about her than he already did.

16

Vik phoned home to let Stephen know it might be a long night, then paged through the reports on his desk, trying to look busy. Marti and Lupe were both on the phone. They had a name now, Missouri New. It might not be the mummy's name, but it was a name not easily forgotten. He had been avoiding the hard questions for several days now, but once the mummy was identified, he would no longer be able to. He felt a need to talk with Mildred, but that would have to wait until she was feeling better. Maybe he would just take a walk. Marti looked up when he put on his coat, but she didn't say anything.

It was cold outside, a calm, windless cold that cut right to the bone. Vik wrapped his scarf around his face, covering his nose, pulled his hat down, shoved his gloved hands into his pockets, and headed for the corner. He wanted to walk back in time. He wanted to go to Curly's old house and smell the hot apple strudel Clara used to make. He wanted to pretend Clara was his mother, as he had when he was a child. He wanted to pretend that Curly was his father. Curly didn't drink. Curly had paid attention to him. Curly had taken him places. Dad had just sat in his room night after night and remembered, or drank until he forgot. Vik was the youngest; his brothers, Greg and Mark, had had things to do that didn't include "the baby." By the time he was in high school and Dad's heart began giving him trouble and he finally had to give up the Wild Irish Rose, it was too late. Dad wanted to be a dad, but Vik had found a replacement.

One night, he was awakened by Dad and Curly arguing. After

that, Curly didn't come to their house anymore. He and Curly still went to Cubs and Blackhawk games; he just didn't tell Dad who he was going with. He didn't invite Dad to go, either. Dad never said anything, but he knew.

Vik stopped for a red light and realized he was three blocks from the precinct. The gray stone church where he and Mildred attended Mass was across the street. Snow began flicking at his face like grains of sand. His feet were cold. He wasn't ready to go back to the precinct, but he turned anyway and headed in that direction.

Why did Dad and Curly have to be so different? Dad had never done anything that seemed important. The only time he'd made the newspaper was the day some lady got her foot stuck in a revolving door and he took the door apart. Now that Vik understood the old way—free meals while on duty, a few dollars changing hands, a little coercion to get a confession—he could appreciate his father's honesty and try to be a man of integrity, too. Back then, all he could see was the shine on the badge, the bulge of the gun, and the swagger that came with the headlines. Curly was all flash and style. Even now, he didn't want to look beyond that. He didn't want Curly to become just a man, or even just a cop. Damn. Everyone was entitled to a hero.

Instead of going upstairs, Vik walked over to Records. The heat hit him full in the face. He shivered.

"Nineteen sixty-three," the uniform complained. "Give me a break, will you, Jessenovik? Can't this wait for first shift?"

"Sorry, pal, I need those records now." He was going to have to find out if Curly had taken a bribe from the Cheneys. "How long does it take you to put things away? What I need is in that box on the table. I'll just pull up a chair."

It didn't take long to look through Curly's files. As in the Farland case, the data was scant. As he looked through them, Vik began sorting them into two piles, not because he wanted to but because the differences between cases in each file required it. One pile was nine files deep. He took another look and cut it to four. Like Farland, the defendants were black. There were a few other similarities, as well. None of the men could afford an attorney and Daniel Randell was appointed by the court. Old Judge Hendricks was on the bench, and all four were bench trials. Two were capital cases, Farland and a man named Willis.

He had come here expecting to read the files of a good detective—notes and confessions and follow-up—and Curly was good. Trouble was, he hadn't bothered about all that if the perp was black. Then it didn't seem to matter at all. Vik pushed the chair back and stood up. He picked up the files and took aim at the wall; then he slammed them down on the table. Why in the hell couldn't Curly just have been dishonest? Same judge, same lawyer, same detective, same skimpy case notes, same verdict—guilty. Justice sure as hell wasn't blind.

Over time, Vik could probably live with a bribe. What he couldn't live with was knowing that Curly was prejudiced. No. It wasn't even that. Curly and Dad had been best friends. If Curly was prejudiced, then Dad—but despite all the drinking and all the long silences between them, Vik knew his dad had always been bigger than that. If Curly went down for this, nobody would look at a case that happened the year before. But Vik had found not just one case, but four. He knew that Willis and at least two other men had received the same kind of justice as Farland. And that was what stuck in his craw. If Farland was seeking revenge now, after thirty years, it was almost his due.

He ignored the elevator and walked upstairs. He wanted to go home. He wanted to close the file on the Willis case, the Farland case, and never open either one of them again. It was too much like looking into a closet and finding not just a skeleton, but a father. Toward the end, when Dad's heart was bad and the booze was gone, he tried to make up for lost time. "My dad was a copper," he'd said one night. "Just a beat cop, like me. He didn't do anything that ever made the newspaper—he never even got an award—but he kept the people he served safe. He kept things out of their lives that didn't belong there. He made their kids believe he had eyes in the back of his head. He kept the peace, Vik. He kept the peace."

He knew, even then, that his dad was talking about himself, as well. And when the time came, Vik remembered. "He kept the peace." He'd had that chiseled into Dad's gravestone.

He kept the peace. Nothing was that simple anymore. Not with gangs and drugs and deteriorating neighborhoods. Hell, they couldn't keep gangs and drugs out of the best neighborhoods. He could remember those days, those times. He knew what his father was talking about. Honor. A man's honor. A cop's honor. What was left when that was gone? What would he see if he pulled his father's arrest records—two codes, two standards? If Dad and Curly turned out to be the kind of cops he was beginning to believe they were—the kind of cops who judged men differently if they had brown skin—was he that kind of cop without knowing it? Had he ever done the same thing?

He pushed open the door to the office. "So, Torres," he said, "what have you got on this Missouri New?"

"Nothing yet, just a name. She worked at the theater for only five weeks."

"Five weeks. If she's our Jane, then she was pregnant when she came here. Let me take a crack at it." He felt a pain in his chest as he spoke, sort of like a knife being stuck in and quickly withdrawn. He began with the obvious, anyone by the name of New who lived in a large city in Missouri. With luck, when Dr. Pickus examined the three victims' necks, she would be able to prove that Taborn, Jane Doe, and Logan had all been killed by the same perpetrator. Then they could arrest Farland again, give him a fair trial this time, and Curly would be vindicated. Was that what Vik wanted? He didn't know. Half an hour later, Marti gave them a thumbs-up. When she hung up the phone, she said, "Both Laura DeLang and George Jamison remember seeing one black woman in the audience. She attended only one performance in Antioch and one here before *Godot* went to Chicago. But she was the only black woman there, and their descriptions, although vague, are pretty much the same."

"That's a start," Lupe said.

Poor kid, Vik thought. You either choose this line of work to watch people bow to the badge or to be useful and have people look up to you. Lupe was the "I'm useful; look up to me" type. Too bad they were all only human, and you were always looking up to someone with clay feet.

Marti could not believe it when Justine Kerr said, "Oh, her" into the phone when she mentioned Missouri New's name.

"What about her?" Justine asked.

Marti could tell by the sound of her voice that Justine was still upset over her unannounced visit, and now because Marti was calling her so late at night. "How did you meet her?"

"Our church sponsored her trip up here from Mississippi and she only hung around for about a month and a half."

"Do you know what happened to her? Where she went?"

"No, and I really don't care to. Not many people did. Most of us were glad to see her go."

"Why?" Marti asked, working to keep the excitement out of her voice.

"She just wasn't what we expected."

"How so?"

"Well, you pay someone's way from the South, see that they have new clothes, a job, a place to stay, and tell them you'll pay for their education, and you expect . . ."

Marti waited, then said, "What?"

"I don't know. It was as if . . . I can't explain it. She just wasn't what we thought she would be. We were glad to see her go."

"Where did she go?"

"Home, I assume. She at least had the decency to leave quietly without asking any of us for money."

"Justine, did this Missouri New have a preference for white men?"

The silence was answer enough. After a few moments, Justine cleared her throat. "Black people brought her here, black people did for her, and all she could do in return was suck up to the white man. She just wanted to get out of the South. She used us."

"Miss New came here from the South," Marti said when she hung up. "Courtesy of the folks at Second Baptist Church. From the sounds of it, those folks were happy to see her go.

"That doesn't tell us a hell of a lot," Vik cautioned.

Marti looked at him. The bags under his eyes were dark, heavy pouches. The expression on his face was grim. His complexion was a pasty kind of gray. For the first time since she met him, he looked old, years older than he was. But why? It was too late to cite his friend Curly for dereliction of duty if he had arrested the wrong man, and that was still a big if. Unfortunately, it seemed like Curly was more than just a friend to Vik, and this was costing him. What if he wouldn't work with her when this was over?

She dialed the Reverend Cleotis Jones's number next, then checked her watch and apologized for calling so late.

"Not to worry," the minister said. "The missus and I never go to bed until after we watch the Oprah late-night rerun. We watch something else in the morning."

When asked about the girl, he said. "Missouri New? I haven't heard her name mentioned in years."

"Do you have any idea how I could contact her? Her pastor in Mississippi, maybe."

The reverend cleared his throat. "Well, now, that could be a problem. She didn't exactly come from a church, even though we told folks she did. She joined a church down there, but she hadn't been a member all that long when she asked for help to come north."

"Where is she now?"

"Why, I have no idea. It was one of those situations where the mother was alone and she sort of left her with a neighbor and just didn't come back. The neighbor, childless and unmarried, thought Missouri was a gift from God until she grew up. Those teen years are hard for most of us. This neighbor was seventy years old. I imagine she was glad when Missouri left. She was quite a handful."

"How so?"

"Here. I'll let Mrs. Jones talk with you. When we got those young women who were a little on the wild side, I tended to keep my distance."

"Whatever has caused you to ask after Missouri New after all these years?" Mrs. Jones asked when she came on the line. "Someone must have told you she was fast. I thought she was more like a breath of fresh air."

"Why is that?"

"Oh, everybody gets in a rut sometimes. Missouri sure enough wasn't going to let that happen to her. We had all these young church sisters chasing after all these church brothers in the hope of catching a ring, and here was Missouri, with her nose up in the air and her eyes on a college education. That was enough for the girls to decided that she was stuck up, but I never found her to be that way. Independent, that's all. We were talking to our children about getting an education, but those young'uns had other things on their mind. Not Missouri. Of course with her background . . ." Mrs. Jones's voice trailed off.

"Oh?" Marti said.

"Well, her mother being a honky-tonk singer and taking off with that saxophone player and all. Some girls might have thought they wasn't no better, but Missouri thought more of herself than that. She intended to be somebody, and I sure hope she succeeded."

"Did she tell you where she was going?"

"No, just up and left. Same as her mother left her. Didn't take anything with her but whatever she had on. Proud, that one. We like to say that pride goeth before a fall, but sometimes pride is what keeps us going, and there's nothing wrong with that. You must have talked to someone about her before you called here."

"As a matter of fact, I did."

"Well, let me tell you, Missouri just did what those other young girls were afraid to. She struck out on her own. We didn't do anything wrong, bringing her to Lincoln Prairie. There was no way that child would have stayed in the South. She thought this was the Promised Land. It was hard for her when she found out it was not. That's more than likely why she left."

"Mrs. Jones, did Missouri ever date a white man?"

"Well, sister, there were rumors. Someone said they saw her in the movie theater sitting beside one; someone else said the same thing, but that she was in a car. I sure couldn't say who it was who told me, nor whom she might have been sitting with. It was just gossip, most likely. You know how it is when folks get jealous, and not just young people, either. Anyway, it seems that all that talk was enough to convince her to leave."

"Did you ever hear from her?"

"Not a word. Can't say as I expected to. Independent, that one, with a mind of her own. Why are you asking about her now?"

"I'm afraid I can't answer that, Mrs. Jones."

"Well, if you get a chance to talk with the child, please give her my phone number. It would be so good to hear from her. I always did believe she went on to make something of herself. It sure would be nice to know."

"Can you describe her?"

"Lord, child, it's been so long. . . . Well now . . . she wasn't too tall, kind of medium height, and her hair was kind of short, but not too short, not quite to her shoulders. There was something odd about it now that I think of it. Longer in the front than in the back." She paused. "I can't really think of anything else. Missouri was a pretty girl, but not unusual, except for the way she wore her hair." She chuckled. "I think the other girls wanted to wear their hair like that, too, but they had made such a big deal of not being like Missouri that they couldn't."

"Why didn't they want to be like Missouri?"

"Because she had come here from a little town in the South and she had big ideas. She wanted to marry a rich man. As if we knew any rich colored men back then. Speaking for myself, I hope she did both."

"Mrs. Jones, there is one other thing. Did you ever notice Missouri wearing any rings?"

"Just that one she wore on her little finger. Just chipped glass, with the middle stone shaped like a heart. Something her mother gave her."

Marti typed up the notes she had taken while she was talking with Mrs. Jones. She made two copies and handed one to Lupe and the other to Vik.

"I can't believe it was this easy," Lupe said. "It's like it was right under our noses, but we didn't know the right questions to ask. This is awesome. Wow."

"This is the result of nine days of work," Marti reminded her. "And we're not there yet. I'm satisfied that we have identified the mummy, though I'm not sure if we'll ever be able to confirm that with any conclusive evidence. We still have to determine who killed her, and who killed Cheney and Logan. This is just the beginning, Lupe, and we've been investigating these cases for days."

"Yes, ma'am," Lupe said, but Marti could see that gleam of satisfaction in her eyes. It was amazing how one breakthrough could make up for hours of coming up empty. Torres would make a good homicide cop someday. Patience and persistence and the ability to forget how long it could take to get anywhere were 90 percent of the job.

Marti checked her watch. It was almost eleven ten, she had been up since just after three this morning. Her body had gone beyond being tired to that euphoric state where she thought she could remain sleepless forever. It was time to call it a night. For once, she wished there was another shift of detectives who could take over and keep the momentum going.

"We're packing it in, Jessenovik."

"Good day's work," he said. He sounded sad.

Marti went over to him and put her hand on his shoulder. "Sometimes the job is a bitch."

He looked away from her and nodded.

The phone rang as they were leaving.

"Feast or famine," Vik said. "With our luck, they've found another cold one."

Marti took the call. It was Mrs. Stazlowski.

"Please understand, Detective MacAlister, I do not want to see either of you ever again. However, I just read in the newspaper that you found another body near Evan—Mr. Armstrong's place of business."

Marti waited.

"And I thought there was something I'd better tell you before anyone else comes to harm."

Smart lady, Marti thought, looking out for herself.

"Evan . . . Mr. Armstrong said he had a silver picture frame that was over a hundred years old."

"When did he tell you this?"

"Oh, over a week ago. It was a Saturday night. We had just come from a silent auction for some charity or other. I had been outbid on something I really wanted. He said he would make it up to me as soon as he could."

Marti thought for a moment. "You never saw it?"

"No."

If she could see Mrs. Stazlowski's face, she would know if she was telling the truth. After the way Vik had acted, she was lucky the woman was talking to her at all.

"Did he tell you why he couldn't show it to you?"

"He said he had put it someplace for safekeeping but that he would show it to me as soon as he could."

And it took two bodies before she called.

"Ma'am, when was the next time you saw Mr. Armstrong?"

"Well, he was supposed to come the following Wednesday. When he called Tuesday night from Milwaukee, he was all excited, but by Wednesday . . . well, little man, small mind. I didn't really expect him to produce. And now, why, he hasn't even called."

Vik didn't say anything when Marti told him. He sat with his chin in his hand and looked out the window. "Snow's picking up."

Armstrong now had motive and opportunity. What was wrong with Vik now?

"We're going to have to talk with Armstrong again, Jessenovik."

"I know."

Something Stazlowski said . . . "He called her from Milwaukee Tuesday night, Vik."

"And . . . damn . . ."

"Right, our anonymous call came from Milwaukee Wednesday morning."

"Armstrong must have panicked after he killed Cheney. Then, when he had time to think about it, he decided he wanted the body out of there before he went back, so he called us."

Vik rushed to get his coat. "What are you waiting for? Let's go."

There was no answer when Marti rang Armstrong's bell, but there was an upstairs light on on Armstrong's side of the duplex and an old Dodge van parked out front. Vik ran a make on the license plates. It was Armstrong's. Marti leaned on the bell. Nobody answered, but the Hispanic man otherwise known as "the alibi" opened the other door.

"What you want?" he asked. He had been drinking. "Ain't nobody there. My VCR stays fixed for a week and then it breaks, and that bastard is not there. He had better come back soon. The smell from his place is making me sick."

"Smell?" Marti said.

"Yes, smell. You want to smell it? If he doesn't come back by tomorrow, I'm going to break down the door and throw out whatever it is."

"Can we come in and take a whiff?" Vik asked.

The man held the door open.

Two hours later, Armstrong was removed in a body bag. Marti and Vik waited outside while evidence techs did what they had do; then she got out the Vicks Vapo Rub, applied some to her nostrils, and passed the jar to Vik.

"What a way to end the day," Vik said. "With a ripe one. Man had the heat turned up full blast. What do you make of this one?"

"I think he had something somebody wanted."

"Like?"

"Like a watch and a key."

"Logan," Vik said. "Where in the hell does this fit?"

"Damned if I know."

"Armstrong was your strongest suspect," Lupe said. "Now who do we look at?"

"Farland," Vik said. "The only one left now is Farland. Let's have him brought in."

Marti didn't give him an argument this time. The body count was getting too high.

Dr. Cyprian wouldn't even guess as to how long Armstrong had been dead, but rigor mortis had come and gone. Marti was willing to bet that he had died before Logan. What worried her was the blood, splattered in an inkblot pattern on his bedroom wall. Their killer was losing control, and they didn't know who his next target might be.

"We've got a real nutcase on our hands," Vik said. "I sure as hell hope that it's Farland, so we can wrap this up now."

Marti didn't answer. If it was him, and they had brought him in sooner, maybe this could have been prevented. Armstrong and Logan might still be alive. And she would always know that she'd been the one who'd said no.

Farland was sitting quietly in one of the interview rooms when they got back to the precinct. His bald head glistened with sweat. Muscles bulged beneath his long-sleeved knit shirt. Marti was struck by his compact strength and his quiet intensity as he watched them.

"Mr. Farland. I'm Detective Marti MacAlister. We haven't met, but you've seen me at Stover House. This is my partner, Detective Jessenovik. Please sit down."

232

"Yes, ma'am."

"Mr. Farland, where were you last night?"

"Same place I been since I got back here. Don't go no place much, unless I have to. Town's changed too much; I'd get lost."

According to the manager at the facility where Farland was living, it was extremely difficult to get Farland to go anywhere, but that didn't mean he hadn't sneaked out. The building was secure, but she hadn't checked the place out yet to determine exactly how secure.

"Tell me about Missouri New."

He blinked, cocked his head to one side, and looked at her. "What about Missouri?"

"When's the last time you saw her?"

"The night before—" He stopped, looked away.

"Where?"

"It was my night to clean the Geneva Theater, where she worked. Next night, I was over at the Rialto. Took turns."

"Was she with Barnabas Cheney?"

"No. She was with a white man, but it wasn't him." There was an edge to his voice, but he wasn't belligerent.

"Did Cheney see her that night?"

"I suppose so. He was there."

Marti thought for a minute. Could Cheney have seen her with another man and become jealous, or angry? If so, what had happened to the other man? Had Cheney killed them both? Whom had she been with? Whoever had killed her had had to know that theater well enough to hide her body. Could Farland have done it? But why?

"Did you see her leave?"

"No, Mr. Cheney told me I could leave early, right after the movie was over, so I went home before the theater was closed."

Had Cheney killed both of them? It would have been two against one. Marti stifled a yawn. She needed to wait and ask these questions tomorrow morning. She was getting confused. Vik looked as exhausted as she was. She touched her eyebrow with the tip of her finger. He nodded.

"Mr. Farland, I'm going have to keep you here for the night and talk with you in the morning."

"I wasn't really expecting to leave."

Vik sat at the kitchen table with Stephen. The ceiling light was off and the small lamp on the table gave off just enough light to eat and read the newspaper by. Vik liked the room in semi-darkness. He had sat here with Mildred many nights talking about the children, the job. He wanted to talk with her now, but she was sleeping, and she had enough to deal with, coping with the MS. She was doing okay with a cane and a walker, but it wasn't getting any better, and the doctor couldn't promise that it would.

He was so tired. He let Stephen fix his dinner. Mildred had cooked a beef brisket, boiled potatoes, and carrots, along with some dumplings. She was cooking. That was a good sign.

"How's your mom doing?"

"Tired, according to Aunt Helena, but otherwise okay."

"She needs lots of rest," Vik agreed. He ought to say something nice to Helena, even if she was a pain in the ass; thank her for helping out.

Stephen fixed himself a plate, too. "Good stuff," he said. "Lori likes sauces and gravies and little curlicue carrots and the vegetables all sliced and diced. I like Mom's cooking best."

Vik smiled. Even though Stephen was twenty-six, he could could still see the boy in him. "Is Lori okay with you coming over here every night?"

"She came over after work and stayed for a few hours. She's worried about Mom, too. It seems like with college and marriage, I've been away from home forever. I like being here again."

Vik ate slowly, enjoying the food, enjoying Stephen sitting across from him, remembering old times. "I'm gone a lot." He had never given it much thought until now, when he wanted to be home. Mildred sat alone in this kitchen many nights, too many nights. His children had spent too many nights without him. They were good kids, thanks to Mildred. He had never spent as

234

much time with them as he should have. He ran his fingers through his hair. "I've always been gone a lot."

"The job," Stephen said.

"The job," he agreed. How did you explain to your kids that the job wasn't more important than they were? It always came first. It had to. "I think it's a compulsion, Stephen, the job. I *have* to find the one who did it. I'm looking at some dead person who I never knew in life and there is something in me that insists that whoever did it has to be caught."

"That's kind of like what Mom told us. She always made your job seem so special, like being the president or something. She told us you were so good at it that nobody else could do that job but you." He ducked his head and scooped up half a potato. "It was like, um, it was like I had this one-of-a-kind dad, like nobody had a dad like mine." Stephen looked up at him. "So, if you ever think that maybe you should have been home more or something, you did the important stuff. You made it to a lot of my football games, graduation, confirmation, all of that. You were only five minutes late for my wedding. And we did get in one fishing trip and at least one Cubs game every summer. Now band concerts, nah, but I don't think you liked the music and I didn't play that well."

He speared a dumpling with his fork, holding it in the air. "Look, Dad, don't think I ever thought your job was more important than I was. I didn't. Krysta didn't, either. Some kids have dads in the military who are gone for months at a time. That's just what their dads do. Being a cop is what you do. And you do it better than anyone else I know. I don't know how important it is to a mother, or brother, or child of a murder victim, that someone will not give up until the killer is caught, but it's important to me. Having your dad home every night might be pretty neat; I don't know. Having you for a dad is better."

Vik reached across the table and patted his hand. "Thanks, I needed to hear that."

"You have been kind of down lately. What's up? It's not just Mom, is it? You've been through this before with her."

"Oh, it's just this case."

"When have I heard that before? You've never gotten like this over a case."

Vik got up and rinsed his dish and put it in the dishwasher. He poured some coffee, changed his mind, and got out the jar of instant decaf.

"Decaf for me, too," Stephen said.

"I'm looking into this old case," he said when he sat down. "I think a friend of mine screwed up."

Stephen poured cream and measured two teaspoons of sugar and stirred it up. "It's either Grandpa or Uncle Curly."

Vik nodded.

"Grandpa?"

"No." Not that it made that made much difference. "Curly and I go so far back."

"How bad is it?"

"My guess is that they'll cover it up, but that's not the point. Someone did thirty years for it."

Stephen whistled. "I'd be pretty pissed off about that."

"Well, he's out now, and maybe he's killed a couple of people."

"So, what do you have to do?"

"That's a good question, Stephen. I've been asking myself that most of the day."

"I remember the times that you told me you did the right thing because it was the right thing. It feels good saying that to you now, but I wish it wasn't Uncle Curly. Still, if you get this straightened out, and they don't make a big deal over what he did, is there more to it than that?"

"Have I ever said or done anything that made you think I was prejudiced against other people?"

"You? No."

"You're sure?"

"Yeah, I'm sure."

"I always thought that being prejudiced was something you wore right up front, that anyone could see it right away. But it isn't always that way, is it? How can something that wrong go unde-

236

tected for so long? How can you look right at it and not know that it's there? How can you be around it and not become that way yourself?"

"Dad, I've heard you complain about stupidity, ignorance, laziness, and some of my report cards, but I have never heard you say anything based on prejudice in my life. And, if you don't believe me, ask Mom."

Ask Mom. He was right. Mildred would know. But he had to take care of this now. He couldn't wait until Mildred was feeling better. Tomorrow. He would get to the bottom of this tomorrow.

17

When Vik got up Friday morning, he went down to the basement and sat at the worktable that had been his father's, and he looked at the leather pouch filled with his father's tools. He thought about those long afternoons when his father had shown him how to use a level and plane and measure a piece of wood. He thought of the sanding, a monotonous task that seemed to take forever. He thought of the cold homemade cider they drank while they worked. It never quite chased away the scratchy feel of sawdust in his throat. He thought of the smell of the sawdust. "An honest smell," his father would say. Honesty had been important to Dad. Or so he thought.

He went back upstairs, made a few phone calls, then waited until Mildred was awake. They had breakfast together, something he could cook, instant oatmeal, applesauce from a jar, and toast. Mildred was looking better. Her face wasn't as drawn. Her eyes weren't as tired. Her hair looked like it had before the MS kicked in. She seemed to be weathering the storm again. He wasn't going to think any further ahead than now. Just today. Today she was better.

"You look tired, Matthew, and something is bothering you. What is it?"

"We'll talk about it in a few days. I've got to work a few things out."

"Good. I miss our talks."

"You're feeling better."

"Much better. Maybe after all that trouble moving the bed downstairs, we can move it back upstairs again."

The doctor had cautioned against it, but Vik didn't have to tell her that now. Maybe the strength would return to her legs soon.

"We take it slow, okay, *moja serce*. We take it slow."

"Slow," she agreed. "For once I am not in a hurry."

Vik called in to say he would be would be late and drove over to a redbrick Georgian on Sherman Avenue. The housekeeper admitted him.

"Mr. Quinn is expecting you, Matthew. Things have been much too quiet lately. He needs a little excitement, but try not to tire him."

She took his coat and showed him in to a room where a half a dozen chairs were arranged around a fireplace. Logs crackled. An elderly man with thick white hair was waiting for him. John Quinn had been the state's attorney here in Lake County before becoming lieutenant governor of Illinois. Quinn had also gone all through elementary and high school with Vik's dad.

"Vik! Where is that beautiful woman you work with?"

"I came alone."

"Too bad. Try not to do it again."

"I'll try not to, sir."

"What brings you here so early in the morning?"

Quinn listened with avid interest as Vik told him about their cases, and he asked an occasional question. "So," he said, when Vik stopped talking. "The Cheneys. Interesting family. But you want to know who is putting pressure on your lieutenant. Hold on for a minute."

The telephone was concealed in a carved mahogany box. Quinn held the receiver with a hand that had veins as thick and knotted as cord. He was eighty-eight years old. The number he called was programmed.

"Quinn here," he said. "Who asked you to lean on Lieutenant Dirkowitz about the Cheney homicide?"

He listened, thanked whomever he was speaking with, and hung up.

"Interesting," he said, then added, "Up front, it is the Cheneys, but behind them, Curly Smith."

"Curly?"

"I think you better talk with Dan Randell. He's had a couple of strokes, but from what I hear, he can still communicate. Talk with him, and Vik, remember—Curly was like a father to you, but Gus was your dad."

Daniel Randell lived in an older Tudor on the far northeast side of town. He was an old man now, too, sitting in a wheelchair by a window with a view of the lake.

"Jessenovik," he said. "Gus's kid." The deep baritone that Vik remembered was little more than a whisper and one side of his face drooped. "Nobody comes anymore. It's good to see you."

"I came to ask you about the Farland case. Do you remember it?"

"I remember all of my cases."

Vik wondered about that. "We found a dead body in the Geneva Theater last week. Black female, about eighteen. We've placed the time of death at about the same time as when Dawn Taborn died."

"Taborn, Farland's girlfriend."

"Maybe."

"So, how can I help you?"

"Curly Smith was the officer of record on the Farland case. His notes are so sketchy that I'm not sure how you got a conviction."

"We got a conviction because the man was guilty."

"Yes, sir, I know. That's what Curly said, too. But usually in a court of law, your word on that isn't enough. We can't even get much from the trial transcripts."

Randell's hand trembled as he wiped a thin stream of spittle from the side of his mouth that sagged.

"Son, that was 1964. A colored woman was found dead in the janitor's closet in a movie theater. A colored man was the janitor. He ran. Now you tell me who did it if wasn't him?"

Was that all it took to be guilty, even in a court of law? It hadn't happened that long ago.

"Sir, could you tell me two things without getting angry because I'm asking?"

"I can guess one of the questions. Collusion. Yes, Curly Smith, Judge Hendricks, and I did discuss this case before it came to trial. What are you going to do about that now? Curly's an old man and retired. Hendricks is dead."

"Sir, if Farland was guilty, then the evidence should have been there to support that. If the evidence wasn't there, you were Farland's attorney. It was your job to defend him."

"Jessenovik, this wasn't that important."

Was this how they'd all thought? Was this what Dad had thought, too? When he got to the bottom of this, would he lose Curly *and* Dad?

"Did Farland admit to killing the girl?"

"Of course not. He did say enough to indicate that he lusted after her and she rebuffed him."

"That doesn't seem like reason enough to kill her."

"Boy, what more did the man need? People kill for less. Now what is this about another body?"

"We found her at the Geneva."

"The Taborn girl was found at the Rialto. One death has nothing to do with the other."

"No, sir, it doesn't, not unless your father owns both theaters, you have complete access to both theaters, you're mentally incompetent, and you have a preference for black females."

"You're saying that Barnabas Cheney . . . Damn but I would have liked that."

Vik stood up.

"Son, don't tell me we let the Cheneys get away. Are you going to get them now?"

"I can't answer any of that."

"Damn," Randell said again. "Damn, damn, damn. Who would have thought . . . The Cheneys . . . Damn."

"What if the accused wasn't guilty?"

"Son, you sound just like your father. You're sure about this involving Cheney?"

"That's the way it's beginning to look."

"But if you can figure that out thirty-odd years after the fact, why couldn't Curly?"

"Maybe he did," Vik said. He knew that was more than he should say, but he needed to hear it out loud.

"Curly put one over on me? And kept the reward for himself? Double damn."

The old man called for his housekeeper and demanded a brandy. Too early in the day, he was told.

"Too early? Look at me, woman. How much time do you think I have?"

She was bringing the drink in as Vik left.

Marti woke up with a headache. She took two Tylenol before she left the house, but she still had a headache when she arrived at the coroner's facility. The dull throbbing at her temples continued throughout Armstrong's autopsy and still had not abated by the end. Armstrong had been beaten to death. When she asked if pressure had been applied to his neck, Cyprian couldn't tell.

Now she tried to ignore the headache as she went through her notes, looking for inconsistencies. When she got to the conversation she'd had with Aunt Lindy about Cheney liking "colored" women, she stopped. Justine. Did she know who had threatened the lawsuit? She had loved Barnabas—would he have told her? Marti picked up the phone and called the high school. Justine was in class.

"I don't care where she is, or what she's doing. Please get her on the phone now."

Marti knew she should go over there, but if she didn't like what Justine had to say, she could pay her another visit at home.

When Marti asked about the lawsuit, Justine switched the call from the secretary's desk to an office.

"It wasn't like that," she said, voice low. "It wasn't like that, but I couldn't tell them that. I couldn't tell my mother. . . . Barnabas said it was all right. He . . . he wanted to do something. I wanted to go to college. His parents gave me the money; that's why I'm here. And Barnabas wasn't angry. He understood. He wanted it that way. I think . . . I think it made him feel better about . . . things."

After she hung up, Marti fixed another cup of coffee and sat looking out the window. The one consistency throughout her notes was that Cheney wasn't violent. There was no question in her mind that Farland could become very violent. According to Farland, two white men had been at that theater that night with Miss Missouri New, and one was her companion. However that had played out, Missouri New was dead. What else did Farland know? She wasn't ready to talk with him again. That could wait until Vik came in.

The phone rang. It was Dr. Pickus. "I'm sorry I took so long to get back to you, but I had to send the photos of the three victims' necks to Dr. Gless. He just got back from England yesterday. He's just given me a conservative yes. There's at least a seventy-five percent possibility that the neck injuries were made by the same person. I can't guarantee that that will hold up in court."

Marti wasn't sure about that, either. "Is there anything else he can do or anything we can send him?"

"I'm afraid not. The chokehold isn't unique, and he can't be absolutely certain that the thumb size was the same in all three cases."

It had to be Farland. "If I send you a set of prints, would that help?"

"I don't know. Dr. Gless is the expert."

"I'll send them. Do what you can. And thanks."

She put in a call to have Farland's prints sent to Pickus; then she drove over to the men's residence.

The man who opened the door was not pleased to see her. Worse, one of her church sisters was there and looked angry.

"Marti MacAlister," the sister began. "How could you do something like this, and without even calling me first?"

"We don't call first." She could not remember the woman's name and wasn't going to ask.

"Well, I'm in charge of this program, and Mr. Farland is doing just fine here. Just because he's got a record and he's out on parole does not mean that you can harass him."

"I'm not harassing him."

"The man is in jail. What would you call it?"

"My job. Look, I need to take a look at this place. I need to know where Farland was a week ago Monday and Tuesday, and the night before last, and I need to know if anyone can vouch for where he was on those nights."

The woman glared at her. "We have a night supervisor. I'll ask him to come in." As she walked away, she muttered, "I think the reverend needs to have a talk with you."

The day supervisor gave her a tour. There were three possible exits, none of them alarmed. Based on what her guide told her, the only reason Farland couldn't leave was that the desk sat at the foot of the stairs. He would have to get past the night person going *and* coming. The church sister came up while she was searching through Farland's belongings.

"Once you get locked up for something, you never are your own person again, are you? I'm going to look into this. I know you wouldn't be here if it wasn't legal, but the man has to have some rights. Poor man ain't nothing but a number now."

Marti thought of Curly's notes and the trial transcript. "You're right," she said. "And if it makes you indignant, I'm glad. He is a man, not a number. I would never look at him that way. But he is a man with a number, and that makes him a suspect anytime this type of crime is committed. That also gives me certain rights, which I will exercise if I have to."

She turned back to the items in front of her. Farland's possessions were meager: three changes of clothes, six pairs of socks and underwear, a pair of shoes. The toiletries were minimal, too. There were lots of snapshots, though, pasted to poster boards and tacked on the walls. An older woman, two children, a boy and a girl. "Who are they?" she asked.

"His daughter and grandkids. The grandchildren are grown now. Both in college. They came to see him over the holidays."

"What's he like?" Marti asked.

"Is this the cop asking the question?"

"It's always the cop asking the question, even when I want to know what the weather's like outside."

"And you're not afraid I'll give you a biased answer?"

"That doesn't matter. I expect that. I just want your impressions. They're as valid as anyone else's."

She didn't want to antagonize this woman, not because they attended the same church, but because another cop might come here one day, someone like Curly, and these men needed someone like this church sister to defend them.

"Mr. Farland is a nice man. He's too quiet, too timid, jumps at loud noises, watches his back, has nightmares, never says anything to offend anyone. I don't like to see that in man, especially not a black man. It worries me, your taking him in like this. I don't think he has what it takes to fight you."

"Then you fight for him," Marti said.

"Oh, don't you worry, Marti MacAlister, I will."

The night manager was there when she went downstairs. He insisted that Farland had not left the house. "It's hard enough getting him to go out when he's supposed to. One of his goals is to go shopping by himself, and he just isn't there yet. He doesn't even ride the city bus."

"He doesn't want to leave the building for anything," the church sister said. "It's like he still wants to be in jail. You'd think it would be hard to keep him in here after all those years of being locked up; instead, it's almost impossible to get him to go out."

Marti had Farland brought to an interview room. He stood up when she came in.

"Sit down, Mr. Farland. Can you describe the white man that Missouri New was with?"

"No, I can't."

Or he didn't want to.

"Did you know who he was?"

"No. That was something I was better off not knowing."

But he did know—she was sure of it.

"Mr. Farland, you and Dawn Taborn and Missouri New attended the same church, Second Baptist. How well did the girls know each other?"

"They was friends. Liked the same things."

"White men?" Marti asked.

He shrugged.

"Why did you kill Dawn Taborn?"

He shook his head.

"Why did you plead guilty to the murder of Dawn Taborn?"

"Didn't have much choice."

"Why not?"

"Lawyer said wouldn't nobody believe me."

"Why did you believe that was true?"

"My momma thought I done it. My wife."

"Why did they think so?"

He thought for a minute. "Because I was a man, a black man, and that's what black men did."

"Kill their women?"

"No, sleep with them."

"Did you sleep with Dawn Taborn?"

"No."

"Did you want to?"

Farland rubbed his forehead with the back of his hand. Was he trying to erase a memory or recall one? When he spoke, his voice was distant.

"Pretty little thing, Dawn was," he said. "She used to come to the theater a lot. She was one of the few people from church who would talk to me."

"So, you wanted to sleep with her. According to the Reverend Cleotis Jones, wasn't thinking and doing the same thing?"

He nodded.

"Did you tell anyone that you had not been intimate with her?"

"Course I did. Lawyer said nobody would believe me if my family didn't. Lawyer was right. He was doing the best he could, trying to cut my time down."

"Did you kill Dawn Taborn?"

"No, ma'am."

"Then why didn't you say so?"

"Lawyer said I was better off just saying nothing, that maybe then I'd get off, or get a lighter sentence. Besides . . ."

"Besides what?"

His hands trembled. He looked down at them and said nothing. The other white man. He knew who it was.

"Why were you afraid of the white man Dawn was with?"

"Man could kill me."

"Can he still kill you?"

Farland nodded.

"Is that why you're afraid to leave the residence?"

He nodded again.

"Please tell me who it is."

"Be dead if I do."

Was thirty-four years in jail the trade-off?

"What about your family?" she asked.

"Them, too."

"All right, Farland. I respect that. But you've got to understand—times have changed now; things are different. I can help you, but only if you tell me what I need to know."

He looked at her for a moment, then said. "You black, just like me, and we're talking about the white man. Ain't that much ever going to change."

Marti stood up. "Where will you feel safer, in the infirmary or with the population?"

"I don't think I'm safe nowhere, ma'am. I would feel better back at the residence."

With that church sister.

"Will you run?"

"I ain't got no place to run to. Things have changed so much, I'd just get lost."

"I'll arrange it."

Vik still wasn't in when she got back to the office. She needed to talk with him. Then again, he was so touchy about all of this, maybe she couldn't. For whatever the reason, she could not quite believe Farland had killed anyone, although she had no doubt that he could. She could not understand the mentality that had allowed him to go to jail for thirty-four years, but she could understand his fear. She didn't see anything in him—anger, rage, hatred—that would allow him to stalk and kill two men. Square one, again. If Cheney had killed both women, and Farland hadn't killed him or Logan, what did they have here? One killer? Two? Three? Four? And what had happened to the man who was with Missouri?

The evidence was slim. They had recovered one weapon, the lamp. They had no witnesses. Dr. Cyprian couldn't tell whether or not pressure had been applied to Armstrong's neck. Cheney definitely wasn't strangled. Why? Because one blow killed him. For whatever the reason, one blow did not take Logan out, so the killer reverted to his method of choice, pressure on the neck. Then he got angry because he had done something he hadn't planned to do, and he struck Logan repeatedly. That much made sense. She wasn't sure how Logan or Armstrong figured in. What did they know, or what had they seen that they shouldn't have?

There were so many things that still didn't make sense. Why thirty-four years between killings? What triggered it? Farland's release? The discovery of the mummy? The last time Farland saw Missouri New was the night before Dawn Taborn died. Nobody had seen New since that night. Now the restoration group was going into the theater. Whoever had killed Missouri knew she was there and thought she would be found, either while they were poking around or when they began renovating, or when they tore the place down. Cheney was killed before anyone knew about the mummy. Why did someone fear Cheney *before* the mummy was found, or fear what they thought he could remember?

What did Curly know that wasn't in his notes? He was a cop. He had to know more than he was telling them. There were a lot of questions she would have asked him when they went to his house if Vik hadn't been there. Lincoln Prairie was still a relatively small town in 1964. Policing, politics—there wasn't much distinction. People were practically related to one another. Hell, look at all the families Vik knew. Just last year, an alderman had been found buck naked with a little lady of the night in the city council chambers, and it never made the local news. It could have been the mayor. Hell, the mayor could have been with Missouri in the Geneva the night she died. Who would tell? Curly knew something. She was going to get him to talk.

18

There was a stillness about the log cabin when Marti and Lupe pulled into the driveway. She was glad she had called Lupe in instead of coming here alone. Off to her right, in the distance between a stand of fir trees and the house, she could see an uneven dark spot in the white snow. The dark spot surrounded by snow held her attention. She stopped and took the binoculars out of the glove compartment. An animal had walked there. She could see its tracks. Curly must have shot it. Seeing blood spattered on the snow was unsettling.

"Doesn't feel right," she said.

"There's nothing out here," Lupe said. "It's too quiet. I'd go nuts."

They approached the house on foot. Not even a bird's call interrupted the silence.

"This place is spooking me," Marti admitted. It had to be the blood on the snow.

Lupe stayed at the foot of the steps while Marti walked to the porch. She went to the window instead of the door. The gray-and-white cat looked out at her and blinked its yellow eyes.

Curly opened the door when she knocked, but as she entered, there was an odd silence, as if the noise had been cut off abruptly. The place smelled of cleaning solvent. A workbench with a heavy-duty bench vise had been placed in front of the sofa. Two handguns, a Smith & Wesson and a Glock, were lined up beside an old Winchester lever-action shotgun. As she watched, Curly picked up the Smith & Wesson and pulled out the clip. He put the weapon down without bothering to check for a bullet in the firing chamber.

"Where's your partner?" he asked.

"Following through on some leads."

"Then it's just the two of us." He reached for the Glock. "Bet you don't know what this is."

The question was so silly that she didn't think he expected an answer.

"This is an easy one to use if you want to learn how to repair them."

"Is that what you're doing?"

"More or less. You'd be surprised at how people neglect their weapons. Most just need a good cleaning." He took out the cartridge and stroked the barrel. "It would be just as easy to send this one back to the factory to be worked on, but what the hell, I've got nothing else to do."

Up close, she could see where Curly's buzz-clipped gray hair was thinning. His face was etched with fine lines. He needed a shave. How old was he? She thought he must be at least seventy-five. She hadn't thought of him as old until now. When Vik spoke of him, he was talking about a much younger man. She looked at Curly's hands. The joints were knobby and showed his age unmistakably.

Curly broke down the Glock and began cleaning it. At first, Marti thought it was dirty, then she realized that the residue coming off on the cleaning pads was just lubricant. When she first came on the force, her lieutenant had yelled at her for ten minutes for leaving too much lubricant on her service revolver. It wasn't the way she had been taught at the Academy. It was the way some of the old-timers cleaned theirs.

He put the Glock down and began working on the Smith & Wesson, one of her favorite weapons, even though it wasn't what she carried.

"It looks like you killed a deer or something out there."

"So; what can I do for you this morning?"

He looked at her. His smile seemed forced. His eyes were as gray as flint, his expression just as hard.

Marti moved closer to the couch. The calico cat jumped up and hissed at her. She decided against sitting down. There was a chill in the air and frost on the window with the northern exposure. The logs on the hearth had burned down. "I need to ask you some questions, Curly."

"About what?"

"We need to talk about the Farland case."

"That one? Again?"

"The killing hasn't stopped."

"Because Farland is out. He's killing them."

"Why?"

"Look, there weren't any other suspects when the Taborn girl died. Who else would have killed them?"

Them? Did he mean Taborn and New? "That's what I need to talk to you about. Other suspects."

Curly's shoulders tensed. "You're making too much of this."

"I don't think so. The Cheneys owned that theater. Now Cheney is dead. Why?"

"Revenge, jealousy. Why does that seem so far-fetched? That's always sounded like one hell of a good motive to me."

"Farland's been out on parole since November. Why now?"

"The man's slow-witted. Maybe it took him this long to figure out who to kill."

"Why Cheney?"

"Cheney?" He gripped a tool. "Can't say."

"I think you know a lot more about the case than what's in your reports."

"And here I thought you came to see your partner's old friend, talk about the old days when cops were real men." He smiled. "A good cop never tells everything he knows."

"And doesn't write it down, either."

He wiped his hands on his jeans. "Look, this happened over thirty years ago. What the hell is so important about a couple of dead ni—colored girls now?"

252

Marti tensed. She had heard worse, and from cops. She was not going to let him distract her. "What do you know that you didn't put into your reports?"

"You need to put this in perspective."

"That's what I'm trying to get, a little perspective. The Taborn girl died thirty-some years ago with thumb indentations on her neck. Now I've got another body with those same marks." Not to mention a mummy.

Curly paled. "They're dead." His voice was quiet. "Give it up. You're not going to catch the one who did it. You're not smart enough."

"Then it wasn't Farland or Cheney."

Curly smiled, or at least the muscles near his mouth moved. "Did I say that?" The color returned to his face. "I suppose it could have been Cheney. He was a nutcase."

"But if it was him, how could Logan have the same marks on his neck as the girl did? Cheney died before Logan was killed."

Curly paled again, and started backtracking. "So, Farland did it. We got the right man. Cheney knew what happened. That's why he flipped out. He saw something he shouldn't have." The veins in his neck bulged. "Who would kill two colored girls but another colored?"

Two. He was connecting the deaths of both women. Was that what he knew? That there was a connection? And, if there was . . . Taborn and New had been friends, hadn't they?

Which one was killed first? One must have been killed because of what she knew. And the other one?

"Did you ever go to the Geneva, Curly?" He must have. He would have been what? Mid-forties, she guessed, and nice-looking, from what she could see now. Taborn had liked white men. Had she liked older white men? If her primary interest was money, or security, she would have been smart enough to stay away from anyone too young to provide that.

"What the hell is so important about any of this now?"

"I've still got a killer out there."

"Why would he kill again?"

253

"For the same reason he did in the first place."

Curly smiled. His hand rested easy on his leg. "And why is that?"

"To cover his tracks."

"Can't you leave it alone? How many folks are there who would care about a couple of colored girls dying so long ago?"

Every time he said "colored," he smiled. If he was trying to get to her, why didn't he just say the *n* word? Because he knew she would make the inference. Smart man. Clever. Smart enough to ask interesting questions. Why was the killer killing again?

"I could accept Cheney as the killer if he hadn't died before Logan," she said.

Curly made a fist. What was he reacting to? *What did he know?*

"Logan had the same marks on his neck as the women. We've got a forensic pathologist on it. One who can match the indentation on Missouri New's neck with the marks on Taborn's neck, and Edward Logan's neck, too." With just seventy-five percent accuracy, but Curly didn't have to know that. "He can match all of them to the thumb," she lied.

"Missouri New?" Both fists were clenched.

"We've got a positive ID on the Jane Doe."

Curly's whole body went rigid. "So, Farland offed two women instead of one."

"And then he killed Cheney because you framed him? Why didn't he kill you?"

"I'm a cop, he's a ni—I'm the Man. Back then . . . A colored man born when he was knows better."

Back then. It wasn't *that* long ago. Just a few years before the *Miranda* ruling. A few years before everyone's constitutional rights were articulated and required to be spoken aloud. Did that really make such a difference? As much as people complained about the perps knowing their rights . . . Farland was arrested before *Miranda*. He must not have known that he had any rights.

"It's Logan," she said. "This could all be explained if it wasn't for Logan."

254

."Maybe he's the coincidence."

"You're too good a cop to believe in them."

"Look, Logan lived on the street. Cheney did, too, just about. And Logan hung out right across from the Merchants building. Even if he didn't know who Cheney was, he must have seen the watch, set Cheney up as a mark."

Logan had the watch; Armstrong had the portrait. What if Armstrong had had the watch, too, and the killer needed it to frame Logan for Cheney's death? If it wasn't for the marks on Logan's neck, everything Curly had just said was believable . . . and those marks were there only because the killer didn't succeed with that first blow to the head.

"No, Logan's the problem here, Curly, not Cheney or the two females. It's Logan's death that's got me asking questions. I think I could tie up everything else."

"But why, for God's sake? The man knew Cheney. I read that in the newspaper. He had Cheney's watch. He had his key. . . ."

The key. Careful. Don't react. Nobody knew about that except the cops and the killer. Was it a leak or . . . She looked at Curly. It was him. He was the white man Farland wouldn't ID; he was the killer.

In the moment that it took her to put it all together, Curly picked up the Glock.

"Bitch," he said. "Bitches, all of you."

The gun clip was on the table. Was there a bullet in the chamber? The Smith & Wesson wouldn't fire if the clip wasn't in, but the Glock would.

"Was that what Missouri New was, a bitch?"

"Damned right, thinking she could trick me by getting pregnant."

"Why Taborn?"

He pointed the Glock at her. "New's stupid, nosy friend. She wanted me to help her find out who did it. Can you believe that? She knew all about us, still thought some other guy got jealous and killed her. She wanted me to help her find who it was." He laughed. "The stupid bitch didn't think that a cop would do it. But not Farland, he knew. He was one hell of a lot smarter. Smart enough to know that jail was a whole lot better than being dead. But you, you're even smarter than that, aren't you?"

"Smart enough to know that gun isn't loaded."

"And smart enough to notice that I didn't check the chamber. Want to go for it?"

"You don't think I came here alone, do you?" She focused on Curly, not what he was saying. Curly's eyes would tell her if he was going to pull the trigger.

"Who'd you bring along? Your partner, Vik? Gus's kid? Wasn't he man enough to come in here and confront me himself? Like father like son. Sellouts, both of them. At least Gus had enough cop in him to keep his mouth shut."

What was he talking about? Would he turn to look at the window if he thought Vik was out there? She might not have time to unholster her weapon if he did, but maybe she could get that one split second she would need to avoid a full hit. "No, Vik isn't with me, but I didn't come here alone."

Vik drove out to Curly's place alone. This was something that was between the two of them. It didn't involve Marti, and he didn't know how, or if, he was going to explain any of it to her. Once he got this out of his craw, he could focus on their cases again, be a cop. At least he hoped so.

There had to be a word for the way Curly's place looked as he approached it—horses grazing, barn in the distance, tall trees, log cabin with just a wisp of smoke curling from the chimney—but he didn't know what the word was. How much of this was bought by Cheney money? He didn't want to know.

He saw Marti's car as soon as he turned into the driveway. What was she doing here? He had to park behind her. As he approached the house, he saw Lupe, gun drawn, standing by the window. What the hell was going on?

Lupe turned, put her finger to her lips, and motioned him forward.

"What the hell—" he whispered. He looked over her shoulder

256

and into the room. Curly was holding a gun on Marti. He unholstered his weapon.

"I brought Lupe along, Curly. Lupe Torres, a female cop, Hispanic. She's looking in at us now."

Curly turned toward the door, then the window. The Glock was pointed away from her. In the moment that he was distracted, Marti drew her weapon. Curly turned to her as she was aiming at him. The sounds of gunfire, glass shattering, and a cat yowling came all at once. Marti hit the floor, surprised that she didn't feel any pain. She must have taken a hit. She smelled the gunpowder and sneezed.

"Marti, Marti, are you all right? Are you hit anywhere?"

"Vik? Where did you come from?" She got up on one elbow. Curly was on the floor a few feet away from her. There was a hole in his neck. She didn't look any higher. "Lupe?"

"I'm with Curly. I'm going to call an ambulance. Just stay where you are. Are you hit?"

"I'm not sure. Nothing hurts. I'm wearing a vest."

"No bleeding," Vik said.

"I think I'm okay."

"Good, stay put."

Marti sat up. Vik sat on the floor beside her.

"He did it, Marti, didn't he?"

She nodded. "I'm sorry."

"Where's Clara?" he asked.

"Just stay where you are," Lupe said. "I'll check on her."

"Curly . . ." Vik said.

Lupe shook her head. "No."

Marti heard a siren in the distance.

Marti slumped in a chair at the kitchen table and tried to ignore what was happening around her. She tried to remember the last time she had been without her Beretta. She had been checked by the paramedics and pronounced okay. Her gun, along with Lupe's, Vik's and Curly's, had been confiscated.

She called Ben, wanting to explain what had happened before he heard it from some other source.

"Everything okay?" he asked.

She filled him in.

"That was you? We picked it up here, but they didn't give names."

She was glad she'd remembered to call.

By the time Lupe came downstairs with Clara, an older cop on the local force was processing the scene. Curly's body had not been removed. The older cop directed Lupe and Clara to the kitchen. Marti gasped as Clara came toward them. The entire left side of her face was one massive bruise. Her left eye was swollen shut, there was a cut on the bridge of her nose, and her right eye was little more than a slit. Some of the bruises were new; some were healing.

"Clara," Vik said. "My God, did he do this to you?"

She nodded and began to cry.

"Clara, why didn't you tell me? We meant to come visit you, Mildred and me. . . ." His voice trailed off. Clara fell into his arms, sobbing.

"We'd better let someone take a look at you. What's this?" There was bruising on both sides of her neck.

Clara put her hands to her face. Her whole body shook.

"It's going to be all right now," Vik said. "We'll get you to a doctor. That cut looks infected. I'll get hold of your brother. He's still in Crystal Lake, right?"

Marti could see tears in his eyes as he called out to one of the paramedics.

After they gave their statements to the locals, Lupe agreed to drive Vik's car back to the precinct.

"You're sure you're okay?" Marti asked.

Lupe nodded.

"Is this the first time you've fired your weapon at someone?"

She nodded again.

"You might feel a little shaky when your adrenaline levels go down. Try a couple of candy bars."

They would have to wait for the coroner's report to find out which of the three of them had taken Curly down. Marti wasn't sure how she would feel if it turned out to be her, but right now she didn't feel too bad about Curly being dead. Vik would feel a lot worse if they found out it was his bullet that had killed his friend.

She turned to Vik. "Let's go."

Her adrenaline high was beginning to dissipate. She needed to get out of here before she was too tired to drive.

Vik still seemed shaken. She had never seen him look so pale.

"Thanks," he said after she started the car.

"For what?"

"Putting up with me."

For the first time all day, she noticed that the sun was out.

They drove without speaking until Vik said, "They were all in collusion on the Farland case, and a few other cases, too."

"Who?" Marti asked.

"Curly, the lawyer, the judge."

He was silent for a while, then said, "John Quinn said the Cheneys were the ones putting pressure on the department, but Curly was behind it. I think he took a bribe from them."

"The brother seemed like a nice-enough guy."

"A lot of people seem nice," Vik said.

Curly had meant a lot to Vik. He had been like a father, too much like a father maybe, and now he was also a bad cop.

"I don't know what Curly meant by this, Vik, but he said you were too much like your father, that you were both sellouts, but that your father had at least been enough of a cop to keep his mouth shut."

Vik didn't answer. He didn't speak again until they were in Lincoln Prairie.

"I think I'll go home for a while."

"Are you okay?"

"No."

"Can I help?"

"We'll talk about it later. I need to see Mildred first."

Mildred was in the den. She was sitting in his recliner with a magazine in her lap. He went over and stood beside her and looked out the window. At least a dozen greedy sparrows were squabbling over a suet ball. Santa Claus was still in the back yard with Rudolph. Maybe now he'd have time to put them away.

"It sure seems like a long time since Christmas."

"You sound tired," Mildred said.

He sat down in her rocker. "Dad didn't do it."

"I'm glad. What didn't he do?"

"He didn't help Curly, except for keeping his mouth shut. He didn't agree with what Curly did, or why he did it."

"Do I want to know what that was?"

"Not now. It can wait."

"Is Curly the reason for the mood you've been in?"

"I haven't . . ." Yes, he had.

"Curly and your father stopped being friends at least a year before Curly retired."

"I know. Because of me."

"No, it was because of some capital case."

The Willis case? "Are you sure?"

"Real sure. Poppa even mentioned it, and he missed a lot."

"I'm glad," he said. Later he would tell her what had happened. Right now, he just wanted to sit with her. "Are you feeling better today?"

"Helena took me to the doctor this morning. He thinks I'm getting some of the strength back in my legs."

He reached over and hugged her. "Thank God." It seemed like such a long time since he had heard any good news. "Thank God."

The house was filled with kids when Marti got home. The boys next door were there. Theo and Peter were in the middle of a chess game and Mike and Patrick were on the computer. Joanna was there with a boy. He was two inches shorter than she was, with the clearest brown skin, not one zit, and muscles. He must lift weights, Marti thought. They were in the kitchen and he was eating a fruit and vegetable concoction that included bananas, sunflower seeds, and broccoli. From the expression on his face, he was enjoying it.

"Want some, Ma? It's good."

"No. Who's this?"

"This is Tony. Tony, my mom."

Tony smiled and held out his hand. Marti squeezed hard so he would know she was not impressed with the bodybuilding.

Tony winced. "Nice meeting you, ma'am."

"You okay, Ma?" Joanna asked. "You're not coming down with something, are you?"

"What makes you ask that?"

"It's kind of early for you to be home, and you're cranky."

"You'd be cranky, too, if you weren't carrying."

"You don't have your Beretta? What happened to it?"

"I might have shot somebody."

"Wow! Anybody I might know?"

Marti shook her head.

"How long will they keep the Beretta?"

"Damned if I know. It's just some small-town department. They might lose it."

"What are you going to carry while they test it?"

"Hell if I know."

"I like the Colt Commando Special, Ma."

"I don't know, I think I'll go with the Smith & Wesson."

Tony looked from one of them to the other. Joanna smiled at him and passed him the salad.

Before she went to bed, Marti got out the locked box where she kept her weapons.

"This one's a beauty," Ben said as he picked up the Colt and aimed it at the window. "But I don't know. Things just won't be the same without the Beretta."

261

"Tell me about it," she said.

"What happened out there today? I always thought that if you shot someone, you'd be a little upset."

"It depends on who you shoot, and if you shot him, which I don't know yet. I didn't like this guy anyway, and if I did take him out, it was because he was about to kill me."

Ben whistled. "Damn, baby, what kind of a day did you have?"

"Actually, it wasn't too bad. But I am worried about Vik."

"Are you sure you're okay?"

"I might as well be—I don't even have all the details. How was your day?"

"It was just a bad-health day. I did a little rescue breathing, got one heart started, and we managed to get a new momma to the hospital before she delivered. I am concerned about how much hot water there will be if we aren't the next ones in the shower."

"I like the after-the-shower part the best."

She decided on the S & W, and locked up the guns.

Later, Momma decided the three women in the family needed a lady's night in. For Momma, that meant facials, shampoos, pedicures, manicures, and woman talk. Ben took the boys to a hockey game in the city.

"So," Momma said as she rolled Marti's hair on large rollers, "looks like I'm the only one here without a man. Now, Marti, you got yourself two men, not one. From the sounds of it, that partner of yours needs looking after, too. And Joanna, Tony's okay, considering his age. I'm proud of both of you. But then, the women in our family always did know how to choose a good man."

"I don't remember seeing Tony hanging around anywhere," Marti said.

"He's not a jock," Joanna said.

"Oh?" Momma said, eyebrows raised.

"Tony likes sports; he's just not on a team."

"Sounds like he might not be around too long," Momma said. "You two have to have more in common than broccoli salad and tofu."

"Well, he's in a couple of my classes and it's kind of neat, doing homework together. He's thinking about becoming a vegetarian. And we're going to the symphony next month. I can't believe how long it's been since I've done that."

Marti couldn't, either. All Chris had ever wanted to do was watch "the game" on TV, no matter what the sport.

"Sounds like you two might have a few things in common," Momma said.

"I hope so. I don't want my whole life to be about sports." She sniffed one of Momma's facials. "Ummm, apricot." She began smoothing it on her face. "Now look, you two, this isn't a lifetime commitment. Right now, we have fun together and lots to talk about. Tomorrow," she said, shrugging, "who knows?"

Momma made a circle with her thumb and index finger. "Way to go," she said.

Vik came in late the next morning. Marti wasn't sure what she expected, but the pouches that had been under his eyes were little more than dark smudges and some color had returned to his face. He offered her some bubble bread, still warm from the oven.

"Mildred's better."

"Thank God."

"Heard anything?"

She knew he meant Curly.

"Not much." She hesitated, then said, "They found some clothes in Curly's basement. The bloodstains match Logan's blood type."

Vik hunched forward in his chair until he seemed huddled into himself.

Marti wondered if she should tell him about the old Oldsmobile in Curly's garage. The description matched that of the car that had been following her. "And Jeremiah Cheney called," she said instead. The car could wait. Maybe she wouldn't tell him at all.

Vik walked to the window. "Cheney paid Curly off, didn't he?"

"He told them Barnabas killed Dawn Taborn. That's why they sent him to Europe, to the institution."

When the phone rang half an hour later, Vik took the call. When he hung up, he took a deep breath and let it out really slowly. "That was the coroner's office. The bullet that killed Curly came from the Glock. The clip was out, but he must have forgotten to check the chamber, and somehow in all of the confusion, he accidentally shot himself."

Was it accidental? Marti wondered. Or did he know the bullet was there and turn the gun on himself on purpose? She thought of her gun. "I hope this means someone is on his way over here with my Beretta."

Vik ran his fingers through his hair. "At least I didn't kill him."

After a few minutes, he said, "When my old man was in the hospital after his heart attack, Curly told everyone I was a tenth-generation Pole, a second-generation cop, and Gus Jessenovik's son. That didn't seem like much to be proud of them, being Gus Jessenovik's son, not with . . ." His voice broke. "Not with Curly around. Now I thank God."

The anger was gone from his voice. There was no tension in the set of his shoulders. The scowl on his face was dear and familiar. Vik was back.

Read on for an excerpt from Eleanor Taylor Bland's latest book

SCREAM IN SILENCE

Available in hardcover from St. Martin's Minotaur

He gripped the rough bark and peered around the trunk of the tree. Puffs of smoke hovered like gray clouds in the evening sky. The Warren place was burning. It had been a fine house years ago when the Warrens owned it. Now most of the paint had peeled from the clapboard, and half the shutters were missing. The steps were rotting, and the screen door in the back hung off its hinges. Cardboard and plastic had replaced several windows. He smiled as flames began licking the edges of the roof. People who didn't take care of their homes didn't deserve to have them. Sirens sounded in the distance, nudging him. As he made his way out of the underbrush, dense scrubs scratched at his arms and legs.

He was humming as he jogged along the mile-and-a-half trail, deserted now because it would soon be dark. He ran away from the sound of the sirens, circled around, and then came closer again. Part of the preserve abutted the Warrens' property. He followed the road, which veered toward the burning building, until he was close enough to see the orange-red flames pouring from the roof, the streams of water from the firefighters' hoses ineffective. There was a deep roar, as if the fire was rolling through a tunnel. The smell of wood burning made him tempted to leave the trail and walk through the trees to get a closer look, but he did not. He inhaled deeply and felt a familiar swelling at his groin. The smoke was not close enough to sting his eyes. The heat could not sear his lungs, but the flames—he could see the flames. He leaned against a tree taking in deep gulps of air, savoring the taste of smoke. There was a sudden loud crackling, then a whoosh as a huge plume of smoke rose above the treetops. The pleasure these sounds brought made him moan aloud.

When he returned home it was a little after nine. He went into the kitchen and in the light from the refrigerator made two roast beef sandwiches. He topped them with mustard and tomatoes and looked out the window as he ate in the dark. He was always hungry after a fire. He fixed himself a piece of cake, some cookies, and a bowl of ice cream.

He used to come home from a fire, eat, and go to bed—not to sleep, at least not for a while, but to remember. It had been different the last few times and tonight. He felt . . . dissatisfied somehow. He wanted more. This fire had burned longer undetected than any he had set in a long while. It was so powerful—flames leaping above the treetops. He should be happy, but he wasn't. And now that he had eaten, he should be tired, but he wasn't. He felt like running for another two hours. He felt as if he could run all night.

He went to the basement and unlocked the door to his workshop. He had built the heavy table in the center of the room, soundproofed and paneled the walls, and put tile on the floor to make it easier to clean up spills. Locked cabinets were filled with chemicals and supplies. There was a folding cot and sleeping bag for those times when he worked until he was too weary to go upstairs.

His journal was still on the table, open to today's date. He made detailed notes about the fire: which combustible materials he had chosen; how he had sealed the area to restrict the oxygen; the length of time he had stood on the hill and waited before he'd shot the pellets that shattered the windows and caused the backdraft and explosion of fire. That done, he opened the combination lock on an old metal footlocker. He took out a wooden box and sat on the bed with the box on his lap. The box was made of oak, polished to a gleam. He opened it with a small skeleton key that he kept taped to the underside of a lamp on the table. It was filled with newspaper clippings, most of them brief and yellow with age. There was only one with a picture, the obituary of a police officer who'd died in a house fire. Setting fires could be dangerous. Sometimes the wrong people came around asking questions. He had never allowed anyone to stand in his way.

He closed the box. There would be another clipping tomorrow. Tonight's fire was so beautiful, it might even make the front page. He felt sad as he returned the box to the footlocker. As wonderful as the fire was, it wasn't the same anymore. It wasn't enough. He unlocked one of the cabinets, removed a shoe box, and put it on the worktable. As he looked at the contents, he felt a surge of excitement. Yes, this was what was missing in his life. Tonight he would find out if that book he'd found in the secondhand store was any good. He would read the directions again, compare them to the checklist he had drawn up based on those instructions. He would make sure he hadn't overlooked or misunderstood anything, then find out for certain if he had succeeded in making his first bomb.

Det. Marti MacAlister parked as close as she could to the area where the bombing had occurred. It was a dark night in an isolated part of town. Dense stands of burr oak and bushes sheltered this part of the road where it ran along the northern perimeter of the Lincoln Prairie Municipal Airport. Branches overhung the street lamps, and few and far between, the houses across the street were further isolated by their distance from the road. Just ahead, red and white lights flashed, blinked, and whirled. No fatalities, the dispatcher had told her, just a mailbox blown all to hell. Just a mailbox—but damned close—not just to some small jets, but also to their fuel source.

Marti rolled down the window as her partner, Matthew "Vik" Jessenovik, approached the car. Vik was four inches taller than her five-ten. He had lost weight during his wife's recent illness, and at 145, was twenty pounds lighter than she was. Almost fifty, he was nine years older than her.

"Vik, what have you got on?" He was wearing a lightweight overcoat over what looked like pajamas.

Wiry salt-and-pepper eyebrows almost met across the bridge of his nose. He had a tendency to lean over and look down at people. Marti called it his vulture look; his craggy face and his beak nose, broken long ago, brought those birds to mind.

"Marti, some idiot set off a bomb thirty feet from the airport. For some reason, that sounded important. What took *you* so long to get here?"

She ignored that. After being a widow for more than four years she had remarried four months ago and Vik was still adjusting. Lately his remarks seemed to imply that she might not be giving the job enough priority. Maybe he was right this time. She and Ben *had* been right in the middle of something.

"What have we got?" she asked.

"There wasn't much damage. I don't know if that's because it was a small bomb or because the mailboxes are out here by the road and away from the houses. I guess we'll find out more about that when the bomb squad and the ATF are through. If they can tell us. The property owner is out of town. Only one neighbor heard anything." He pointed toward the only house with lights on. "There are half a dozen houses along this part of the road, with about a half a mile of undeveloped land behind them. I haven't talked with the people who reported it yet—I was waiting for you—but I woke up everyone else. So far, nobody up late; nobody out late. From the looks of it, they're not your average nosy types. As far as I can tell, everyone has gone back to bed. You'd think they would at least have some outdoor lights on. Maybe they don't want the pilots to mistake the street for a runway. Oh, apparently there is one barking dog—belongs to that house back there." He pointed to the house to the left of the blown-up mailbox.

"Why isn't it barking now?"

"The neighbors wondered about that too, but they were more pleased than concerned. Barking is definitely not encouraged, although I don't know why else anyone would want a dog."

Marti stifled a yawn. She glanced at the clock on the dashboard: 11:57. "What time did the call come in?"

"A little after eleven."

"Maybe we should check on the dog first." She got her flashlight out of the trunk.

They found a small mixed breed under some bushes about fifty feet from the house. The dog was lying in a thicket, like it had been tossed there.

"It looks like its neck was broken," Vik said.

Marti shivered and looked away. People who harmed animals disturbed her.

"Think we should tell them about their dog?" Vik asked. "The place is dark. It looks like they've gone back to sleep. Maybe the people who reported this can tell them in the morning. After all, they're neighbors."

"Whatever. It can wait." She didn't feel much like breaking the news either. Pets were like children to a lot of people.

Yellow tape marked off the area where the explosion had occurred. The mailbox had been attached to a post that was sunk into the ground near a long, gravel path leading to the house. All that remained was one jagged shaft of wood pointing upward. There were indentations on the hard-packed dirt where the force of the explosion slammed pieces of metal and wood into the ground, but nearby bushes and trees were undamaged. Marti had worked a car-bombing case when she was on the force in Chicago. She was glad there were no bodies this time. This one hadn't done much more damage than a large firecracker.

"Hell of a place for a bomb," Vik said, gesturing in the direction of the airport. "Too many corporate jets hangared there. Too many politicians flying in and out. It could be some fool playing a joke, or an irate neighbor, or somebody who's ticked off with one of those corporations."

"Or one of those politicians," Marti said. It was warm for the end of April. Spring had come with quiet rain and a slow greening. The mailbox in front of the house next door had petunias planted at its base. A light wind ruffled her hair. She unbuttoned her jacket. Too bad Vik couldn't take his coat off. Pajamas. This had to be his first experience with a detonated bomb; they did respond to calls reporting threats occasionally and she could remember him talking about one that hadn't gone off.

"Just what we need," Vik said. He kicked at the dirt. "Innovation, creativity, stupidity. If this was some damned fool prank . . ."

"And if it wasn't?"

"Come on, MacAlister."

"Nobody's home, Vik. Why do you blow up a mailbox when nobody's home?"

"So they won't get hurt?"

"Then what's the point?"

"How the hell do I know? You think this was political?"

"We'll have a better idea of that when we see the day's flight list."

"Dammit, MacAlister, this is Lincoln Prairie, Illinois, not Belfast or Nairobi. We don't have any terrorists here. No skinheads, no neo-Nazis, no paramilitia."

"No?" she said. "Like hell."

This bomb and a fire earlier this evening, both without injuries or fatalities, along with a drive-by Saturday night with no injuries, made her uneasy. There was such a thing as too much luck. It tended to come in bunches—like trouble.

There was a light on in the den when Vik pulled into the driveway. Mildred was waiting up for him. She must have had a good day. More and more now the days were good. MS wasn't fatal, at least that's what the doctor said. But it leeched away so much of her life. He could remember how she had loved to ice skate, and dance, and take long hikes in the woods. Now she couldn't walk more than ten minutes without her legs becoming weak. And, over time, there would be more changes, more restrictions. Now it was a just a walker, perhaps soon it would only be a cane, but one day it would be a wheelchair.

He let himself into their home and walked toward the light. His den was now their bedroom. As he walked, he heard the thump of Mildred's walker, and before he reached the doorway she was coming into the hall to greet him.

"Matthew!"

In his mind's eye, she was always the girl he'd married. When

270

she smiled, the years fell away and she seemed as young as a bride.

"*Moja serca*," he said in Polish, going to her. "*Moja serca*." My heart.

He listened to the police band on his CB until daybreak. What a stroke of luck, finding that old book in the secondhand store. He had been looking for something to add to his World War I and II collection. All he could see was the spine when he pulled it from the shelf, Bombs Away. He almost put it back when he saw the condition it was in, but the diagrams caught his attention. Step-by-step instructions for making all kinds of bombs. He had to wear latex gloves when he handled it because the cover was so soiled it must have been handled by many people. The pages were dog-eared, and wrinkled and stained where someone had spilled coffee. It wasn't until he called the publisher to order another and was told it was no longer legal to own that he realized how valuable it was. That was two summers ago. Now, after assembling everything he needed, he had built and detonated his first bomb.

At eleven o'clock Tuesday morning, Marti and Vik met with Lefty, the sergeant in charge of Lincoln Prairie's bomb squad, and an agent from the ATF (Bureau of Alcohol, Tobacco and Firearms) in Lieutenant Dirkowitz's office. The two of them would have been in court if it wasn't for whoever had blown up the mailbox. The judge agreed that meeting with the ATF took precedence over their testimony in a murder-two case that had been pleaded down to second-degree manslaughter.

The lieutenant's office was at least as big as the one she and Vik shared with two vice cops. Even so, it seemed crowded with three extra chairs. Marti recognized Lefty, though she had never worked with him, and nodded. Lefty was a tall, beefy man with the tip of the index finger on his left hand missing because of some handyman mishap at home. The young man sitting beside him with scraggly, dirty blond hair pulled back in a ponytail and wearing faded jeans had to be the ATF agent.

Dirkowitz was drinking his usual can of diet pop. "Coffee?" he asked. The Pyrex pot and Styrofoam cups were there as a courtesy to the ATF. The lieutenant wasn't big on the amenities.

Marti reached for a cup and wished for sugar as she inhaled the aroma of coffee that was almost as full-bodied as hers. She took a seat and smiled at the ATF agent.

"Dirty Dirk" Dirkowitz ran thick fingers through close-cropped blond hair. He had played football with the Southern Illinois Salukis and still had the build of a linebacker. He made introductions all around. "Sorry to have to bring you out here with something so minor."

"No problem," the agent said. "Especially since it was already detonated. I don't know if I'll come back though, unless you get a live one I can play with."

Marti caught the humor and smiled as Vik scowled. "What have we got?" she asked.

"Nothing sophisticated; just your average homemade toy."

Vik's frown deepened.

"How much did they have to know?" she asked.

"Just the basics." The agent explained the composition of the bomb, how it was assembled, and what detonated it.

The sergeant interrupted occasionally to ask for clarification on a few technical points, but otherwise just listened, nodding his head.

"This sounds sophisticated enough to me," Vik said, when the agent stopped talking.

The agent shrugged. "It doesn't take a degree in chemistry. There are recipe books around, if you know where to look for them. The materials are commonplace, harmless even until you get the right mix. Nothing was used that we could identify as being imported by paramilitary groups."

"The fuse is what concerns me," the sergeant said.

"Why?" Marti asked.

"He used a chemical fuse," the agent explained. "It has just enough instability to be somewhat unpredictable."

"You mean maybe we'll get lucky and this idiot will blow him-self up?" Vik asked.

"Possibly," the agent said. "The fuse does improve those odds. It also improves the odds of doing something the bomber doesn't intend—it goes off too soon. . . . Usually, we can get an ID on the victim, but we find miscellaneous body parts all the time and never know who the bomber was. One time we found two right feet."

"Does this nutcase have enough information to build a bigger bomb?" Vik asked.

"Sure. My guess is this was practice. And I'd guess this guy was a loner rather than part of a group."

"Why?" Vik asked.

"A mailbox?" the agent said. "Groupies own property in isolated areas. They bring their families along and have cookouts and blow up old cars and trees and small buildings."

"You're kidding," Vik said.

"Nope. Wish I was. Then again, this could be some kind of a practical joke."

Lefty distributed some reports and walked the others through them. "If we're lucky, this is an isolated incident, some asshole having fun, and I've told you more about this than you'll ever need to know. The problem is the incident's proximity to the air-port and the clientele who have access to it—and not just the politicians. You've got CEOs with companies that manufacture all kinds of things that could piss someone off. You also have cor-porate types from other countries flying in for tours and meetings. Bottom line—security is going to be damned tight there for a while. If we get real lucky on this one, even if we do have a seri-ous type on our hands, he'll get discouraged and take his action someplace else. On the other hand, if he has a specific target, he might try again."

"Two CEOs flew out of that airport yesterday," Lieutenant Dirkowitz said. "A party of five legislators came in, including a congressman and some executives from a company in the Republic of China. If this isn't an isolated incident, who is he after?"

After Lefty and the ATF agent left, the lieutenant swiveled around in his chair and looked out the window. He had a limited view of Lake Michigan. Today the sunlight made glittering highlights on the blue water. "How long has it been since that kid made that goop stuff and we thought it was nitroglycerin?"

"Last summer, sir," Vik said.

At least a minute passed before the lieutenant spoke again. "I hope it's not a kid," he said. "Let's hope it's not a kid."

"Oh no," Vik said. "It's some prankster or a nutcase."

It presented them with one hell of a choice, Marti thought.

"Damned shame about where it went off," Vik said, as they walked back to their office. "This would have been a lot less complicated, MacAlister, if we didn't have to bring in the ATF."

"Anything that involves the post office involves the Feds."

"Hell, there wasn't even any mail in the box. Besides, our guys can handle it. You heard the ATF agent. This didn't take much expertise. It was just some idiot trying to make a better firecracker."

"You wish. It was a bomb, Vik. A real bomb, not some Silly Putty recipe some kid mixed together."

"I know," he admitted. "Just when you think it's safe to go to sleep at night, we get some damned lunatic on our hands."

"Maybe it's not that bad."

Vik gave her a look that suggested she was the one who had problems with wishful thinking.

A MYSTERIOUS PLAGUE
AND A VICIOUS KILLER STALK NEW ORLEANS—
NOW THE CITY'S MOST BRILLIANT FORENSIC TEAM
MUST STOP THEM BOTH DEAD IN THEIR TRACKS.

LOUISIANA FEVER

An Andy Broussard/Kit Franklyn Mystery

D.J. DONALDSON

A lethal virus similar to the deadly Ebola is bringing
body after body to the New Orleans morgue. As
Broussard and Franklyn try to uncover the source of
the virus, they come up against another killer—and this
one is human. Now they must stop a modern-day
plague and a malicious murderer before Kit and Andy
become statistics themselves.

"His writing displays flashes of brilliance...Dr.
Donaldson's talent and potential as a novelist are considerable."

—*The New York Times Book Review*

"A dazzling tour de force...sheer pulse-pounding reading excitement."

—*The Clarion Ledger*

LOUISIANA FEVER
D.J. Donaldson
0-312-96257-6___$5.99 U.S.___$7.99 Can.

Publishers Book and Audio Mailing Service
P.O. Box 070059, Staten Island, NY 10307
Please send me the book(s) I have checked above. I am enclosing $_____ (please add
$1.50 for the first book, and $.50 for each additional book to cover postage and handling.
Send check or money order only—no CODs) or charge my VISA, MASTERCARD,
DISCOVER or AMERICAN EXPRESS card.

Card Number_____

Expiration date_____Signature_____

Name_____

Address_____

City_____State/Zip _____
Please allow six weeks for delivery. Prices subject to change without notice. Payment in
U.S. funds only. New York residents add applicable sales tax.   LF 8/98

In all of New York's Chinatown, there is no one
like P.I. Lydia Chin, who has a nose for trouble,
a disapproving Chinese mother, and a partner
named Bill Smith who's been living above a bar
for sixteen years.

Hired to find some precious stolen porcelain,
Lydia follows a trail of clues from highbrow art
dealers into a world of Chinese gangs.
Suddenly, this case has become as complex as
her community itself—and as deadly as a killer
on the loose...

China Trade

S. J. Rozan

CHINA TRADE
S. J. Rozan
_____ 95590-1 $5.99 U.S./$7.99 CAN.

Publishers Book and Audio Mailing Service
P.O. Box 070059, Staten Island, NY 10307
Please send me the book(s) I have checked above. I am enclosing $_____ (please add
$1.50 for the first book, and $.50 for each additional book to cover postage and handling.
Send check or money order only—no CODs) or charge my VISA, MASTERCARD,
DISCOVER or AMERICAN EXPRESS card.

Card Number_____

Expiration date_____Signature_____

Name_____

Address_____

City_____State/Zip _____
Please allow six weeks for delivery. Prices subject to change without notice. Payment in
U.S. funds only. New York residents add applicable sales tax.   CT 1/99